REPLAY

Toronto Blaze Series
Book 3
by
Kim Findlay

To smart women and the men who love them

"'If you ever get a second chance for something, you've got to
go all the way. '– Lance Armstrong

TORONTO BLAZE ROSTER

#	Name	Nickname	Country	Position
1	Ivan Petrov	Petey	Russia	Goalie
8	Cliff Royston	Royster	Canada	Winger
10	Devin Oppedisano	Oppy	Canada	Winger
12	Corwin Cashman	Crash	US	Defense
17	Josh Middleton	Ducky	Canada	Winger
18	John Deeker	Deek	Canada	Center
22	Gerber	Gerbs	Switzerland	Winger
23	Brian Barnes	Barnes	US	Winger
25	Phin Collins	Bongo	Canada	Center
32	Braydon Mitchell	Mitch	US	Goalie
33	Lars De Vries		Netherlands	Goalie
38	Daniel Astrom	Fitch	Sweden	Center
44	Justin Johnson	JJ	Canada	Defense
57	Whittaker Cooper	Coop	US	Defense

Coach Osgood	Canada
Coach Salo	Sweden
Scout	Trainer
Carlos	Trainer

A NAKED RUSSIAN STANDING IN FRONT OF ME

JOSH

THE LOCKER ROOM was always crowded in the preseason. It was noisier too—players chirping over each other while skates and sticks hit the floor. Also, lots of sweat. That was kind of gross, but it was part of the game. The air buzzed with the bodies and noise and something that was just hockey.

I grinned, still standing in my skates, because this was fun. So many guys, all excited about the possibilities ahead of them. I remembered when I was one of the hopefuls in preseason games. Playing my ass off, trying to impress the coaches and the other, established players.

My first training camp had been in Nashville, with the team that drafted me, and I'd been sent down to the farm team after. It had been a big disappointment. I was one of the shorter players, and all the pundits had questioned whether I could make it with the larger guys, so I'd had some doubts. Then, halfway through the season a couple of injuries to players on the big team got me called up, and the time I'd spent on the farm team had upped my game. I'd stayed up, and never looked back. A year later I was traded to Toronto. Now I was one of the established players, not one of the wannabes.

Training camp and the preseason were way better this way.

I'd gotten to know most of these new guys and kinda wanted them all to make it, but we weren't allowed that big of a roster. Thank all the hockey gods I wasn't in charge of making the decisions. Word had come down that some of those cuts were coming through tomorrow. We were a week into preseason games, and the coaches had to let some players go.

"Hey, we should go out tonight!" I yelled into the noise.

A couple of the new guys looked at me, eyes kind of big like they weren't sure I was talking to them.

"Anyone who wants. Let's go out and enjoy that we're here." I got a few yeahs back, mostly from the newbies.

Fitch, whose stall was down one from mine, asked, "Is that a good idea?"

I didn't care. "We don't have to go crazy. Like, maybe not a club. But we can go out to a bar, meet some people, do something more than watch hockey tape and worry."

That had the new guys nodding. I wasn't worried, at least not about whether I'd make the team. I played right wing on the top line last year, and at the end of the season, the second highest point scorer on the team was me. This summer I'd worked hard with the teammates who'd stayed in town to prep for this year. I'd have to majorly screw up to miss making it, and I wasn't doing that.

Fitch shrugged. "Okay, I'm in."

I was surprised he wanted to come. He'd been traded in from Edmonton over the summer. Cooper had suggested

Fitch and I could be roommates and he'd moved in a couple of days ago, but I didn't know him very well. He was older and didn't talk about himself much, but he gave off quiet vibes. Nice, but not a guy who'd party much. Maybe I was wrong.

I circled my hands like a megaphone in front of my mouth. "Okay, who's in for the Top Shelf tonight?"

About five of the new guys raised their hands. So did Royster. He was one of the regular players, part of our shut down line. With Fitch and me, that made eight, which was probably a good number. The three of us could watch out for the others.

"This is not good."

Oh fuck. I had a naked Russian standing in front of me with his arms crossed.

Petey, or Petrov to his face, was our starting goalie and, as far as I was concerned, a cyborg. He never lost his temper, never shirked a practice or workout, and never had fun. He'd been part of the group training together this summer, so I'd spent a lot of time working out with him and yeah, perfect cyborg.

"We're not going to do anything crazy. Just go have a few drinks, meet people we haven't been sweating with all day, and clear our heads for a bit."

Petey frowned. "Not late."

I wanted him to move, because if I sat down, his junk would be in my face. "No, I promise."

He jerked his head in a nod. "Okay, I come." Then, thankfully, he stalked off.

I dropped on the bench to unlace my skates. Petey coming with us would certainly keep the rooks in line, but I wasn't sure it was worth it.

"Is he always like that?" Fitch asked.

I looked up. "Like what? Naked? Or the cyborg thing?"

He grinned. "Both. Either."

"He might be a Terminator, except he stops goals instead of killing people. The other thing? My guess is that his family back in Russia are nudists. Because he never bothers with a towel when he's walking around the showers and locker room." I straightened up to work off my skate. Didn't want to give Fitch the wrong impression. "He's always dressed anywhere else though."

"Good to know. I've got some stuff arriving at the condo from the freight company, so I'm not staying for lunch. I'll see you later?"

"Later!"

He headed for the shower while I pulled off my jersey.

"So, 'meeting people' is hooking up, right?"

I looked up at…Foster, I think his name was. One of the new guys. He'd taken off his pads but still had his under-layers on. "Yeah, I guess, but be careful."

He nodded. "I carry protection."

"That's good, but I meant be careful that no one gets hurt, right?"

He narrowed his eyes at me. "Hurt?"

"Don't promise shit if you don't mean it. Don't say you'll call when you won't."

He rolled his eyes. "Yes, Dad."

Like that, was it? "No means no."

He shrugged. Fine. I'd tell Petey to watch out for him, and I couldn't imagine a better cockblocker.

* * *

THE NINE OF us had snagged the usual tables at the back, under the second floor of the Top Shelf. The bar was close to the arena downtown, so we usually met up here after games.

The place was popular with the local athletes since there

was a sign out front: *No selfies, no autographs, or no service.* Management kicked out patrons who bothered us. Not that we didn't do some pics and stuff, but people were discouraged from crowding us.

That didn't include the puck bunnies though. There were now fourteen people squeezed around our tables. One brave woman had tried flirting with Petey, but that didn't last long. Royster was cozied up with another. And two of the newbies, not Foster, were flirting with a couple of cute blondes.

Fitch was talking hockey to the other wannabes who'd come out with us, and some of the girls were listening in. Fitch wasn't wearing a wedding ring because he was almost divorced, but he somehow deflected the women without saying anything. Awesome superpower. I had a woman sitting tight beside me, leaning over so her boobs were right there. A sure thing, a nice way to end the day.

But my dick just wasn't interested.

I hadn't hooked up much over the summer. I'd been training hard, but it wasn't just that. Maybe it was the end of last season. Losing in overtime in the Stanley Cup finals had kicked us all in the balls, and something, I dunno what, had just taken away my urge to hook up as frequently as I used to. Maybe I was getting old. I was twenty-four now.

In any case, this woman wasn't doing it for me.

"Uh, I'm going to—" No, I couldn't say go to the head, or she'd offer to blow me back there. "The bar. Can I get you something?"

She looked over. It was crowded and it didn't look fun. Normally I'd wave for a server, but the puck bunny didn't know that. Fortunately, she didn't offer to follow me.

"A cosmo?"

"Sure." I'd bought a few of those over the years. I wouldn't have trouble remembering her choice.

I slid out of my seat, a little faster than was probably

polite, but I needed some space. From her. It wasn't like I would get space at the bar, but I wouldn't be pressed up against someone hoping to bag a hockey player for the night. Hopefully.

There was a reason I normally flagged down someone to take my order: I wasn't tall. Officially I was the shortest guy on the team, but I think Barnes fudged his height. It took a few minutes before I got close enough to ask for a cosmo and a Keith's ale. The bartender recognized me and promised to add it to my tab.

"I didn't take you for a cosmo drinker." The voice beside me was husky, feminine and amused.

I turned to see a redhead sitting at the bar. She was hot, but older, watching me with a little smile. "It's not for me. It's for—"

"Your date?"

I shook my head. "Someone I'm trying to get rid of, honestly."

The woman laughed. "Not sure buying her a drink is going to do that."

I sighed. "It got me away from the table though."

She leaned forward so we didn't have to speak so loudly. "What's your plan?"

I looked over my shoulder. Cosmo Girl was moving in on Foster now. "If I wait long enough, she'll go for someone else."

"Waste of a cosmo."

"Worth it. Um, do you want it?"

"Not my drink, but thanks."

The bartender was still working on the pink concoction. I tilted my head. "You don't look like someone who hangs out in a sports bar." She was wearing a suit, an actual skirt and jacket that looked expensive as shit.

"I'm not."

"Got lost?" I grinned at her.

"No. I was meeting someone and he picked the place. It didn't work out."

Now my dick perked up. She was something different. Maybe I was just bored with the usual choices. "His loss." The cosmo was set on the bar in front of me with my beer. "Sure you don't want this?"

"You're welcome to it. I'm Madeline, by the way." The redhead held out her hand. It was smooth, not like my callused palm.

"I'm Josh."

She dropped my hand after we shook. "Here's what I'm looking for. It's been a long couple of weeks, and I just want someone to fuck me. Then I'll kick him out. I won't call and I don't do repeats. Are you good with that?"

My dick now lost interest. What was wrong with me? I wasn't looking for a girlfriend. One night was all I wanted.

A sudden crash when a server dropped a tray of drinks attracted my attention. I caught a glimpse of light brown hair on a short woman and something inside me leapt. *Katie?*

She turned around, and no, it wasn't Katie.

Was that my problem? I'd heard from friends of friends that Katie was going to school in Toronto this year. Was I hoping to see her again? *Ugh.*

Losing the Cup. Losing Katie. I had to get myself together and out of this funk.

I turned back to the redhead. She was attractive and knew what she wanted. I could get my dick onboard, and better her than the bunny back at the table.

"That sounds great. Just let me tell my group that I'm leaving."

CHAPTER 2

LIKE A HOBBIT AFTER AN EXTENDED VISIT TO MORDOR

KATIE

STAYING up to watch one more episode of *Outlander* was a mistake. The hall light almost blinded me, dragging me out of Scotland and back to the condo. Madeline was home. I quickly hit pause and pulled out my headphones. Someone crashed into the wall, and I heard the sounds of kissing and moaning.

Shit. She'd brought someone home, and here I was, sitting in the living room like a voyeur. If they took some time—another moan—I could still make my getaway. I quietly closed my laptop and pulled out the power cord. With my free hand I pushed back the afghan I'd been curled up under. I shoved my feet into my slippers.

"Katie?"

Damn. Not quick enough. I looked up at my roommate/landlord, a half smile on her face, hair mussed and lips kiss swollen. She was standing at the corner where the hallway reached the kitchen, open to the living room. No sneaking away now. Her hookup stood in the shadows behind her. Not my business and I'd intruded enough, so I dropped my gaze. Laptop in my hands, I stood, ready to hide out in my room. With earphones in.

"Sorry, I should have been in my room already. I'll just—" I threw a thumb up in a dorky move toward my room.

"Katie?"

I froze in place. This voice wasn't Madeline. It was male and impossibly familiar. I never thought I'd hear it again in this lifetime. I'd been counting on that. My eyes opened so wide I must've looked like Bambi. *What the fuck?*

Hookup guy stepped around Madeline and I immediately regretted every life choice I'd made that brought me to this moment. Most especially the ones that resulted in the hobbit slippers and baggy sweats I was wearing, as well as the hair that needed washing and the lack of makeup. *Damn it.* If I was going to meet Josh again, I was supposed to look hot, in a skintight dress with heels, perfect hair and makeup, not like a hobbit after an extended visit to Mordor.

And damned if that devastated, heart-ripped-out feeling wasn't trying to make a replay in my chest. *Fuck no.*

"You two know each other?" Madeline leaned back against the breakfast bar. Even tousled, she was sleek and put together. Josh was wearing a short-sleeved button-down with jeans, his brown hair a mess. He was taller than I remembered him, and the shirt didn't hide how broad his shoulders were or the biceps stretching the sleeves or the sweetness in those brown eyes...

Ugh.

I needed to salvage this situation. I'd only been rooming with Madeline a couple of weeks so far, and I liked this place, especially the discounted rent. Housing prices in Toronto were stupid. If Josh messed this up for me, I'd throttle him with my power cord.

"Yeah. We knew each other in high school." There was no reason to tell her that we'd dated for two years.

"We went out for two years and then broke up."

Thanks, Josh, for making it as awkward as possible. Madeline looked between the two of us, eyebrows raised. I, however, got stuck on that phrase. *We broke up.*

I didn't want to drag this out. I wanted to hide in my bedroom and try to pretend he wasn't about to hook up with my roommate. But some things I couldn't let slide. "No, Josh. *We* didn't break up. You broke us up. I didn't get a say in it, remember?"

His brow scrunched in his *I'm thinking* expression. I snorted.

Madeline chuckled. "Oooh. Drama. I'm here for it."

I didn't know her that well, and I didn't want to air my dirty laundry in front of her. I took a step to slink away, but no. Josh was busy rewriting history and not thinking about my situation at all.

"Katie, it was the right thing to do."

I exerted admirable control by not throwing my laptop at his earnest, confident face. It was a close call though. My knuckles showed white as I reminded myself of the cost of a new laptop.

"Was it, Katie?" Madeline asked.

I couldn't let him congratulate himself on his wisdom. I'd just clear that up so I could leave, Josh and Madeline could get back to what they'd been doing, and I wouldn't find myself looking for a new place to live.

I narrowed my eyes at my ex, hoping to laser my displeasure into him with my glare. "Josh thought so. He was being scouted for the NHL draft, so I guess he didn't need his tutor anymore."

He made a hurt noise in his throat.

Madeline turned to him. "Wanted to be free to fuck around, Josh?"

I could have cheered. Madeline was on my side, even though I wasn't the one planning to give her orgasms. Maybe I should, because right now I loved my roommate.

"No!" He almost shouted, which was pretty rich. He was here precisely to fuck Madeline.

The only reason the two of them weren't already naked was because of Claire and Jamie and my stupid decision to watch one more episode. "Oh, really?"

With me and Madeline staring at him, he finally realized just how precarious his position was. He ran his hands through his hair and rubbed his face. I didn't let the familiar gesture fool me into lowering my guard. Or my laptop.

"Okay, this looks bad. And yeah, I've hooked up. But that's not why we—" A growl from me had him course-correcting. "Not why I broke up with you."

Madeline looked like she only needed popcorn to be having a full movie experience. "Why, then?"

He looked at me, as if asking for permission. I lifted my chin. *Up to you, buddy.*

He turned back to her. "It was our senior year of high school. Katie was accepted to a bunch of schools, and some of them were offering her scholarships. I didn't want her to make a decision on a school because of me."

There was a moment of silence. Madeline looked at me, and I nodded. "Yep, that's what he said. *In a text.*" The pain of reading that still hadn't faded as much as I wished.

Madeline's eyes rounded.

"Because obviously, having a vagina, I couldn't have made a decision in my own best interests."

"Oh, Josh. You didn't." Madeline shook her head at him.

Josh's cheeks flushed. "I— Okay, yeah—I should have

talked to you. I was afraid I couldn't go through with it if you were right there."

Now I was really angry, and all that hurt and rage could finally be unleashed on the guy who was the source. I no longer cared that I looked like I spent my free time reading romance novels and accumulating cats between visits to the shire.

"Yeah, Josh, you *should* have talked to me. It's not like I didn't know you were going to be drafted. And maybe we could have decided on a long-distance relationship, or maybe we would have broken up. But you could have respected me enough to let me have a say in a decision that affected me."

Josh's jaw fell open. He swallowed. "You would have wanted to break up?"

I rolled my eyes so hard it hurt. "We'll never know because *you didn't bother to talk to me.*"

I reminded myself that Josh wasn't cute, he looked like a goldfish. "I just— I never thought—"

Before I could explode again, Madeline patted his arm. "You're not irresistible."

His cheeks heated up as he stared at the floor. "I know."

That seemed like my cue. "Well, I'm going to my room. Have fun."

"Katie?" Josh was wearing his kicked-puppy expression. "I'm sorry."

I stopped in my tracks. I deserved an apology, damn it, but the right one. "What are you sorry for, exactly?"

"That I didn't talk to you. I thought I was doing the right thing."

"Really?" I wanted to cross my arms or put my hands on my hips, but I was still hanging on to my laptop. Instead, I let my tone show just how much I doubted that. "And that's why you started going out with Rhonda?"

He looked down again. "Mom said I needed to make it real."

"What a bitch!" Madeline said the words, but they were exactly what I was thinking.

"Yeah, I knew she never liked me." There was an unsettled feeling in my stomach. When he took Rhonda out, I'd been angry and hurt and mortified. Convinced he'd really wanted to fuck his way through the puck bunnies when he got to play hockey. Not that his "best for you" argument was any better. I didn't want to think his mother had manipulated him, that maybe he'd really believed breaking up was in my best interests. I wanted to keep hating him.

"That's not right. She liked you."

I rolled my eyes again. Madeline tilted her head in a question. I shook mine. "You dodged a bullet, Katie."

There was an awkward pause. I wasn't going to discuss Josh's mother, and Madeline was waiting for us to entertain her.

"Uh, I'm going to go." Josh's eyes were flicking from me to Madeline to the hallway.

Madeline nodded at Josh. "Good idea."

"And again, I'm sorry, Katie. I didn't want to be an asshole." He turned and headed to the doorway.

Madeline followed and locked the door behind him. "Wine?" she asked when she came back.

I nodded and finally set my laptop down.

She pulled a bottle out of the fridge and reached for the corkscrew. "They never want to be an asshole, and yet…"

"Exactly."

CHAPTER 3
I'VE LOST THE STORY HERE

JOSH

I WAS STILL THINKING about Katie when I opened the door to my condo. She was here, in the same city as me, and now I knew where she lived. That gave me ideas. She'd blocked me back in high school, on her phone and social media, so I'd had no way to get in touch with her. Now I could find where she lived again… But the way she'd looked at me?

I'd never seen that expression on her face before. After we broke up—no, after I broke up with her—she'd moved to stay with her grandmother and attend another school. I'd been glad I didn't have to see her again, because it hurt too much, but I'd missed her. If I hadn't had hockey to focus on, I don't know what I'd have done.

If she'd stayed around, I wouldn't have been able to resist trying to make up with her.

Damn it, I'd messed up so bad.

There were lights on in my place, which worried me for a moment till I remembered my new roommate. Fitch sat at the kitchen island, drinking a beer and scrolling through his phone.

He turned and raised a brow. "That was quick, Ducky."

I frowned, working through my conversation with Katie. "What are you talking about?"

"The redhead you left the bar with. I thought you'd be gone for a couple of hours."

"What? No, I mean…what?" I'd been so focused on Katie I'd forgotten about…what was her name again?

Fitch got up and opened the fridge. "We should talk—I'll get you a beer. The way to make a woman happy takes more than ten minutes."

I stared at him. "I know that. Well, unless it's a quickie. But I know how to get someone off. *And* make sure it's good. Tonight was different. Things happened."

He passed me a bottle. "It happens to everyone, is that what I'm supposed to say? I wouldn't know myself, but—"

I swallowed a mouthful of beer, ignoring my roommate and his chirping. I needed to figure out how badly I'd screwed things up with Katie and how to fix it. Back in high school, I'd done what everyone said was the right thing. But she was still super pissed, and maybe she was right.

"Ducky?"

I blinked at Fitch, who was smirking. What had he been talking about? Right, sex. But that hadn't been a problem. It never had, unless you counted tonight, but that wasn't a performance thing. "I have no problem with my sex life. It's just, when we got to her place, her roommate was there."

He kept his mouth straight, but I could tell he was having fun because his eyes were smiling. "Don't tell me you said no to a threesome."

For a moment, that idea bored into my brain. The roommate was hot, obviously, since I'd gone home with her, but it was thinking of Katie that got my dick perking up. "I didn't say no. I didn't say anything but hi to Katie."

Fitch took the beer away from me. "I've lost the story here. Tell me what happened."

I grabbed for my beer, but he kept it out of reach. No problem. I swiped his instead and took a long swallow.

He rolled his eyes. "You've heard of germs?"

I shrugged. "I'm thirsty. And I'm trying to figure out what happened."

Fitch sat down again and set his chin on his hands. "Okay, tell Dr. Daniel the problem."

Who? Oh, right. Daniel was his real first name. I wanted to tell him there wasn't a problem, but I needed to get someone else's take on what had gone down. I was good at hockey, but I'd never done well in school or other things that smart people did. And tonight? I'd never had a hookup go sideways like that. The last time I ran into a roommate when I went home with someone, we'd gone the threesome route. It had been a lot of fun. But that wasn't what I wanted with Katie.

"So, the redhead and I got to her place, and we were making out. Like, kissing, and I was getting my hand under her shirt, and she was rubbing my dick. But her roommate was there, and she said she'd go to her room and leave us and that's when I realized she was Katie."

Fitch held up his hand. "Let's see if I've got this straight. The redhead's roommate was Katie, and you know her? Previous hookup? Did things not go well with her? That would be awkward."

I shook my head. "Katie wasn't a hookup. She's my ex."

He stared at me like that was a hard concept to understand. Not sure why, because he'd said he was getting divorced so he now had an ex, if he hadn't before. I shrugged and tried to remember anything my mother might have said to show she didn't like Katie and that I'd missed. Why hadn't I known?

Fitch snapped his fingers in front of my face.

"What?"

"Finish the story. What kind of ex is Katie? Wife? Fiancée? Girlfriend?"

People didn't know about her because it had been a long time ago. Fitch wouldn't know anyway, since he was new to the team. "Girlfriend. We were together for two years."

"Sorry, Ducky. I didn't know. I thought you were one of the fuckboys on the team."

I shrugged a shoulder. "Well, yeah, but that's because I didn't have Katie."

Obviously. If I had a girlfriend, I didn't cheat. Those were the rules.

"How long ago did you break up?"

"Senior year, high school."

"And you're what, twenty-four now? So six years ago? You haven't had a girlfriend since?"

I shook my head. It was five years ago. His math was off because I'd had to repeat a grade, but it didn't matter. I'd never been serious about anyone because I hadn't found anyone like Katie.

"Huh." Fitch took a swig of my former beer. "So, you saw the ex and that killed the mood?"

"Well, yeah. Especially when they were talking about me and all the things I did wrong." I picked at the label on the beer bottle. That was the part that had me stumped. I'd been sure I was doing the right thing.

"What did you do?"

I gave Fitch a quick recap of everything I remembered. When I looked up, he was shaking his head at me. My beer was empty but I didn't think I should get another, even though it was an optional practice in the morning.

"When you want to end a relationship, you need to talk."

I let out a long sigh. "Yeah, I get that now. I was just afraid that I couldn't do it if I was looking at her."

"Why did you have to break up? And why then? You could have waited till you were drafted, in case you ended up somewhere near her. Or broke up then if you didn't think long-distance would work."

"So she would pick a school for the right reasons. Her parents said—"

"Wait, her parents were in on this?"

Oh yeah. They'd asked to talk to me and explained that Katie had to make important decisions and I was a distraction. They were afraid she might decide not to go to school until I was drafted so she could follow me.

Fitch frowned when I told him. "Seems they didn't like you. Or that Katie was easily influenced."

"I thought they liked me." Had I been wrong about that too? "And no, Katie can be a hard-ass. She wouldn't do my homework for me, always insisted I could do it myself if we found a way for my brain to figure it out." And she did. She was brilliant.

"Then maybe they were wrong. Sounds like Katie could have decided on her own."

Fitch made a good point.

"I messed up, really badly."

"I'm afraid you did. That's too bad, because it sounds like you really cared for her."

I did. In high school, there had only been two things that mattered to me: hockey and her. "Katie—she's the best. She's so smart, and I don't know what she saw in me."

Fitch fought back a grin. "Me neither."

"And she said my mother didn't like her, and I'm trying to see if I missed something. If Mom didn't like her. I mean, Mom always said she did, but people lie." I'd always respected my mother and other adults. That was how I was raised. I never thought Mom would lie to me. But damn, these people had played me.

"That is true."

"Yeah, I'm going to have to figure that out."

"Good to know before you get serious about someone else."

I picked up his empty bottle and crossed to the recycling. "What do you mean?"

"Well, if your mother interfered with Katie, she might do it again. And if you find someone else, someone you want to be with, you don't want your mother to cause problems."

"Why do you keep saying 'someone else'?"

Fitch threw his empty bottle into the recycling. "Don't you want to have a girlfriend again? You've obviously blown it with Katie. And with the redhead."

"I wasn't serious about Madeline." I frowned. "And she wasn't serious about me. But I'm going to get Katie back, now that I know I made a mistake in high school."

He turned around slowly. "I don't think that's on the table. Sounds like she's still pissed at you, with good cause."

"But that's a good sign, right?"

He blinked at me. "You think it's a good sign that she's pissed at you?"

"Yeah. Because that means she didn't forget me. And she's still thinking about me."

"That's—well, that might be a good point."

I nodded. I wasn't a genius, but I wasn't stupid either. Well, not always. "I know it won't be easy. But I'm used to working hard. I didn't get to play hockey by taking things easy. I'll just have to work on getting Katie to love me again."

"How do you think you're going to do that?"

"I don't know. But I did it once. I'll just have to find a way to do it again."

It would be harder this time. Katie was pissed at me, and she wasn't my tutor so she didn't have to spend time with me. Or maybe...no. No way I could convince her I needed study help now.

But I wasn't the kid who hoped to make it to the NHL anymore. I was here. And in Toronto, where people loved hockey. I had money, and I had connections, and all the determination in the world. That should make up for everything else.

I was going to find out.

CHAPTER 4
COOL WAS NOT IN MY WHEELHOUSE

KATIE

I WOKE UP, light sliding into my room around the edges of my blinds. Memories of the night before flooded my brain. I cringed. How embarrassing. Josh. Fucking Josh.

How was I going to face Madeline again, after last night's drama?

This condo had been an incredible score and I wanted to keep it. Originally, before I'd moved here, I found a couple of women to room with through an online site. That didn't work. Turned out they were looking for a roommate because no one would stay with them.

One of the first people I made friends with at the University of Toronto was Andrea. She was a second year TA and was kind enough to take me under her wing. Andrea had been roommates with Madeline last year before moving in with her girlfriend. Madeline was a special auditor, worked for the federal tax department, and traveled across the country to work on cases. A lot of the time her condo was empty. She liked to have someone there to keep an eye on things and preferred grad students since they were past the partying stage.

Andrea had sent her a message on my behalf to see if she was looking for a roommate. Fortunately for me, she was. Madeline and I met at her condo to discuss rooming together. As soon as I walked in, I hoped we could make it work because the place was amazing. Not a student apartment, but a real home—expensive furnishings, security at the doors, and it was right downtown, making commuting a breeze.

We'd sat at her dining room table to discuss the details. She liked her place to be tidy. I did too, so that wasn't an issue. She worked long hours, and didn't need someone to chat with or plan her life with. She didn't want to be set up with nice guys or told she worked too much. Just someone to keep the place occupied, keep on top of the garbage and take deliveries if needed.

I was tidy, didn't want to get involved with anyone either, and would be happy to do a lot of my studying here, so there'd be someone around.

She cautioned me that she was likely to bring home her hookups, but they wouldn't spend the night. I had no problem with that. And if it hadn't been for Josh—fucking Josh—there would have been no problem ever.

I pulled on my housecoat, shoved my feet in my fuzzy slippers, and left my room quietly, aiming for the coffeepot. I didn't want to talk about last night or remember it if possible. With any luck I could avoid Madeline until her next trip. And after that, hopefully enough time would have passed that this became a funny story.

Madeline was already up. *Damn it.* She was dressed in yoga wear that looked expensive, with her hair pulled back in a smooth ponytail. And was that makeup? On a Saturday morning when she wasn't working? Life goals, right there. But not till I had coffee.

"Coffee's ready."

Okay, having a roommate with her life together wasn't always a bad thing. I pulled out my *Second Breakfast* mug, dumped milk and sugar in the bottom, and poured coffee into the cup.

"No wonder you don't care what kind of coffee you drink. There's hardly any coffee in there."

She sounded amused, and I refrained from giving her the finger. I liked my coffee sweet and creamy. Take me to Tim Horton's for a double double and I was happy. But my roommate? "Do you even drink Timmy's?"

She shuddered. "Sometimes it's all I can get."

I swallowed a mouthful of caffeinated goodness and did my best to keep my moan inside. Madeline bought expensive coffee and included it with the rent. She might ruin me for bad coffee.

With the caffeine hitting my veins, I began to qualify as awake. I tried a pleasant smile. "I want to apologize."

"What for?" She was holding back a smile.

Damn it. She knew that this was about last night. "I'm sorry I messed up your plans for the evening."

She waved her free hand. "Not a problem. He's a little young for me anyway, and he was more interested in you."

Well, it wasn't because of how I looked, that was for damn sure. "I knew he was playing in Toronto. Anything he does is news back home, but I thought in a city of six million I'd be safe."

She rested her hip against the countertop. "Safe? Was he abusive?"

"No, no. God no. I just didn't want to run into him."

"The odds of the two of you meeting up like last night

were pretty low. But if you really want to avoid him, skip the Top Shelf, especially when the Blaze play."

"That's where you…" I wasn't sure the right way to say *picked him up*.

"Yeah. I had a date there." My mouth dropped open and she laughed. "Not Josh. It was a setup by a coworker. I wanted something short and sweet. But he told me he was looking forward to kids—lots of kids. So that wasn't happening. I bumped into your hockey player at the bar, and he was cute. I asked if he wanted one night, and he was down for that." She shrugged. "Wasn't my night."

"You're not upset?"

"Why would I be? There are a lot more men out there."

I felt like a country rube around Madeline. She was the definition of sophisticated. "I'll make sure to be in my room when it gets late."

"Don't be silly. The place is yours to use. I'll send you a text if I'm bringing someone back next time, okay? Maybe you can do the same if I'm in town."

"Sure." I hoped my cheeks weren't red. This casual talk about bringing a guy home for a night wasn't something I was used to. Until my senior year at Dalhousie, I'd lived at home, and there was no way I'd bring anyone back there. Even at university, I'd only slept with guys I was dating, and that just seemed so unsophisticated next to my roommate's style.

Ah well, I was a geek. A math student with a *Lord of the Rings* obsession. Cool was not in my wheelhouse.

"And just to let you know, if you wanted to call Josh, I'd…" I'd what? Hide out in my room? Find somewhere else to stay for the night? Josh and I were *so* over but being in the condo while he and Madeline had sex would still hurt. Logically, I had no reason to feel that way. We couldn't be more over, but I'd been with him longer than any boyfriend since.

She shook her head. "I don't even have his phone number. I think I can survive without getting involved with my roommate's ex."

That was nice, but I didn't want to set down rules for her.

She moved over to a stool at the island. "I've never met anyone who was close to one of the city's hockey players before."

If she thought I had some kind of connection to local athletes, I needed to set her straight. "We went to the same high school. I lived in the same place my whole life, but he was drafted to the city's junior hockey team, and he and his mom moved to just outside Halifax. I was one of the smart kids, especially with math. My parents wanted me to concentrate on my grades instead of having a part-time job, but they were okay with me tutoring. Josh was already some kind of hockey prodigy, but he was struggling to keep up in class. It just happened that I became his tutor."

We had nothing in common—I wasn't athletic, and he wasn't a keen student. But as we spent time together, we found common ground. He loved *Star Wars*, I was a Tolkien fan, and we were willing to share each other's interests. For a long time he made me believe I had more to offer than my brains.

Oh well.

"Then we started dating, until he broke it off. That was hard. I really loved him. I refused to go to school and see him with Rhonda, or anyone else. I planned to homeschool myself to finish the year. My parents finally sent me to my grandmother's for the rest of senior year. I was moping around like my life had ended, and the school near Gram's place had a good AP program. They were distracted with some stuff going on with my older sister, so it worked out."

"And that was it?"

"He was drafted and went away to play hockey, and I

went to university. I hadn't seen him for five years till last night."

And what a way to run into him again.

Madeline watched me, using that analytical brain of hers. I wished she'd focus on something else. "I'm trying to picture the two of you together."

Not necessary, since we were so *not* together now.

"You're smart. Intense. He's pretty laid-back. I would have said he was not very bright, but…"

I frowned. People always thought Josh was dumb. He didn't do well on tests, and wasn't a great reader, but he wasn't stupid the way people assumed. There was more to him than hockey. He had other things he used his brain for. He loved *Star Wars*, and on that, he had *opinions.* Very well thought-out and endlessly argued opinions.

Plus, he was hockey smart. I had never been a big hockey fan and avoided the sport altogether after Josh and I broke up— Damn it, now he had me doing it. After *he* broke up with *me*, I avoided hockey. But before, when scouts were watching him and people wanted to talk about Josh and hockey all the damn time, they talked about his hockey intelligence. He understood the game on an intuitive level. I did not. Which was fine, because I was done with hockey.

"He's not just a dumb jock. Ask him about *Revenge of the Sith*. He'll give you a dissertation."

Madeline frowned, and now I knew she didn't use Botox. Just looked naturally perfect. "What's that?"

"*Star Wars* movie. Josh had big opinions on that."

She fought back a smile. "Hmmm."

Thanks to Josh, I loved *Star Wars* too. For a while, after he'd cut me off, I'd had to set aside my love of the Force because it reminded me too much of him. But time passed, the hurt faded, and I'd reclaimed *Star Wars*. I'd even stopped my stupid tendency to rehearse conversations with him about some of the new shows. In my head, obviously, since he was gone, but he'd been my *Star Wars* and *Lord of the Rings* buddy. Not relevant here, obviously.

"Two years," she said. "Was it just tutoring and sex?"

The coffee flew out of my mouth and over the counter as I choked. "Gghh." I tried to speak but coughed instead.

Madeline laughed and grabbed a cloth to wipe up what I'd spewed out. "No sexy times?"

I grinned at her. "Two horny high school kids? Oh, we made time for that."

"Did you make him study? Or just do the work for him so he'd pass?"

I almost swallowed more coffee. "I did *not* do his work for him! He needed to know this stuff." I'd warned him that hockey wasn't a sure thing. He could get injured. He might not make it. And shockingly, he'd been willing to put in the work.

"Maybe he needed that. Someone who didn't let him get by on his athletic skills."

I bit my lip, letting my brain return to a time I'd mostly blocked out. "Maybe that was it. Most people only talked hockey to him. I knew some, but my family had never been big hockey fans."

"I'm sure, if he was talented—and he must have been to be where he is now—a break from that was good for him."

"Well, Dr. Madeline, I think you've now figured out why we lasted as long as we did. But we had different paths to follow. We'd have broken up eventually. Though it would have been nice to have some say in that."

"You absolutely should have had a say in that decision. If Josh hadn't cared about you or didn't want the relationship to continue because *he* didn't want to, then he has the right to initiate that discussion and make his own decision. But to decide for you? I'd be furious."

She would. She was angry on my behalf, five years later.

I should have pushed, five years ago, and asked questions. I'd been so insecure that Josh breaking up with me had seemed inevitable. I hadn't asked why or demanded answers. I thought I knew them—I wasn't pretty enough, fun enough, any kind of enough except smart.

He hadn't needed smart to get drafted.

Had I learned? Gotten any better? Did I think I was enough now?

CHAPTER 5
SO, WHAT'S MY PLAY?

JOSH

"HEY, MOM." My mother and I talked a few times a week, and for this phone call I had something to ask.

"Josh, how are you? How is training camp going? Did management make the final cuts?"

I sat on a stool at the breakfast bar. "I'm doing okay. We're playing preseason games, and the last cuts are coming. I'm glad that's not up to me. But the team looks good. We should go all the way this year."

"I'm sure you will, hun. We're all rooting for you. I wish you could have been home for longer this summer. I miss you."

I rubbed the back of my neck. Yeah, Mom always wanted me at home, but it wasn't the same now. A lot of people had moved away, the ones I knew, and the rest were interested in Ducky, the hockey player, not Josh, the person I was when I wasn't playing hockey. They wanted to talk about hockey all the frickin' time and expected me to pay for everything. I didn't mind, but it would be nice if maybe someone just had me over for beer and talking about *Star Wars* or something like that.

This summer, we all, the whole team, had promised to work hard and be in great shape so that this season we could go all the way. Losing in overtime at home in the finals had been super shitty. I knew Mitchy, our backup goalie, thought it was his fault for letting in that goal. He was in net because of an accident with Petey, our starter, and JJ blamed himself for running Petey down. Petey thought he'd have stopped the shot if he'd been playing, and Cooper and Crash missed a pass that led to the goal—hell, if I'd scored when we'd been down in Minnesota's end, we wouldn't have needed Mitchy to stop anything. Lots of blame to go around.

"Josh?"

"Uh, sorry, Mom. Got distracted there."

"I asked how things were going with your new roommate." Her tone was disapproving. She didn't think I needed a roommate; I was an adult and it was my condo. But I liked having people around so I didn't feel all alone. Plus, with someone in my spare bedroom, I put Mom up in a hotel when she visited a few times a season. She'd been a single mom, and I appreciated how hard she'd worked to raise me. I just needed some space.

"Fitch is great so far. He's kinda quiet, but he's nice. He's going through a divorce so sometimes he gets a little down, but I help cheer him up."

I didn't like people being sad. I was a goof, but if it helped someone feel better, that was all good, right?

"Does he bring home women?"

My face heated up. I hooked up more than Fitchy, at least so far, but I did not want to talk about that with my mother. She had to know I wasn't sweet and innocent. I was twenty-four, and I'd been playing in the NHL for years now. Distraction was in order. "So, guess who I ran into?"

She sighed. I wasn't subtle. "How would I know who you ran into?"

"Well, you know her. Katie."

She didn't say anything.

"You know, Katie. Katie Baker. My old tutor?" And my old girlfriend, but something told me not to mention that to Mom.

"How did she manage to track you down?"

I stared at the fridge in front of me. Why would she think Katie found me? Katie did *not* like me, not now. She had to know I played in Toronto, but I hadn't heard anything from her after she moved here. She could have found someone to tell her how to get a hold of me if she'd wanted. Most everyone knew where the teams hung out.

"She didn't 'track me down.' She wasn't even happy to see me. It was an accidental thing."

"I doubt that."

I was never going to tell my mom that I went home with a woman I picked up in a bar and found Katie that way. It would prove Katie hadn't planned it, but I didn't need another lecture from my mother on using protection and being careful.

Mom had never spoken like this before about Katie. Like Katie was out for what she could get. Maybe Katie was right, that Mom didn't like her. "Why would you even think she'd want to see me after the way I broke up with her?"

Could rolling eyes make a sound? "Joshua, don't be naïve. You're successful and wealthy. The Bakers would love to get their hands on you."

What the fuck?

"I don't think so. She was super pis— I mean, she was not happy to see me."

Mom sniffed. "Well, I hope you don't run into her again."

No need to tell her I was planning how to do just that. "Did you know she was in Toronto?"

"Why are you asking me?"

I shrugged, but she couldn't see that. "Just, someone from back home, you know. Figured people would talk, mention that she was here."

"I don't listen to gossip, Joshua."

That was a flat-out lie. Usually half of our phone call was her telling me about people she knew and what was going on with these strangers. "Why don't you like Katie?" Cause yeah, she didn't. Katie was right.

"I don't think she was good for you. She took advantage of you, when she was tutoring you in high school. You needed to keep your focus on hockey back then, to make sure you made it."

Was that what she really thought had happened? "I wouldn't have made it through math without her." Katie was a math genius.

"She was an adequate tutor, but it should have stopped there."

I was the one who'd pushed for us to be more than tutor and dumb jock, but I didn't say that. If I didn't get Katie to agree to see me, Mom would be happier if I just let it go.

"Have you been dating?"

I bit my lip. Not going to mention Katie's roommate, the hot redhead. Mar...Mag...*Madeline*. Mom would want to know every little detail about any woman I mentioned. Me not knowing her last name would shock her and start that speech I just wasn't interested in. "No one special."

"That's good. You have lots of time. You'll know when you meet the right girl. When that happens, she'll be the one you want me to meet."

I bit my lip harder. "Sure, Mom. Well, I need to get to practice. Just wanted to check in."

"You're so sweet, Josh. Take care. I'll have to check your schedule, see when I can come for a visit."

"Can't wait." Did I sound sincere enough? I must have, because she said goodbye and let me go.

I set the phone down and dropped my head in my hands. Katie was right. Mom didn't like her. Which meant that Mom's test for the right girl was all wrong. I knew the right girl, and Mom definitely didn't want to meet her.

Now I just had to figure out how to get my girl to let me see her again.

* * *

COACH HAD LISTED the surviving roster at the practice arena. Only a couple of the guys who'd gone out with me last night were still around. Practice was more focused, since there were fewer of us on the ice, and the coaches worked us a little harder.

Training camp was always tough, but this year we'd all come back in good shape and ready for the season. *Our* year, this year. Fitch was fitting in well, and everyone seemed ready to give it their all.

After practice most of the team hung around for the free food—nutritionally balanced and full of good shit for us. Some of the married guys left to spend time with their families which was unfortunate for me. They might be the best ones to answer my questions. But I would make do with the guys who'd stayed and had partners or girlfriends.

Normally I hung out with the single guys who were my age, but I needed wisdom here and that meant someone who was older and had found their woman. Found and kept her.

Cooper raised an eyebrow as I sat at the table with him

and Mitch and Barnes. "Sure this is where you want to sit, Ducky?"

I nodded, picking up the bottle of ketchup. The pasta smelled great, and some ketchup would help the plain chicken breast go down.

Cooper shuddered. "You're a heathen."

I grinned at Cooper. "Yeah, I like ketchup."

Mitch frowned. "Ketchup is full of sugar."

"Exactly!"

"Is that why you honored us with your presence today? To give us all nightmares about your eating habits?"

I shook my head, my mouth full of pasta. I held up a finger and swallowed. "No, I need some advice."

"What kind of advice?" Barnes asked.

"Romantic advice." I shoved some more pasta in my mouth while they exchanged looks.

"You met someone?" Mitch asked.

I shrugged and moved my head sort of up and down and sideways. "It's someone I knew back in high school, but I just found out she's in Toronto now."

"Did you call her?"

"I don't have her number, but I know where she lives." I was still blocked, according to my searching last night.

"Stalking her?"

I felt heat moving up my neck into my cheeks. "I ran into her."

"At a bar?"

"Not exactly."

Then Fitch slid into a chair beside me. "Oh, let me tell."

I sighed and took a bite of chicken. Might as well let him.

"He hooked up with a redhead, went home with her, and found out his ex is the hookup's roommate."

Everyone stopped to look at me. "So, threesome?" Barnes asked.

Fitch shook his head. "No. Apparently there's a roommate code when it comes to exes. Instead of a threesome, the two of them ganged up on Ducky."

Yeah, it didn't sound good, and I was going to get chirped so bad. But if they could help me with Katie, I'd take it.

"Wait." Cooper held up a hand. "This is the ex you're interested in? Because that makes a big difference."

Good to know. "Why?"

"Because she already knows you. And for some reason, it didn't work. Not sure if you can change things. Why did you break up?"

Fitch answered for me. "The key isn't why, but how. He ended a two-year relationship by text."

The whole table groaned. Yeah, I got it. I wouldn't do it again, assuming I could get Katie back. If I got back with Katie, I wasn't going to let her get away.

"Why did you break up with her?"

I waved at Fitch to continue, since he was enjoying it so much. Might as well finish my meal.

"It was the end of high school and he was heading to the draft. She was getting scholarship offers for universities."

"You wanted to sample all the puck bunnies."

"No!" I blurted out. "Why does everyone keep saying that?"

"It's kind of obvious."

"Well, it wasn't to me. My mom and her parents thought she'd give up on school to follow me. I didn't know how long I would play or if I'd make it, so that would have been a bad thing to do. She's really smart. She should go to the best school for her."

"Her parents didn't like you, huh?" Cooper smirked.

"Wait, why wouldn't they?"

Barnes pointed a finger at me. "I don't know, but they wanted you to break up."

"Your mom too, eh?" Mitch added.

I shrugged. Mom had made it clear this morning that she really didn't like Katie. I guess her parents didn't like me either. There was a lot I'd missed back then.

The parents not being on board made this more difficult. But I wasn't giving up. I was here with the Blaze, and I was succeeding. I'd worked hard to make it in hockey, and I'd work hard to get Katie back too.

"So, what's my play?" These guys had their women. Time for them to share the advice.

Barnes frowned. "This isn't going to be easy. Not like you can send her flowers, ask her out for dinner."

Not when I didn't have her number.

Cooper narrowed his eyes as he looked at me. "What does she do?"

Had she said anything last night? "I don't know. She was going to major in math when she went to university, and I heard she was going to school here. So something like that?"

"Then you're not going to run into her through work."

"No way."

Cooper nodded slowly. "I think, first, you're going to have to get her to be your friend."

"My friend?"

"You did more than just fuck around back then, right?"

"She was my tutor, but we had a lot of fun together." I held up my hand. "Not just like that. She's cool. I liked being with her."

"Then that's your play. Get her to agree to be your friend. No way will she go out with you after a text breakup. Get to be friends. And if you're lucky, maybe then you can try for more."

I considered that. Hanging out with Katie, even as friends and nothing more, would still be great. But if she started dating someone, that would be hard.

Wait, was she dating someone? How could I be friends with her if she was with someone else?

I couldn't ask my mom, or her parents, so I'd have to be her friend, find out what was going on, and prove to her that I was the right guy for her. The only guy, for the rest of our lives.

Yeah, that was going to take some work.

CHAPTER 6

EVERYONE WOULD WANT TO BE HIS FRIEND

KATIE

THE AIR FELT COOLER as October grew close, and I was down for it. The city absorbed heat in a way I wasn't used to—walls of high rises, bumper-to-bumper traffic, and no breeze. I was looking forward to winter when sweating wouldn't be a problem anymore. I loved the life of the city, but the heat made going out less appealing.

I walked home from class rather than taking the subway. Living this close to the university was good for my pocketbook, and my fitness. I was careful with my money. Mom and Dad were covering my additional costs, and I would hate to ask them for more. I'd never had a job other than tutoring, so I didn't have an easy way to increase my income. Plus, being a TA while working on my master's was going to be demanding as it was.

Thanks to the afternoon sun, my shirt was sticking to my back as I approached my new building. I shifted my bag on one shoulder so I could grab my keys. How did the damned things always fall to the bottom? I'd just managed to hook the key ring on a finger when I heard my name.

"Katie!"

The keys fell as I jerked. *What the...Josh?*

I turned around and there he was, weaving through people in the crosswalk as he made his way across the street toward me. I blinked, but no, he was still there. *What the hell?*

"Were you meeting Madeline?"

After that awkward night and the conversation in the kitchen the next day, I'd assumed she wasn't interested in Josh anymore, but maybe she'd changed her mind. She might not have his number, but she knew the bar where the players hung out. Josh was out of luck though. Madeline worked long hours, and I rarely saw her before eight on weeknights.

Josh pulled his brows down into a frown. "No. Why would I be meeting her?"

"Because..." Never mind. Wasn't going to ask Josh about his hookups. I didn't want to think about them. Or anything Josh-related. I waved a hand. "Okay, then why are you here?" Was there someone else in the building he was hooking up with? Had I accidentally found myself in hockey hookup central? Would I be running into Josh constantly as he visited the puck bunnies?

Damn, I knew it. There was always something when a rental was too good to be true.

"I came to see you," he said, as if that was a thing.

"Why?" We damned well didn't have any plans together. I hadn't thought I'd see him again. Except, for example, on the bus that had just passed by behind him with his face on it. Damned hockey players.

He held up a bag with the name of a pizzeria on it. "Thought you might want this."

"Pizza?"

His big grin crossed his face. "Nope. Donairs."

On cue, my stomach rumbled. "Donairs? Real donairs?"

He nodded. "Some people from Nova Scotia run this place. It's the real thing."

How had I not known about this? I was new to the city, but *priorities*! I eyed the bag in his hand, noting the name for future reference. "And you brought me some?"

He bit his lip. "I was hoping we could share them? I wanted to talk to you."

What did he think we had to talk about? But...donairs. The smell was wafting into my nose, and god, I'd missed them.

But did I miss them enough to ask him up to talk? I wasn't afraid of him. He might have hurt my heart, badly, but he wasn't a bad guy. I'd tried to hate him, but it was difficult. He was like a golden retriever, all happy and friendly, and just didn't understand why I was upset he'd peed on my bed.

That analogy was getting weird fast, so I nodded and opened the door. He followed me, and in the elevator the smell of the donairs filled the small space. I almost grabbed the bag from him to start scarfing down some of that back-home goodness but was proud of my restraint. We reached the eighteenth floor and the doors opened. He followed me to our condo and waited while I opened the door.

Once inside, I kicked off my shoes and headed to the kitchen. This time, Josh wasn't mouth-locked with my room-mate and knocking into the wall. Instead, he toed off his own shoes and followed me to the island separating the kitchen from the living room.

I dropped my school tote on the island and pulled out some plates. "What do you want to drink?"

He unwrapped the food bag and reached inside. "Oh, whatever. Water's good."

I shrugged and pulled out a beer for myself. Not everyday

I got to eat a donair. Josh set two wrapped sandwiches on my plate, and two on his.

I passed him a water bottle. "So how did you find this donair place?"

"I looked it up."

Well, duh for me not doing the same. Hadn't even occurred to me. I'd seen gyros and shawarma, but though they were close, they weren't the real thing. Then I moaned as I took my first bite. It was sooo good.

I looked up, wiping sauce from my chin, to find Josh staring at me. I rubbed my chin again. "Sorry, I should be more careful."

He cleared his throat. "Nah, it's fine. I've missed them too."

There was silence while we enjoyed the first of our sandwiches. I took a long swallow of beer and sighed. There wasn't much better than a donair and a Keith's.

I pulled back the paper on the second one. "Have you been back home often? To enjoy these?"

He licked sauce off his thumb. "I was back for a week this summer. You?"

"I ended up going to Dalhousie, so I lived at home till my last year. Just moved to Toronto in time for this semester."

His head tilted. "You stayed—and you're still in school?"

I shifted, sitting a little taller. "Doing my master's now."

That big grin was back. "That's great, Katie. How long will that take you?"

"I'm working as a TA, so I'm going to spread it out over two years. This is my first year."

"The University of Toronto is the top school in Canada, right?"

I nodded. I was proud that I'd been accepted at U of T. I'd done well at Dalhousie, back in Halifax, but this was a more competitive degree. Plus, the distance from family was good.

They loved me, but sometimes the expectations were smothering. "How did you know U of T was the best school?"

"I remembered you talking about it. You didn't get in before? I was sure you would."

I set down my sandwich, appetite gone. "I did. But there was a lot going on back then. It wasn't a good time to leave."

He stared at me. His mouth dropped open and I knew he was going to ask. Not something I wanted to discuss.

"So, why are you here, Josh?"

His mouth closed and his shoulders lifted on a long sigh. He picked up the wrappers from his donairs and smoothed them out before folding them again. I waited.

When there were no more papers left to deal with, he rubbed the back of his neck and finally gave me a sheepish smile. "I came to apologize some more."

"You don't have to."

"Yeah, I do. I called my mom. And when I mentioned you, she wasn't very nice."

As I would have predicted. Still, the donairs didn't sit as well in my stomach.

"She didn't talk like that before, when we were going out, but you were right. She doesn't like you. So, I'm sorry I didn't know. And that I did something stupid, breaking up with you like that."

It had been more than five years, and I'd moved past that whole agonizing time. But there was something warming in my chest after that apology. Josh believed me.

He was super close to his mother—his father had died when he was young, and he didn't have siblings. It was to her credit that she'd done a pretty good job raising Josh on her own, but she did work the guilt and "poor lonely me" thing a lot. Josh was too nice to see anything but love when his mom overstepped, but I'd seen her through clearer eyes.

I wasn't sure she'd like anyone Josh dated. Not unless it

was someone quiet, meek and willing to settle near Mrs. Middleton. If someone asked her, she'd say she would be happy to see Josh settle down with a nice girl, but she wouldn't want to be usurped or replaced. She hadn't liked me because she thought I was a threat back then. I wasn't biddable, and I didn't plan to stay. She would not be happy to know Josh was here with me, even though we were no longer dating. Which the petty side of me liked.

"Thank you," I said. "I appreciate that you checked it out and let me know you believe me."

He nodded. Looked down. "And your parents don't like me?"

Again, golden retriever puppy, shocked that someone had slapped his nose. "What are you talking about?" My parents had always been kind to Josh. They hadn't been thrilled that I had a boyfriend—what they called *a distraction*—but they had nothing against him personally.

"It wasn't just my mom who told me it would be better for you if we broke up." He held up his hand. "Sorry, I meant if I broke up with you."

"What the— Are you saying my parents were in on this? They talked to you?" My voice got loud and high.

His eyes skittered around the kitchen. "Um, they didn't tell you?"

I was feeling violent again, but this time I didn't want to throw anything at Josh. I had different targets in mind. "No. They just told me I could go stay with Grandma and finish up at a different school." I'd refused to go to the same school as Josh. I wasn't going to expose myself to Rhonda and her gibes. Seeing Josh when I wasn't with him? I couldn't face it. "They talked to you?"

He huffed out a sigh that almost moved the mangled donair wrapping papers. "Yeah. They talked to me, said you were making a very important decision, and they were afraid you'd choose based on me instead of what was best for you. I talked to my mom, and she agreed." He swallowed. "When I told them I'd do it, for your sake, they said they'd explain it to you. So I sent you that text."

I dropped my head in my hands. It was all making sense now. "No, they didn't talk to me."

I'd been hurt. Badly hurt. Devastatingly hurt, the way it is when you're a teenager and everything is new and your hormones are going at warp speed. And my parents had let me live with that, feel that horrible rejection and inadequacy, because of their own agenda.

"I'm sorry, Katie." Josh's voice was soft. "I would have explained, if I'd known they hadn't. But I don't get why they didn't talk to you."

I blew out a breath and lifted my head. "Did you hear about Nora?"

He frowned. "Your sister? Did something happen to her?"

"She got pregnant."

"When? She was in med school, right?"

I nodded. "Yeah. Mom and Dad were big on education. They had to drop out of school when they got pregnant, and they wanted to be sure we could finish our own degrees. Nora was supposed to be a doctor, so getting pregnant was a big bump in that road."

Josh watched me, waiting for me to continue. He'd always been a good listener.

"Anyway, it was right around the time that you—" I flapped a hand his way. "She announced she was pregnant and was dropping out of school to have the baby. Mom and Dad were freaking out. They were really upset about it, and that Arlo wasn't the one dropping out of school."

Josh cocked his head. "Arlo is the father? And did they think that would happen to us? That you'd get pregnant and drop out? We were careful." He bit his lip. "Mostly."

"I know. But Nora was too."

"Huh." Josh's brow was creased. "So, they lied to me?"

I shrugged. "Kind of? I mean, they'd already been talking to me about how what school I picked was a big decision, and I shouldn't let other factors influence me."

"Like me."

"Like you. And then when Nora got pregnant? That gave them something else to worry about. With Nora pregnant, I was the daughter left to make the family dreams come true."

His shoulders drooped. "I'm sorry. I shouldn't have texted you like that. I should have talked to you."

But he wasn't the only one. I'd been so insecure in how I looked and my lack of social popularity that I hadn't asked him any questions. "I'm sorry too, Josh. I should have asked you why you were doing it. I was just too hurt. And then when I heard you were with Rhonda…" That had convinced me my low self-esteem was correct.

"Mom said it would make sure you didn't choose a school for me."

"It worked."

"Fuck."

Exactly. And I was going to have a long chat with my parents. I'd been so pissed that Josh had taken away my autonomy, but they'd done the same thing. They were the new targets of my anger. Apparently I wasn't totally over what had happened back then.

"So, are they happy now?" he asked. "You got your degree, you're getting your master's—they must be proud of you, huh?"

If only it was that simple. They weren't happy that I moved to Toronto. They wanted me to get my degree but also stay home where they could feel part of my success. I needed some distance to feel free.

I had to process all this new information. And for that I

needed alone time. I stood. "Sure. Well, thanks for the donairs and the apology."

Josh stayed seated, eyes on the countertop, shoulders tensing. He wanted something else.

"So, Katie, I was hoping…" He rubbed his hand over the back of his neck, looking up at me through his ridiculous eyelashes.

I crossed my arms. "What?" If he thought we could pick up from where we'd been before he smashed my heart, he was *sooo* wrong. I understood he'd been manipulated, but there were years of resentment to work through. And I wasn't in Toronto to find a boyfriend. I had my own dreams, and Nora's life was still an object lesson.

"That maybe we could be friends?"

My jaw dropped. "You want to be friends?" Josh Middleton, star of the Toronto Blaze hockey team, was not suffering from any lack of people wanting to spend time with him. He wasn't lonely, so why?

He nodded. "Yeah, I'd like that. We could be friends, right? We used to like to watch movies and stuff. We had fun, even without sex."

"Why would you want me for your friend?" I'd seen the people wearing jerseys and T-shirts for the team on campus, and a lot of them had *Middleton* across the back. Not as many as Cooper, but still. He was a professional athlete. Everyone would want to be his friend.

"I like you."

There was no reason for that to make me waver, for my defenses to soften. He liked me? How was that possible? It had been five years. He didn't know me. "I'm not the same person I was five years ago. You might not like the me I am now."

But that felt wrong even as I said it. Back in high school, we shouldn't have fit. Yet our differences somehow balanced out and we worked. Those basic character traits, they couldn't have changed that much, could they?

Josh frowned. "Well, some things have changed, obviously. Like, I'm in the NHL now and not living with my mom. And you're not with your family, and you're doing your math thing. But you're still you." His frown cleared as he settled that.

"I might be a total bitch now."

He grinned. "You were a bitch sometimes back then."

"I was not!"

He nodded. "When you talked about Rhonda—" He stopped and shook his head. "I'm really sorry. That was a shitty thing to do. I was so mixed up. I felt miserable, but I thought our parents were smart, you know? And Rhonda, she was a *real* bitch. She kept trying to say bad stuff about you, so we left that Valentine's dance early and I took her home. Then I went driving for a while, just trying to clear my head."

That memory still stung. Especially when Rhonda had hinted, oh so snidely, that she and Josh had left early and gone to her home.

Josh was staring now at the empty donair bag. "I think...I think I kinda knew I'd messed up, and that it had been the wrong thing to do. But I knew you wouldn't forgive me anyway."

I swallowed a noise in my throat. That anger and hurt back then had been the only thing that got me through.

Josh shook his head and looked back at me. "I'd really like it if you'd give me a chance to be your friend." He gestured at the wrappers. "We can do things like this, stuff from home. And..."

"And?"

His grin was back. I shouldn't have given him that inch.

"Maybe watch some *Star Wars* stuff? Have you kept up with that?"

I crossed my arms. "What if I have?"

"And that new *Lord of the Rings* series. I bet you've watched it at least twice."

Three times, actually. "Maybe. Did you watch it?"

"Yeah. We have time to kill when we're traveling. What do you think about that Sauron guy?"

I frowned. "That's not what's in the books."

"No?"

"I know you didn't read them, but in the *Silmarillion...*"

An hour later, Josh left. After he'd suckered me into expounding on my favorite TED Talk, we'd discussed TV shows. And then what it had been like for him in Nashville before he was traded to Toronto. And I finally made him leave because I had homework. I'd totally forgotten about the upcoming confrontation with my parents and just gone with the flow. He'd always been good at that—untangling my worries by just being him.

I still had to work out what I was going to do about my parents, but I wasn't as tense now. My head was clearer. That was thanks to him.

I guessed we were friends now. Were we? He'd kind of Joshed me into it, and I'd given him my phone number.

But without him distracting me, was that what I wanted?

CHAPTER 7
YOU HAVE MUCH TO LEARN, PADAWAN

JOSH

I WAS in a great mood when I got back to my condo. Katie was talking to me, the donairs had been spectacular, and Fitch was making a late dinner. Two donairs didn't fuel a hockey player, so this was excellent.

"Hey, you got extra?"

He rolled his eyes as he turned down the heat. "Of course I have extra. But didn't you say you were picking something up when you were out?"

I opened the cupboard to get out the plates. "Yeah, but it was just a couple of donairs. I'm still hungry."

"What are—never mind. Let's eat."

He plated the stir-fry he'd put together. He was an awesome cook. When Cooper had asked if I wanted another roommate after Bongo got his own place, I'd said yes immediately. I liked people, got along with almost everyone, and didn't like being alone. Once I found out how well Fitchy cooked, I made a deal where I'd get the groceries and clean up if he'd prepare the meals. Even though he was ten years older than me, we were working out great as roommates.

We sat down at the breakfast bar with our food.

"You're in a good mood," he commented. "Did your plan work with Katie?"

"I think so." I took a bite, slightly burning my tongue, but it was worth it. "This is fantastic."

He smiled. He liked to hear when he'd done well. I thought life with his ex hadn't been smooth even before they moved to Edmonton, when apparently things blew up big-time. He didn't really talk about it, but word got around. I didn't know what the problem had been with his wife, but if letting him know he was a good cook helped him, I was happy to do it.

"Thanks. Are you two friends now?"

I swallowed. "Pretty sure. She didn't say it, but she didn't kick me out, even when I mentioned what went down in high school. And I asked her about a TV show I knew she'd watched, and she talked about it, a lot."

"Did you watch it?"

I scooped up more food. "Yeah. It was one of the things we did. Even after we broke up, I kept watching the things we used to watch together. People always said we were different, but we had fun even before we started having sex."

Fitch paused. "Were you… Maybe this is too personal, but were you her first?"

I nodded. "She was mine too." I stopped eating. "It wasn't good, what our parents did. We could have been something really special."

His smile twisted. "Yeah, but it might have gone totally off the rails anyway."

"You're talking about yourself?"

"I am, but it applies to a lot of people."

He'd never mentioned his wife before. Did this mean he wanted to talk? "You're from Sweden, right?"

"I was born there. My family moved to California when I was ten."

"Wow. I didn't know that. That's why your English is so good?"

"Most Swedes learn English."

I scraped the last of the food from my plate. "I don't speak any other languages."

"Most North Americans don't."

That sounded like something that should be fixed. But right now, I wanted to know more about Fitch. "So, was your ex from Sweden too?"

"No, I met her in California. USC."

So he'd gone the college route. I wasn't surprised. "You played in school after you were drafted? Were you college sweethearts?"

He pushed his plate away. "I guess you could say that. We met my junior year." He stopped, and I thought that was it. Then he continued. "I'd been drafted by LA, so we knew I was staying there. I played well, and she enjoyed being a WAG. The women were all pretty tight. But I didn't want to just play hockey, I wanted the Cup."

I nodded. I felt the same. Didn't every hockey player?

"I was in my thirties, a free agent, and LA didn't look like management was trying that hard to win. My agent got an offer from Edmonton, and they're a competitive team. Lost to Minnesota just before Minnesota—well, you know."

Yeah, we knew. They won the Cup by beating us.

"She said she'd give Edmonton a try. Maybe she thought she did, but anything different from LA was a problem. The house, the weather, the other WAGs. We started fighting, about stupid things."

That would suck.

"She visited LA while I was on a road trip. And then, the next road trip, she went back and stayed there."

"Sorry about that."

He shrugged. "Our families were supportive, and I thought we were strong, but apparently not. If Katie's family and yours are opposed, plus with the stress this life puts on partners…well, maybe that's too much opposition."

I got what he was saying, but I wasn't giving up on Katie. Time to move on.

"So did you get a degree? I went from juniors to the AHL to the NHL. No college."

He stood to pick up our plates. "Yes. Just because I was drafted didn't mean I'd play."

People had told me to have a backup plan in case hockey didn't work out, but I'd never listened to them. I'd been sure I'd play, and here I was.

I stood—I was supposed to clean up when he cooked. "Hey, that's my job." I grabbed the rest of the dishes and took them over, hip checking him away from the sink.

"I don't have anything else to do right now."

I shook my head, blocking him from the sink. "You can go play a game or watch TV or something. We've got, like, fifty million channels and streaming sites." I started running the water in the sink, and the sneaky fucker put some dishes in the dishwasher. "Hey!"

He backed off once his hands were empty. "Okay, I'll leave you to it. Anything good out to watch lately?"

Huh. We hadn't spent that much time together in the evening. I was usually out somewhere, or he was. There'd been a bunch of guys coming back for the preseason I'd met up with, and I'd been around for training camp, checking on the newbies and helping out where I could. "What do you like? Sci-fi, fantasy, horror, action, chick flicks…"

He leaned against the island, hopefully not checking on

whether I did a proper job on the dishes. I preferred a room-mate who wasn't a mess, but I didn't want a clean freak who'd be on my case all the time.

"Action. Thrillers and suspense."

"Okay, maybe there's a new James Bond or *Mission Impossible?*"

"I'm going to take a guess here and say that's not what you watch."

I put the frying pan in the drying rack and pulled the sink plug. "No, I'm big into *Star Wars,* loved the Dune movies, stuff like that."

"So, you like baby Yoda?"

I stared at him. "You mean Grogu?"

He stared back. "Is that baby Yoda?"

I wiped my hands and hung up the towel. "You have much to learn, Padawan."

"I don't need to follow your imaginary world."

I crossed my arms. "Because James Bond is so real?"

He grinned. "You got me. MI6 is not quite like the Bond movies."

I wasn't going out tonight and had nothing really to do except try to figure out my next move with Katie. "Tell you what, you find something you like and I'll watch it with you. And then you watch something I want."

He grinned. "Any limits on what I can pick?"

I rubbed my hand on my pants. "I don't like scary stuff. Call me a wimp if you want, but I don't like horror."

"I don't either. What about something just a little scary? Not a lot of blood, but some suspense."

I shrugged. "I'll try, but if I don't like it, I'm not going to keep watching."

"Same here."

"Beer?" I asked.

"Sure."

I grabbed two out of the fridge and followed him into the living room. I had a big couch with lots of lounging space, since I often had a bunch of hockey players here, and a couple of recliners. A huge TV and gaming system with killer sound.

I'd re-signed with the Blaze a couple of years ago, for five years and pretty good money. If I kept playing at this level, I could maybe pick what team I wanted to play with next. Right now, I was happy with the Blaze. And if Katie was here in Toronto for another year…

Fitch settled in a recliner and I spread out on the couch after I gave him his beer.

"So what are we watching? James Bond?"

He waggled his brows. "Have you seen Stieg Larsson's *Girl with the Dragon Tattoo?*"

I frowned at him. "Never heard of that."

"As a Swede, I have to correct that gap in your life."

"THAT WAS SICK, MAN." The movie had definitely been disturbing.

Fitch turned to me, his eyebrows drawn together. "Was it too much?"

"Right on the line."

"What are you going to inflict on me in return?"

"I have to think about it."

He smirked at me. "You've got time. We have a game tomorrow night."

Right. Even if we weren't playing in every preseason game, we needed to watch. See what these newbies were like and how our opponents were looking. Injuries happened, and any of the guys trying out might be playing by season's end. "Yeah. Any of these new guys in particular you think might make it?"

He shrugged. "You'd know. This has been your team for a couple of years now."

"Yeah, but you've played longer than me."

"Calling me old?"

I grinned. "If the gray hair fits."

He threw a pillow at me. Then we talked about the guys who were still battling for a spot. I thought Luke Walker showed a lot of promise on defense. He was Mitchy's old roommate.

Plus, the name was cool. I could call him Skywalker if he was playing with us.

Then it was time to go to bed. It had been a good day—mending bridges with Katie and getting to know my new teammate. Even if that movie was sick.

"Hey, Ducky, can I say something?"

"Sure."

"It relates to what we were talking about before—relationships."

He didn't look like it was a good thing, but I still wanted to hear it. He did have a lot more experience with women than me, since he'd been married.

"I'm glad you've talked to her, cleared the air. But…"

"But what?"

"But there was a reason you two split up."

"Yeah, our parents."

"They played a part, yes, but—"

"Spit it out!"

He sighed. "You're going to have to deal with your mother and her parents if you do get back together with her. They might still want to break you up."

I didn't like the sound of that, but the way my mother reacted? Maybe there would still be things with Katie's parents too. "I'm going to talk to Katie and not just listen to them."

"You didn't before."

"I know, but—" He lifted a hand and I waited. Better listen in case it was something I needed to know.

"The fact that you were convinced to break up with her, and she didn't fight it? I'm just saying, you might have had issues beyond your parents. And if that hasn't changed, the outcome won't either. Relationships aren't easy. Maybe this one isn't going to work out for you."

I didn't say anything, and he went into his room.

Fuck.

I'd thought if I convinced Katie to go out with me, and I didn't listen to my mom and her parents, we'd be good. But he had a point. Why did I believe them so easily? Was I just a dupe? Had I changed?

And what had happened with Katie?

CHAPTER 8

WAS THAT YOUR CHOICE?

KATIE

"I SWEAR—HE thinks I'm just here to get my Mrs." I stabbed my salad to punctuate my point. *"Do you think you can handle this project you've selected?* Like I'll faint away from brain strain."

Andrea picked up a mouthful of hers more delicately. "He's the oldest tenured prof. He'd be shocked to know that women are allowed to vote."

I sighed. "It was just so discouraging. I thought I was used to this—there aren't a lot of women in STEM courses, but there are more than there were."

"I was lucky—I've got one of the younger and female profs. I am grateful every time I hear some other TA talking about their advisor."

"Is it just me or is it worse now that we're grad students?"

"It's worse."

"Thanks." A tomato leapt off my plate and rolled onto the table.

"Take it easy on the defenseless produce."

I shook my head. "Sorry. There's been a lot going on these past few days."

Andrea set down her fork. "Is everything okay with Madeline?"

I stopped, fork in midair. "What? Oh, Madeline is great. I love staying there. I owe you for that."

"Yeah, I love that I'm living with Lisa now, but that place was a pretty sweet score. If it's not Madeline, and not Professor Grinch, what's up?"

I set down my fork and considered. I was dying to talk to someone. There was a lot of frustration and anger burbling inside, and I wanted to figure out my thoughts before I next spoke to my family. We were close, and I needed to express myself without hurting them. Or maybe I shouldn't worry about that. I couldn't talk to any of my friends from back home, because of the Josh factor, and it was a little awkward talking to Madeline because she and Josh had been about to hook up. I was still making friends here at U of T, so if I was going to unload on anyone, Andrea was it.

"I ran into my ex. And I learned some things that are messing with my head."

Andrea shoved her plate aside. "Tell me about this ex—a guy, right? You're straight?"

I nodded.

"What did he do? We can take steps, restraining orders or —you blocked his number and on social media, right?"

I held up a hand. "No, no, it's not like that." When her eyebrows lifted skeptically, I rushed to reassure her. "I swear, I'm not having those kinds of problems. He broke up with me in high school, and I took it hard. I did block him every- where, because I was really angry and hurt. But when I talked to him recently, I learned that my parents manipulated him to do that, and now I'm hurt and angry with them too."

Andrea crossed her arms and leaned on the table toward me. "Are you sure your parents are at fault here?"

"Yeah, after talking to him it made a lot of sense. They were worried he'd distract me from school, as if my boyfriend was the only thing that mattered to me. I've got all this anger inside, and I'm trying to get a hold on it before I talk to them."

"Maybe if they did something shitty, you should be angry at them."

"But we're really close. My family is big on education, and I appreciate that."

"They support you being here."

"With money and encouragement, yes. They're paying for everything my TA money doesn't cover."

"Helicopter parents?"

"Not really. See, when they were going to university, they got pregnant with my sister Nora. Their families freaked out, didn't want them keeping the baby, but they dropped out and raised her and me. They worked long hours to make sure we had an education fund, could take extra classes if we wanted. They didn't hover, and didn't micromanage what we did, but gave us a really good support system."

"So what's the but? Since you're pissed now."

"Nora and I didn't get jobs while we were in high school, just did some tutoring, so we could focus on school. I started to tutor this one guy."

"The ex?"

"Exactly. And that led to dating and falling in love."

"The parents didn't approve?"

"His mom didn't, but she was a single mom and kind of jealous of anyone. But she didn't do anything beyond making comments when Josh wasn't around. I thought my parents were okay—they said as long as I kept up my grades, that was fine."

"Obviously it wasn't."

"My senior year, Nora, who was in pre-med, got pregnant and dropped out."

Andrea's eyebrows rose. "I'm guessing they weren't very happy about history repeating itself."

"They were really upset. I've never seen them like that before." I stared over Andrea's shoulder, not really aware of the rest of the sandwich shop behind her. "I'm not sure why, but it wasn't Arlo who insisted she stay home while he finished his degree. Nora said that was what she wanted."

"This is when your parents started manipulating your future?"

I focused back on her. "Exactly. They convinced my ex that it would be better if we split up. I was getting acceptances from universities, and they thought I'd give up school to follow him or try to pick a school near him. So he sent me a text that it was better for me if we broke up."

"A *text?*"

"Dick move. I know. But when I ran into him again, he said if he talked to me in person, he might not have been able to go through with it. And that my parents told him they were going to explain it to me, but they didn't."

Andrea held up her palm. "Why couldn't he have followed you instead? Where did he want to go to school?"

I paused. Was I sure about sharing this? "He wasn't going to school. He played hockey, and he was good. Everyone said he'd be drafted. Obviously, he didn't know where."

Andrea blinked for a minute. "Oh. You knew all that, right?" I nodded. "So what had you planned to do?"

"We hadn't talked about it. But Josh knew the schools I applied to, and he didn't try to sell me on places that had hockey teams. He wanted me to accept the best school I could go to. We kind of ignored what would happen after graduation."

"You didn't think about it at all?"

"Of course I did. I went through all the options in my head, but we hadn't talked about it together. I think I'd have suggested we try long-distance, but it would have depended on where he was going. If he'd gone to the West Coast, and I couldn't see him for months at a time? That wasn't going to be feasible." And how could I expect him to do long-distance with me when there'd be so many women available to him?

"So, your mom and dad didn't think you'd make the right decision and went behind your back and manipulated your boyfriend to make things work out the way they wanted."

I shifted in my chair. It sounded so bad when Andrea said it out loud. Even though they'd done it out of love.

"I'd say you had perfectly realistic expectations about what was going to happen and didn't need your parents to step in and make a choice for you. Wait, you said you just found out. You met your ex, and he told you?"

I nodded.

"Your parents have kept it secret all this time?"

"I spent all these years thinking he was a total asshole. And that my judgment about guys was shit." That I wasn't good enough.

Her eyebrows rose. "Have they done anything else like that?"

I started to shake my head, but had I even considered that possibility? "I—I don't know. I would have said they'd never do something like that, but now I'm not sure."

"In my opinion, you have every reason to be pissed. What happened with your next boyfriend?"

"I never got really serious about anyone after Josh. But you know, after all those college applications, I ended up staying home and going to Dalhousie."

"Was that your choice?"

"I thought so. With Nora having the baby, and me

wanting to help out, it just seemed like staying home was the best option."

But had that been my idea? I was second-guessing everything now.

Andrea started to put her napkin and plate on the tray. "I should get moving. Another class of first-years to deal with. But here's a thought—see if your ex wants to go out with you again. Just to mess with your parents. He's here in Toronto now, right? Since you just ran into him?" She stood up, throwing her bag over her shoulder.

I nodded. "Yeah, but it's been a long time. Honestly, he's more out of my league now than he was then."

A strange expression crossed her face. "Uh, did he get drafted?"

"Yeah. Nashville. Which wasn't any place I'd applied to."

She stared at me. "And he's in Toronto now?"

"Uh huh."

"Is he, like, one of the players? On one of the fucking NHL teams?"

I eyed her warily. "Yeah."

She ticked off her fingers. "From Halifax. Drafted by Nashville. Playing in Toronto."

My cheeks heated up. If I'd been trying to keep his identity a secret, I'd blown that.

Andrea's eyes widened. "Is that your ex—Ducky?"

I turned to look at the TV, where a team photo of Josh was up on half the screen. The other half had words like injury and treatment.

My stomach dropped. What the hell had happened to him?

CHAPTER 9

TOTALLY WORTH IT

JOSH

I SAT on the trainer's table, trying to keep my knee still while Carlos worked on it. They'd done an X-ray and nothing was broken, but it still hurt like hell.

The rest of the team were finishing practice, getting showers, heading for the airport to play the last preseason game in Ottawa. I was supposed to play tonight. I had a bad feeling about being scratched.

Fuck.

It had been a normal two-on-two drill. But Crash had slid into me at a weird angle and I'd gone down badly on my knee. I'd been lucky so far, never had any kind of major injury, and I was freaking out.

I wasn't supposed to be done with hockey yet. I was only twenty-four, and I'd planned on at least ten more years. Lots of time to stash some cash and figure out what I would do next, since hockey was the only thing I'd ever been good at.

Carlos finally stepped away and came back with an ice

pack. He wrapped it around my knee and I hissed in a breath. It was cold.

"So?" I asked. I needed to know what I was dealing with.

"Class one MCL tear."

"Shit. That sounds bad. Can I play? How long am I out for?"

He rolled his eyes. "You're not playing tonight. You need to rest this for at least a week."

"A week?" I squeaked. That meant missing our opening game as well as tonight.

"Yes. If you do everything I tell you, I might let you back on skates in a week. But if you don't, it'll be two weeks or longer."

"Fuck."

He shrugged. "I know. But this isn't the postseason. If you're going to damage yourself, better now than during the playoffs."

If it had been the playoffs, I'd have told him to wrap it and let me go.

He glared at me like he could read my thoughts. "Remember, your game is based on speed. You need your knee working properly. Ice it regularly, wrap it, and I'll show you what exercises to do. Do not do more thinking it will get you back on the ice sooner. Use the crutches. If you do all that, you should be back quickly."

I collapsed back on the table. Missing tonight and our first game of the season was going to suck, but I'd do everything he told me to do. I couldn't gamble with anything connected to playing.

Carlos emailed me videos on the exercises I was supposed to do and wrapped my knee, sending me back to the locker room on the crutches. Most of the guys had gone, but Crash was waiting, dressed and looking like his dog had died.

Wait, he didn't have a dog, did he?

"Oh, fuck, Ducky. I didn't mean to. How bad is it?"

I was pissed, but it wasn't Crash's fault. I mean, the guy was already beating himself up over that pass from the last game of the finals.

"Gets me out of going to Ottawa." I gave him the best smile I could.

"Shit. And after that?"

"If I do everything they tell me, I'll be back in a week." He'd said on the ice, so that meant playing, right?

"Fuck."

"Not your fault. Just one of those things. You go win tonight's game for me, okay?"

It took a little more reassurance before he wandered away to get ready for tonight. And me? I struggled into a pair of sweats, grabbed my wallet and keys and phone before it hit me.

My car was a stick. And my knee wouldn't let me work the clutch. Assuming I could get into it on my own with these crutches. I'd never had to use them before, and they were stupidly awkward.

I could get an Uber or a cab home. But I didn't want to leave my baby in the lot here. It should be safe, but…I'd ask someone to drive me home. Problem solved.

Except the rest of the team had gone. The trainers and equipment guys were busy prepping for tonight's game. Who was left that I could trust?

An idea flashed. I could ask Katie. We were supposed to be friends now. She might be in class or something, but if she wasn't, I could book her a cab to get here, and she could drive me and the car back to my place. I could pay her, maybe. If she was a student, she'd need money, right? I knew she could drive a stick shift.

Brilliant! It would get me out of a jam, and I'd like to show her my car. She wasn't as expensive as Cooper's Ferrari, or

Royster's Lamborghini, but she was the car I'd always wanted, and I was proud of her.

I wedged myself against the wall and pulled out my phone.

You around?

I tried to get comfortable on the crutch, since I didn't know how long it would take to answer. *If* she would answer. I hadn't even messaged her since she gave me her number because I was so fucking afraid of saying the wrong thing. I'd messed up text messages in the past.

The ring of the phone, with the buzz along with it, almost made me drop the stupid thing. "Katie?"

"Are you okay? Are you in the hospital?"

What was she talking about? "No, I'm at the arena."

I heard the sigh over the line. "Thank god. You were on the news at the sub shop and—"

"They've already got that on the air?" Meant it would be all over the internet too.

"So you are hurt?"

"Yeah, but it's not a big deal." I was trusting Carlos that it wasn't.

"Not a big deal?" Her voice had gone up a little bit.

"Yeah, I'm on IR—injured reserve—for the next week. Which is shitty, but it's just a week. Nothing major."

A pause, and I heard the sounds of traffic. She was outside somewhere, so not in class. "I guess that's good."

"Oh yeah. Could have been something serious, but if I do what they tell me, I should be back on the ice next week." There was another pause. Right, I'd messaged her, and she wanted to know why. "That's actually why I called you. I'm at the arena and I wondered if you'd give me a ride home."

"I don't have a car in Toronto. Can't your teammates help?"

"They would, if they were here. We've got a game in

Ottawa tonight, so while the trainers were checking out my knee, the guys had to leave to get ready to fly out. I don't want to leave my car here, and not everyone can drive a stick, so I thought…" Hoped, really. "That maybe if I sent you a ride, you could come and drive me and her home? And I'd pay for you to get to your place too."

This was the longest pause yet. She probably had shit to do, classes or whatever. It was—I lifted the phone away from my ear and checked—one thirty in the afternoon. Not everyone had my weird hours.

"Her?"

"My car."

"Okay, I could do that."

I pumped my fist. *Yay!* Chance to see Katie again. "Give me your location and I'll send a ride."

"I'll wait for them at the corner of Galbraith and Beverley Street."

"Text me the address, okay? And I'm going to give the driver an answer to the question you should ask, to make sure this is legit."

"I've done rideshares before, you know."

"Don't care. I want to know you're safe."

I imagined her eyes rolling. I'd seen her do that enough times. "All right. See you in a bit."

I called up my rideshare app, waited till she sent me her location, and then booked a ride. I ordered an Uber Lux because I could afford it and she deserved it. Then I told security so they'd let the car into the player lot. I also sent a quick message to Mom to let her know I was okay—if the media was on this, she'd worry when she heard. I'd barely had time to crutch my way over to the player lot before the Mercedes rolled up and Katie stepped out.

She was wearing jeans and a T-shirt. It was black, and I grinned as I read it. *Math puns are the first SINE of madness* with some graph or shit with it. With her black jeans and red Vans, she looked like a math nerd. Like she had been back in high school.

The driver rolled down his window. "You a *Lord of the Rings* fan?"

I nodded, glad that my question and answer had worked. Katie rolled her eyes. "Yes, I asked his favorite meal and he said Second Breakfast."

"Thanks, man. Want an auto or selfie or something?"

The man's face lit up. "Absolutely. Sorry to hear you're injured."

Katie stood back till I had her take the photo with the guy's phone. Then he rolled away and it was just the two of us.

"I've never ridden in a Mercedes before," Katie said. "That's not what you have, is it? I'd be petrified to drive it in Toronto."

I shook my head. "No, I've got a Ford."

Katie looked around the lot, practically empty at this point. Her gaze stalled on the yellow Mustang. "Is that—?"

"Yep."

"That's a freakin' Mustang."

"I know."

"I can't drive that."

"Well I sure as hell can't." What were we going to do if neither of us could drive?

She turned to face me and her shoulders dropped. "Right, sorry. I forgot to ask how you're feeling."

"Honestly, a little tired."

Her gaze ran down my body, landing on the knee that wasn't taking any weight. "And you probably need to rest that. Okay, I'll do my best but I can't pay for repairs if I hit something. I haven't driven in Toronto yet."

I shrugged. "It's just a car. I have insurance."

Inside, I was cringing. The car was my baby. I kept her detailed and parked in the back of parking lots to prevent dings. But Katie was already freaking out and I wanted to calm her down. And as much as I loved my car, Katie was more important.

I passed her the keys. "Would you bring it over? Armpits are getting sore with these crutches." I really wanted to get off my feet. Foot.

She stared at the keys, and then the car.

I nudged her leg with one crutch. "It's not throwing the ring into Mount Doom."

She rolled her eyes but looked a little less tense. "Okay, let's hope for the best."

I watched her walk away, enjoying the sway of her ass, the swing of her hair and the way she hitched up her book bag.

Yeah, my baby might get a ding, but totally worth it.

CHAPTER 10
MY NEW FRIEND

KATIE

YOU CAN DO THIS, I told myself. It was just a car.

I was fine with driving a stick. I'd learned on one and had been driving a standard back home before I'd moved six weeks ago. I just hadn't driven since then, and traffic here was different than I was used to—more congested, more bus and bike lanes, and frantic drivers. Plus, the little Ford Focus I drove was vastly different in power than this.

I threw my bag in the back seat and drew a long breath before settling in the driver's seat. Then I couldn't get a key to pop out of the fob Josh had given me. *What the hell?*

"Just push the button while you're pumping the brake," he yelled at me from where he was standing by the doors.

I did, and the engine rumbled, loud and powerful. Another breath, before I pulled the door shut and put her in gear. A lurch. I hadn't removed the parking brake. *Shit.*

Took care of that, and carefully, so carefully, stepped on

the clutch till I felt it take. I'd seen a sixth gear on the shifter, and hell if I was using that. First gear rolled us gently forward, and I kept it slow till I'd curved around and pulled up beside Josh. I put it in neutral and hauled up the parking brake, then jumped out to help him.

He managed to get the door open, but the crutches didn't want to fit in the opening.

"Turn and set your ass down. I'll throw these in the back." He rolled his eyes at my bossiness, but once he'd gotten in the seat I was able to slide the crutches in the back and get behind the wheel.

Josh played with the display and set up directions for me to get to his place. It wasn't too far—about halfway between the arena and Madeline's condo. I pulled in a long breath, and Josh turned with a grin. "You can do this."

We'd soon find out.

I pushed down on the clutch and shifted into first. The car started forward, reasonably smoothly. No jerking. *Go, me.*

I drove slowly to the exit. The GPS told me to turn right, so I flicked the turn signal and checked for traffic coming from the left. This time of day the streets were less congested than at rush hour. Fortunately.

I pulled out okay. Shifted up through second and third before a traffic light stopped us again. Josh didn't try to talk, since all my focus was on shifting and keeping the car from hitting anything. But in the silence, his stomach growled.

I turned my head.

He shrugged. "I eat a lot, and I missed lunch while they were working on my knee. Mind if we pick something up?"

The light changed, and the voice in the car urged me to proceed forward. "Is there a drive-thru on the way?"

"Um…"

"What do you want?" I knew that tone of *um*. I knew the

Josh of five years ago so well, and that Josh was a lot like this one.

"There's a Greek place a few blocks away. It's in a little strip mall, so you can park. It's not a drive-thru, but it's not too different?"

His stomach growled again. A big part of me wanted to just get to his place as soon as possible so I could relax. But the guy was injured and hungry. I was getting more comfortable with the car. Timewise, I didn't have that much work due before tomorrow. And the Josh I'd known couldn't boil water, so he needed food. It was probably safer to park somewhere than navigate a drive-thru, where I might scrape something.

He played with the display again, and the voice directed me to turn left at the next intersection. Couldn't between four and six, according to the sign over the traffic light, but now it was good.

The place, when the GPS told me we'd arrived at our location on the left, wasn't very prepossessing. There was a payday loan shop on one side and a convenience store on the other. The windows were a little grimy, and I couldn't see anyone inside.

Still, he'd lived here for years, and if this was what he was hungry for…

I stopped the car and pulled on the parking brake again. "What do you want?"

"I can get it." He pushed on the door handle.

"Josh, you need me to get your crutches out anyway if you're going to go in there, and you're supposed to stay off your feet, right? So just tell me."

His shoulders dropped. "Sorry, I didn't think about that. I didn't want to put you out any more."

"Hey, it's okay. This place is good?"

"Yeah. Really good."

"And it doesn't look too expensive."

"It's pretty affordable."

"Then I'll try it sometime. I've just learned a new place to eat. And I'm driving your car. I can mark off the 'drive a Mustang' square on my bingo card. I'm getting something out of this too."

"If you want to get some food, go ahead." He passed me a credit card. "I can at least feed you to say thanks."

I'd had lunch, but hey, I could get something to keep for dinner. See if the place was as good as he said. And I'd take a free meal. TAs weren't exactly rolling in it.

Josh wanted some loucanico and dolmades and pastitsio, as well as a salad. Not things I was familiar with, but I repeated the names to myself a couple of times and headed in.

Once I opened the door, the aroma was divine. I inhaled deeply, and suddenly my salad seemed a long time ago. I ordered what Josh wanted, added souvlaki and salad for myself, and promised I'd return when I could spend time figuring out what some of the more unusual items were to expand my repertoire.

My phone buzzed.

Get two of everything. Then I'll have leftovers.

I expanded the order and scrolled through my messages while I waited for the food. Then a tap of his credit card, and I was able to leave with a couple of bags of incredible-smelling goodies.

Josh was playing with his phone when I showed up. I set the food in the back of the car and got in the driver's seat. His stomach rumbled again.

"If it tastes half as good as it smells, I'm definitely coming here again."

"It does. It absolutely does."

The voice in the console told me to get moving, so I pressed the clutch and followed the instructions.

Daytime traffic was lighter than rush hour, but drivers were slower, dawdling while they figured out where they wanted to go. But eventually we arrived at our destination.

Josh pulled out another plastic card and passed it to me to scan to get into the underground parking. He directed me to a parking spot beside a big Ford pickup.

Tension leached out of my shoulders as I parked the car safely in its slot. I'd done it, without taking on any damage. Driving again had been fun, but also nerve-racking.

"You did great." Josh grinned at me.

"I'm glad I didn't wreck it."

"Nah, you're a good driver. And it's just a car."

The way Josh had talked about Mustangs back in high school, I was sure it was more than just a car, but it was safely parked and no longer my responsibility. I opened the door and got out. I rounded the back while Josh shoved his own door open.

"Give me a sec to get your crutches."

He pulled himself up by his arms, biceps stretching his shirt sleeves as he gripped the roof of the car. I tried not to ogle him and managed to wrestle the crutches out. I shut the back door most of the way so I could pass them to him.

While he propped them under those muscular arms, I grabbed my bag and the bags of food. Josh shuffled forward awkwardly in the tight space between vehicles and closed his door.

I backed away, letting him mostly hop till he had enough space to deploy his crutches.

"Thanks, Katie. Appreciate this."

"No problem." I was about to pass him his food when I realized that he might not be able to handle it as well as the crutches. Plus, the food was jumbled up together. After smelling it all the way here, I didn't want to lose my portion. "Want me to carry this up for you?"

He shot a glance from the bags to his hands, locked on the crutches. "Would you mind? I don't want to take up your time. You must be busy."

Points to Josh—he'd never considered his hockey world more important than my academic one. He had mostly been punctual for our tutoring sessions, even before they became something beyond just studying. "It's okay."

I followed him to the elevator, not far from his car. He hit a button for the eighteenth floor once he'd crutched inside. His stomach gurgled again as the smell of the food filled the elevator.

"You must have nice views."

"Yeah. It was weird when I moved in. My first place, after moving out, was a townhouse in Nashville. And we had that place in Halifax, remember, over the garage of Mr. Musgrove's house? I wasn't used to being this high up."

"Do most of your teammates live in condos? I thought they'd have mansions somewhere."

"More the family guys. Condo works for me. Traffic is always a bitch, so being close to the arena is nice. Plus, with all the traveling we do, no one wants to worry about shoveling snow or mowing lawns."

The elevator dinged that we'd arrived. I held it open while he maneuvered out. Then he led the way down the hallway to the end unit. It looked like there were only a few condos on this floor.

He opened the door and stood back for me to enter. There was a roomy foyer, so I shuffled aside for him and toed off my shoes, putting them on the shoe mat, already covered with discarded footwear.

We went down a hall with a couple of doors off it before taking a turn and arriving in the living room.

"Wow."

Madeline had a nice place. But this place had French doors to a huge balcony, letting in the view. The sun, now on the western side of noon, illuminated the wide spaces. I could see furniture outside—big couches and a table.

"You like it?"

"That view, the windows? What's not to like?" Josh didn't answer, and I turned to see him looking down, bashful. "It's really nice, Josh."

"Thanks. It's not too much, is it?"

Was he embarrassed by his success? "You make a lot of money now. Why shouldn't you enjoy it?"

He sighed. "It doesn't seem real sometimes, you know?"

"But it is, isn't it?" I kept my voice low.

"I'm not sure I deserve it."

Josh had been at the top of my hit list, along with Rhonda, a couple of weeks ago, but he'd dropped down once I'd understood better what had happened. His mom and my parents had moved up in his place. He still bore responsibility, but knowing Josh, my anger was cold and fading. How upset could you be with a golden retriever who gave you those sad eyes?

He was who he was. And we weren't dating, and I wasn't trusting him with my heart. We could probably work out being friends. To his credit, he wasn't forgetting where he came from, and he wasn't arrogant.

He led the way through another doorway that opened to the kitchen. I dropped the bags of food on the counter, prepared to take my portion and go.

"I'm starving. Want to join me?"

I hesitated. Two weeks ago I'd have happily spit in his plate. Was I ready to sit down and share food and chat? I'd come to help him when he was stuck, so it was a little late to try to nurse those previous hurts.

While I dithered, his face fell. "Sorry. You want to go." He pulled his phone out. "I'll get you a ride."

"I can stay long enough to eat."

He looked up, a smile creasing his face. "That's awesome."

"Tell me where the plates are." Because apparently I was hanging out with my new friend.

CHAPTER 11

YOU MAKE ME SOUND LIKE A KID

JOSH

MY DAY HAD TAKEN a shitty turn with the injury to my knee, but now it was so much better. I'd been trying to find the right way to reach out to Katie, and she was here at my place and wasn't rushing off the first chance she had.

Not saying I'd get hurt again to get this result, but I could enjoy it this time.

She set plates on the counter and started to pull out containers from the takeout bag.

"Let me help."

She frowned at me. "You're not supposed to be on your feet, are you?"

Shit. I'd forgotten, too excited to have her here, but I'd better do what Carlos had told me to do. "Okay. I just need to get an ice pack."

She pointed to the living room. "Sit."

I boosted myself up on one of the stools at the breakfast

bar. I leaned the crutches against it and pulled my injured leg up to rest on another stool.

She pursed her lips, but apparently this would do. "Where's the ice pack?"

"In the freezer." I pointed. It was a big kitchen, and I had a fridge and a separate freezer. Her gaze swung between the two appliances, and she shrugged before opening the freezer.

One side had prepared meals. I couldn't cook, and following the nutritionist's guidelines made meal prep more difficult so I used a service. With Daniel around I wouldn't need it as much. The other side had a shitload of ice packs and some vodka. Last season, Bongo had lived with me, and he loved his vodka. I should get rid of that.

"Interesting." Katie pulled out an ice pack.

"You know I don't cook. And the vodka belongs to Bongo. He was my roommate before he got his own place. I'll tell him to come get his stash." She brought me the ice pack and I draped it over my knee.

"You don't have a roommate now?" She passed over a plate filled with Greek goodness.

"Yeah, I do. Thanks, and have some of this stuff too if you want."

She scooped a bit of the loucanico I'd requested onto another plate. "Where's your roommate?"

Anxiety swept over me again. "He's on the way to Ottawa. Might be there now." I pulled out my phone to check the time. "Yeah, the jet's probably landed."

Katie sat down on a stool by my foot. "Another hockey player, eh? What position?"

"He's a center. Playing the second line, it looks like."

"And you?"

I set my fork down, worry interfering with my appetite. "Last season I was the first line right winger. But this season..."

Katie cocked her head. "Did they demote you?"

I pointed at my knee. "I haven't played much in the preseason. And now, when I was supposed to finally get some real time in a game, this happened. They'll have someone else playing tonight, and if that guy has chemistry with Oppy and Deek, well…"

Katie stared at me for a minute. I wasn't sure what she was thinking. I poked at my food, before setting my fork down. Finally, she spoke. "Seriously. Are you really likely to lose your spot after missing one game?"

I fidgeted in my seat, because this idea wasn't totally realistic, I knew. "Probably not. But after last season, coaches and management want to make sure everyone is clicking. I'm going to lose at least a week. I might not play the home opener."

Katie rested her chin on her hand, elbow braced on the counter. "I don't know if you're just worrying needlessly or not. How good are you? You seem to be pretty popular."

I picked up my fork again to have something to do other than meet her gaze. "I'm not too bad."

"Define not too bad." She used her serious voice, the one I heard when she got on my case about math when she was tutoring me. It probably shouldn't be that hot. It told me she wasn't going to let me get away with avoiding whatever we were talking about.

"I had the second highest points total on the team." I looked at her out of the corner of my eye. I hoped that impressed her.

"Goals?"

"Goals and assists."

She pursed her lips, distracting me. "Right. That sounds like you were more than not bad. Did anyone get signed to the team who's a better scorer?"

I shook my head slowly.

"Any of these new guys coming up scoring better than you?"

I shrugged. "Not really. Not yet."

"So why are you so worried?"

I sighed. "Something I've learned, it's that hockey is a business. After our loss, the team could have decided to change things up. They kept most of the team together, but if we don't do well, they might start trading."

"Are you afraid you'll be traded?"

"A bit. I like it here. But what if no one wants me? What if this is it?"

Next thing, Katie was on the stool beside me, my foot resting on her lap. "Josh, from what I've picked up, and what you told me, that's highly unlikely. The trainers said this would heal quickly, right?"

I nodded.

"You're making lots of money, right? So if the worst happened, you're okay financially, aren't you?"

"Yeah, but then what would I do? Everyone said—*you* even said—I should have a backup plan. And I didn't. Hockey is all I know. It's all I can do. What if it's over?"

She shook her head. "We were all wrong. You're here, making millions, right? You've probably made more than you would have in any backup career. And when you're done, though probably not for years yet, you'll find something else to do."

"Like what?" I wasn't just saying this. I had no idea what I'd do after hockey, but I'd thought I had more time to figure it out.

"What do other players do after they retire?"

"Some coach or do commentary on-air. Or go into management. Or business. And I can't do any of that."

Katie raised her brows. "Why not? I told you, back in high

school, that there's more to you than hockey. You're not stupid."

"No one else said that."

"Everyone around you back then was interested in you succeeding in hockey. They were going to make money if you did or hoped for some fame or whatever. They didn't look past the player part. But if someone does, there's a lot there. Trust me, I wouldn't have gone out with you if playing hockey was all you had to offer."

I looked away for a moment, afraid of what she might see on my face. Katie had been different. She'd made me believe I was smarter and could do more. She didn't care about hockey. She'd cared about me.

I'd been so stupid to give that up. To give her up. If she'd wanted to end things when high school was over, well, I couldn't do anything about that. But I'd thrown it away when maybe we could have made it.

She stood, putting my foot back on the stool, and I missed that contact, even through my sweats.

"But we're not going to dwell on something that isn't a real concern. Someone else will play tonight, but they won't play as well as you would. And you're going to be winging on the first line soon enough. Eat."

She was right. My career wasn't over with this little injury. I'd been lucky not to be seriously hurt previously, and I was overreacting. Even if I didn't start on the first line when I got back on the ice, I'd make my way there.

I was short for a hockey player, and I hadn't been drafted till the second round because the experts all thought I couldn't maintain my game at the top level. I'd shown them. I'd made it to the NHL, made it to the top line, made it to game six of the finals.

I'd do it again. And I'd work just as hard to get Katie back. No matter what anyone else thought, she was good for me.

82

The best. And I'd learn to be the best for her too.

Fitch's words echoed. I'd have to do things differently this time. Last time, I'd been worried about making it in hockey since I was short and not as bulky as a lot of players. I'd overcome that by being fast and taking hits and shaking them off. This time, I'd make her more of a priority.

And here I was, when I finally had Katie with me, complaining again, being insecure. Enough of that. "So, what's up with your family and school and everything?"

Katie's eyebrows flew up, but she allowed me to change the subject. "Nora had a boy—Garret, and he's adorable. He's almost five, and she's pregnant again." Katie had a warm smile on her face. I bet she loved her nephew and was good with him. She had lots of patience. "Nora loves her kid and her partner, so they're good. She switched to a nursing program, and I think she's almost done."

I cocked my head. "So, you graduated first? Like, from college?"

She nodded, head lifting. She was proud of that. Bet her parents were too.

"First college graduate in the family, right?"

"Yep. The whole family came out, took a bazillion pictures, had a party."

"That's great. And now you're…"

"Next step is master's. Then PhD."

"You'll be Dr. Baker."

"Yep. I'm in applied mathematics, finance. But I've also thought I'd like to teach."

"You'd be good at that."

"In the math world, the attitude is definitely that those who can't, teach. So that's kind of a backup plan."

I didn't know what she'd do in applied math, finance, but she definitely was a good teacher.

She smiled and then stood up, her plate empty. "That was

really good food. Thanks for feeding me. Want me to put the leftovers in the fridge?"

"That would be great."

My stomach twisted. She was getting ready to go. Which, yeah, she'd stayed longer than I expected, but I'd like her to stay for a while yet. I grasped at ideas to make that happen, but I had nothing. She had her own life and was probably busy with all her school stuff. I'd asked a favor of her to help me, and she'd already done more than enough.

I pulled the ice pack off my knee. It was getting warm, so I'd better get another, and then stretch out on the couch to play a video game till the Blaze game came on at seven.

I grabbed my crutches, balancing my weight on my good leg, and carefully moved toward the freezer.

"What are you doing?" She sounded strict again.

"New ice pack."

She held up a hand and cut in front of me to pull one out of the freezer.

"Thanks." I reached for it, but she moved it away from me.

"Go settle down wherever you're going to rest, and I'll bring it to you."

"You don't have to—"

"I offered. Go, sit or lie down or whatever."

I grinned at her and turned on the crutches and hobbled my way to the big couch in the living room. I was slow. Usually my body was my tool, doing whatever I asked of it. But these crutches were awkward, the movement strange to me.

Katie finished in the kitchen, putting our dishes in the dishwasher and the food away in the fridge before wiping down the countertop. I'd wedged myself into the corner of the couch, leg up beside me, crutches on the floor at my feet.

She brought the freezer pack over and passed it to me so I could put in on the knee again.

"Do you want a water bottle or something?"

"Just a glass would be great, thanks."

She opened a couple of cupboards, then brought out a large glass and filled it up from the fridge. She carried it over and set it on the coffee table in front of me. "What else do you need?"

"I'm good. The remotes are right there and I've got my crutches."

She frowned. "When does your roommate get back?"

"After the game. It'll be late. They'll fly out from Ottawa after."

"And you'll stay put till he gets home?"

As if. "I'll have to eat, and you know, hit the head. Get another ice pack." She stared at me, foot tapping. "I'm good, Katie. I've got the crutches. I'm slow but I can do it."

"The Josh I knew in high school was more likely to do something he shouldn't. He wasn't good at staying still."

I wanted to say I'd changed and wasn't like that anymore, but it was going to be hard to just sit all day on my own. "I've got some games I can play. I don't need to be waited on."

"No." But she still watched me.

"What?"

She looked away for a moment, then back at me. "I can come back. Go home, grab the stuff I need for my classes, and get you through the evening till your roommate comes back."

I liked the sound of that, but... "I can take care of myself."

"I'm sure you can get an ice pack and warm up some leftovers. But you're likely to decide you need to go check something in your car or go get a Coke or ice cream from a corner store because you get bored and restless. I'm not going to take care of you till you're playing again, but maybe today, when you haven't had time to heal."

I pushed down how good that made me feel. She knew me, and she did care about me. "You make me sound like a kid."

She grinned. "Would you rather be alone?"

"Hell no." Especially if the alternative was Katie.

"Okay. Give me your keys."

* * *

SHE WASN'T LONG—ONLY a couple of hours, but it felt like more. I made my own way to the bathroom, because damned if I'd let her follow me there. But after getting another drink, I was on the couch, behaving, when she got back.

We ordered in Thai, because if she was helping me, I wasn't giving her leftovers. She rolled her eyes but didn't say anything. We talked a bit while we ate, about how she was adjusting to Toronto, and how it compared to Halifax. I settled back on the couch while she put the dishes and leftovers away. I was set for food for tomorrow.

"Does your knee hurt?"

I shook my head. "No, it's good."

She jerked her head at the TV. "I think your game is on soon."

Right. I needed to watch, see how everyone did. "Do you mind me watching it? I could use my phone instead of the TV."

Katie smiled. I smiled back, because how could I not?

"I brought headphones. I'll do my stuff, and you can do your job."

She dropped her legs to the floor and picked up her backpack. She brought out a textbook and her laptop and settled back in the chair. She looked up, questioning why I was watching her.

Right. The game. I picked up the remote and found the broadcast. Time to do my job.

CHAPTER 12

THE BEST INCENTIVE I'VE
EVER HAD

JOSH

IT WAS A PRESEASON GAME, so the winner wouldn't matter as
far as points went for the season. But we had a healthy
rivalry with Ottawa, and bragging rights were on the line as
well as the mental game for when we next matched up.

Most of the guys playing were going to be on the roster
on opening day. The coaches were still checking out the last
of the tryout players: recent draft picks, and some guys from
the farm team. I needed to understand the play of the guys
I'd be on the ice with. I was on the first line, but things got
changed up during a game. It was better to know what all the
guys played like for when we would share the ice.

I should have been able to concentrate, despite the knee. I
loved hockey and could watch any game that was on—
women, juniors, even peewees. Usually if there was a hockey
game on, it was hard to keep my attention on anything else.
Now, Katie switched ice packs for me when I needed them

and brought me drinks and some fruit to eat, but the game couldn't keep my focus.

Katie was here at my place. She'd come to help me, and not only did that thought make me happy, I liked having her here. She read her book, made notes on her laptop, and in between chewed on her thumbnail. She used to do that when she was working on her homework in high school and I was trying to work out the math problems she had given me.

Then she'd reward me with a blow job if I got it right, and that was the best incentive I'd ever had to do math. I always made sure she got off too, but we couldn't have full-on sex that often, what with all the parents around. I should have picked up sooner that they didn't like us together.

Thinking of those old study sessions made my dick get hard, so I shifted around so Katie wouldn't see. Sweats were comfortable but didn't exactly help hide an inconvenient hard-on. I was still working on the friends thing.

I needed to focus more on the game and less on Katie. I shifted so the TV took up more of my view.

The team was also having problems with focus. It would be nice to think my absence was making that big a differ-ence, but I was a forward. Our defense was struggling too, and that part wasn't really on me.

Coach had talked to us after previous preseason games. He said we were too in our heads after last year when we lost the final game in overtime. There was a lot of pressure since we'd been one of the last two teams. People expected a lot of us. *We* expected a lot of us. This game? Was not meeting those expectations.

Fitch was one of the few players who didn't look like they were having trouble. He was fitting in with new players and he had our systems to learn, but maybe he just didn't have that same pressure as the rest of us because he was doing better than the guys from last year. Even Cooper was called for holding, which was so not like him.

Despite that, it was a one-goal game and I finally got into it. Petrov, our starting goalie, played the first period, and one of the draft picks started the second. They had Mitch, the guy who'd been called up from the AHL and was in net for that overtime goal, start the third period.

I knew he felt a lot of stress after last season. Even if this wasn't a game that counted.

The forwards were finally applying some pressure in Ottawa's zone. But then there was a breakaway by Ottawa—a two-on-one on Mitchell. Shades of that last game against Minnesota. I held my breath as he stayed up and blocked the shot.

Yes!

Then Ottawa got the rebound and put it in. The goal lamp lit up and that was it. Technically there were still a couple of minutes to play, but the team had lost its mojo, and the final score was 4-2 for Ottawa.

"Damn." So frustrating to be stuck here with my leg up when my team needed me. But being with Katie—

I turned, and saw she'd fallen asleep in the chair. I'd have fallen asleep in seconds if I'd been reading a math book, but she loved that stuff. She must have been tired. And comfortable enough to let herself go with me here.

I liked that.

I flicked off the TV and stared at her for a few minutes. While she was sleeping, I didn't have to worry about what she'd think if she saw me looking at her. I didn't have to make sure I was just being friendly.

She'd changed, but not that much. She had blonde streaks in her hair that looked like she'd been out in the sun. That was new, and I liked it. Her figure had matured, and damn if

I didn't want to see more of that. But I also liked just looking at her face, relaxed and calm.

I'd seen and been with a lot of women. Model types, even. But I'd never found someone I wanted to watch the way I did Katie. Maybe her nose wasn't straight, and her cheeks a little round, but to my mind this was how my perfect woman looked.

Should I wake her up? It was only a little after nine. I could let her sleep till ten. Knowing Katie, she was probably studying stuff a week in advance. She needed her sleep, I told myself.

I didn't want to turn on the TV again and maybe disturb her, so I picked up my phone and scrolled through Instagram.

* * *

KATIE

IT TOOK me a minute to figure out what was going on.

Daylight was warming my eyelids, and I felt pleasantly rested. My mouth, however, felt nasty and gluey, like I hadn't brushed my teeth before bed. My neck was bent, and I was sticking to…leather?

My eyes snapped open, blinking against a sunny fall morning. But this wasn't my bed. This wasn't actually a bed at all. Beside me was an empty leather couch. When I looked down, I saw I was curled up in a large recliner. There was a blanket thrown over me with the Toronto Blaze logo on it.

Yesterday rushed back at me. Lunch, the TV report on Josh's injury, Josh calling me. The relief of knowing he was okay, then going to help him. Driving his car, eating with him, coming back to make sure that restless energy he had didn't make him do something stupid.

I'd been the one to do that instead, falling asleep here. Had he tried to wake me up? Had I snored?

My bladder was insistent that I pay it attention. I cautiously lifted my head but there was no one in the room with me. I heard noises from the direction of the kitchen but couldn't see anyone, so I risked standing up. The blanket pooled at my feet. I picked it up and left it on the chair.

There was a powder room in the foyer that I remembered using, so I tiptoed that way.

Peeing first. Immediate relief. Then I splashed water on my face and stood up to assess the damage.

Smeared mascara, any other makeup long gone. I opened a drawer, found some toothpaste and a comb. I squeezed out some paste and washed my teeth and tongue with my finger before rinsing in the sink. Then I worked the comb through my hair, making it look less like a rat's nest.

The clothes were a wrinkled disaster, but I wasn't going to ask for an iron or to throw them in the dryer. I'd survive.

I cast a longing glance at the door. I'd love to just put on my shoes, right there on the mat, and flee but I didn't have my things. And really, why was I freaking out? I'd fallen asleep. Josh could have woken me up but didn't. Nothing I could do about it.

I walked quietly back to the living room and checked the time on my phone. Still early enough. I could say good morning and goodbye and have more than enough time to go home to clean up and get to my first class.

Josh wasn't alone in the kitchen. He was sitting on a stool at the breakfast bar, left leg elevated and another ice pack on his knee, talking to a stranger in front of the stove. A man, taller than Josh but equally fit. Fortunately, he was the one cooking, not Josh, and the smell was incredible.

My stomach gurgled.

Josh turned, a big smile crossing his face. "Morning, Katie. How are you?"

I cleared my throat. "I'm good. Uh, sorry about falling asleep."

The stranger turned. He was about ten years older than us, with dark hair, green eyes, and a short trimmed beard. Textbook case of tall, dark and handsome, while I was here in rumpled clothes with no makeup. Good thing guys were not on my agenda in the immediate future. "I should probably go."

"You don't have to. Here." Josh pushed over a mug. "Got coffee for you. Do you still take it with double cream and double sugar?"

I nodded. There was no reason to find that charming, just because he remembered how I liked my coffee.

"I'm Daniel, Daniel Astrom," the stranger said, and my cheeks heated.

"Sorry!" Josh shook his head. "I forgot you don't know Fitch. This is Katie Baker, my…friend."

"Nice to meet you, Katie."

He held out his hand and I shook it. Then, since it seemed I was staying, I sat on a stool and took a sip of life-giving ambrosia, otherwise known as coffee. "This is good, but I should get out of here. You guys have things to do."

Daniel—Fitch—turned back to the stove.

"Do you have class right away?" Josh was looking at me with those puppy-dog eyes. "If not, you could stay for an omelet. Fitch is a good cook."

"I shouldn't impose."

Josh's chin stuck out. "You helped me a lot yesterday. Eat something, and I'll call you a ride."

I gave in. It smelled good, and I couldn't say I wasn't hungry, not after my stomach had betrayed me. "If it's okay with Daniel." I wasn't comfortable calling him Fitch, especially when I didn't know what it meant.

Daniel set a plate in front of me, then added cutlery.

"Thanks."

"No problem."

I picked up my fork and tried for conversation. "So, how was the game?" I'd mostly ignored it, and then had fallen asleep before it was over.

The two hockey players shared a glance.

"Let's just say we're glad it's the preseason and doesn't count," Daniel said.

"Sorry." Then I let them talk hockey while I scarfed down the food in front of me. "This is really good," I said when I'd finished and Josh had started his own breakfast on the plate Daniel had given him.

Daniel turned at that, spatula in his hand. He pointed it at Josh. "I'm only considered good if I'm compared to Ducky."

I swallowed the last of my coffee. "Josh's mother wouldn't let him make anything in the kitchen."

Daniel cocked his head. "No?"

I nodded. "She did her best to make him a stereotypical helpless man."

Josh sat up. "What?"

Oops. Josh might have decided I was right about his mother not liking me, but that didn't mean he was ready for my unvarnished opinion of her.

"That explains a lot," Daniel said, turning back around.

Josh stared at me. "You really think that? Why?"

Was he asking why I thought that, or why she'd done it? If he wanted to be friends, I'd be honest. I wasn't going to watch my words, not like I'd done before. "I thought she wanted you to be dependent on her. To need her."

Josh's jaw dropped.

I shrugged. "It makes sense. Your father left, and she didn't want you to leave her too."

Josh's mouth was still open and he was blinking, like that was fueling his brain to work out what I'd said. Had I crossed a line?

"Whoa," he finally said. "You thought about that?"

I set my mug down. "We dated for almost two years. I always knew she didn't like me. Of course I tried to figure out why. She's very…possessive of you."

His brow furrowed. "But she talks about me finding a nice girl and settling down."

Daniel put another omelet on a plate and grabbed a fork. "Think he'll figure it out?" He took a bite, watching Josh like he was the entertainment for the morning.

Josh ignored it. "So, Mom didn't think you were nice?" His voice was high-pitched, incredulous.

"She seems nice to me." Daniel apparently felt he was an integral part of this discussion.

"She *is* nice," Josh stated, as if Daniel had argued the point instead of agreeing with him. "Why doesn't Mom think you're nice? Why doesn't she like you?"

I sighed. "If you asked, she would tell you I'm nice and mean it. But I'm not the nice she wants for you in a permanent partner."

Josh set his fork down and crossed his arms. "Tell me what that means."

This might be brutal, but maybe he needed to know. It would help in case he started dating someone his mother didn't approve of. My shoulder twitched. Someone else.

If this was too blunt, maybe he would decide he didn't want to be friends. But might as well know now. "I don't think she's ready to be a grandmother, or to share you. And when she is ready, she'll want someone different." Even back then I wasn't the imaginary daughter-in-law she pictured.

"I'm not going to go back home to Nova Scotia, buy a house close to her, and let her come over and arrange things and tell me how many kids to have and how to raise them."

Josh frowned.

I stood. "Your mom had a difficult time, raising you as a single parent, and she did a good job. And I'm sorry if what I said sounded mean, because I didn't intend that. She loves you and wants the best for you. This is what she believes is best. Maybe I'm wrong, but that's the impression I got from our interactions."

Josh had his sad face on, but I wanted it all out there.

"Your mom and I are never going to be besties, so you should know that before we try being friends. I'm going to go now. Thanks for breakfast, Daniel, and thanks for dinner last night, Josh."

I grabbed my bag and almost ran out of the condo. I might have just blown things up with Josh, and that upset me more than was reasonable. Not just that it would end our friendship replay—I didn't want to hurt him any further.

Maybe his mother was right. I wasn't good for him.

CHAPTER 13

I DON'T FANGIRL OVER INSURANCE AGENTS

JOSH

WHOA. That was a lot to think about. Had Katie always felt that way? Was she correct about my mom?

"You okay?" Fitch eyed me as he took my plate away.

"Do you think Katie's right?"

"Katie believes what she said is the truth. I don't know if it is."

I sighed. "I don't know either. She's just my mom, and…" I shrugged. She was a normal mom to me, the only one I had. She'd always taken good care of me, but— "Is Katie saying I'm weak? My mom does everything for me and wants to take over my life?"

Fitch shrugged. "I've never met your mother. You seem to be mostly functioning fine on your own, outside of an inability to cook and leaving things lying around the place. Even if Katie is right, when you have only one parent, then you would appreciate them and see them in their best light.

That doesn't mean you're weak or that you can't make your own decisions."

"You're not helping as much as you probably think you are."

He nudged me. "You're how old again?"

"Twenty-four."

"You should be figuring this out yourself, right?"

I nudged him back. Adulting was hard sometimes, but if I wanted to prove I was my own person, not manipulated by my mother, I had to do it. Because Katie was going to learn that things weren't ending the same way this time.

* * *

FITCH DROVE me into practice and I met with the trainers. My knee was only sprained, and already a lot better. They worked on it and I was allowed to do some weights, not stressing my knee, and watched the rest of the team practice on the ice.

Coach was pissed about the game from last night, so I didn't mind being in the stands as much as I would have another time. The guys were winded and dragging by the time they got off the ice.

I waited till everyone was cleaned up and heading to eat. Then I joined Cooper and Barnes and Mitchell again. Fitch followed me, but that was okay. The four of them had gotten me this far with Katie, so I hoped they could help again.

Cooper grinned when I sat down. "Need more advice?"

"Kinda." My mother was always going to be part of my life. And I hoped that Katie would be as well. There were a million jokes out there about people not getting along with their in-laws, so this had to be a problem most relationships dealt with. "Do your girlfriends or wives have problems getting along with your mothers?"

Mitchell looked at Barnes, eyes wide. Barnes gave himself a shake. "You don't ask the easy ones, do you?"

"That's a yes, Ducky," Fitch said.

I knew it.

Mitch held his hands up. "My mom and Jayna get along great."

"Lucky bastard. My mom is barely polite to Mya, and her mother hates me."

Yikes. I wanted to ask why, but Cooper started speaking.

"I can't help you from personal experience. Callie is an orphan, and she probably gets along better with my family than I do, which still isn't great. But you told us your parents —your mom and Katie's folks—were the ones who pushed you into breaking up with Katie. Are those issues still there?"

"With my mom, yeah. And I need to be prepared in case her parents are still the same." There was no longer a problem about Katie picking a school because of me, or not going to school. But that might have been an excuse.

"That's a tough one."

I rested my head on one hand. "So what do you do to fix it?"

Barnes burst into laughter. Cooper and Fitch held it back, but they were grinning.

"There's no easy fix. There might not be any fix." Cooper shrugged.

Some families all got along. Mitch said his did. Surely there was something I could do. "But then, like, do they fight forever?"

"Do Katie and your mother fight?"

I frowned. "Not before. But when I told Mom I met Katie again, she assumed Katie was only with me for my money."

Cooper leaned back. "Does Katie want you for your money?"

I shook my head. "No, she doesn't. You can kind of tell, you know?"

Barnes nodded, but Fitch rocked his head back and forth. "Not always."

"Is it likely your mother will change her mind?" Cooper asked.

"I hope so, but I don't know how."

Cooper cocked his head. "Hmmm. Katie's pissed that your mother wanted you two to break up?"

I frowned. "She must be, but she didn't sound angry this morning when she talked about Mom, did she, Fitch?"

Mitch's eyes went round, and Cooper and Barnes smirked.

"She came over yesterday, to help me since—" I pointed at my knee. "She fell asleep and I didn't wake her up. Nothing happened."

They looked at Fitch, who shrugged. "Pretty sure that's the story. And no, Katie didn't sound angry. But if she's right, I doubt your mother and she will ever be very close."

I still wanted advice. "So you can't fix it when your mother and girlfriend don't get along. What do you do when they both want something different?"

"Then you find out who's more important to you."

Oh, that didn't sound like fun.

* * *

Fitch asked if I was okay when we drove home. "You're very quiet."

"I've got a lot to think about."

"Katie and your mother?"

"Yep."

"So, you're not giving up on Katie?"

I shook my head. "No. We were pretty young when we

dated, but since then—yeah, I'm still not that old, but I've seen a lot of people. I've met a lot of women but there's no one like Katie."

"That's a good point." Fitch used the fob to open the gate to park under the condo. "People might argue you didn't know anyone else when you were in high school, but that's not the case now."

My cheeks heated up. I *had* done a lot of hooking up. I was young and making serious money and playing a sport. I tried to make sure everyone had a good time, and I didn't promise more just to get someone in bed. I'd sort of dated a couple of times, when it hadn't been just a one-night exchange of O's, but it hadn't gone anywhere. A lot of people thought my *Star Wars* obsession was immature.

"What's so special about her?"

"You met her. Can't you tell?" Wasn't it obvious that she was a great person?

He held up his hand. "I'm not insulting her. I just wondered why she was right for you, compared to anyone else."

I frowned while I tried to put it in words. "I'm not smart." Seeing Fitch start to speak I rushed on. "I was held back a grade. I always struggled with school. And I was short, and we didn't have a lot of money, so I wasn't very popular. Until I got good at hockey."

Fitch nodded slowly.

"I still struggled in high school, but everyone wanted me to do well so I could play. I got Katie as a tutor. She was different, from the beginning."

She'd made things so much better.

"She believed in me. Not as a hockey player, cause that didn't seem to matter to her. But she made me do all the assignments, told me I could do it, and I believed her. She even got my math teacher to let me do my exam on the chalkboard so I could walk around while I was taking the test. Since she noticed moving helped me focus."

"Did it work?"

I nodded. "Katie is the only person who made me feel smart about something other than hockey. She believed in me, not the guy on the ice."

Fitch had a soft smile, and I realized I must have sounded pretty sappy.

"Plus, she's pretty and sexy and smart—what's not to like?"

Fitch turned off the car in the parking slot next to mine. "She sounds like she was a good fit with you. But things might be different since you broke up with her."

"I don't think so. I'm the same, and even though she said she might have changed, I don't believe it. We just…work."

"So what are you going to do about your mother?"

"I'll concentrate on getting Katie back, and not worry about my mom and Katie getting along. Cause if Katie doesn't give me another chance, I don't have to pick one."

Daniel shook his head. "I don't know whether to commend you for not obsessing over a problem that might never happen, or caution you for putting off an altercation because you're wimping out."

"I'm going with commend me."

I didn't look forward to arguing with my mother, but if Katie would give me another chance, I wasn't giving her up.

* * *

I TEXTED KATIE, making sure she was okay, but didn't have a chance to get together with her again for several days. We had some team bonding things going on before the season started—dinner at Cooper's, game nights, and a BBQ at Deek's. I was still babying my knee, so any free time I had meant sitting around with my foot up. I wanted to see Katie, but asking her to come over to play video games wasn't the progress I wanted. I wanted us to spend time together in a way that didn't say "high school hangout." I had to up my game and make sure this replay wasn't a repeat of that. This time I was doing it right.

Unfortunately, I couldn't figure out the perfect next move.

Fitch watched me make my protein shake the day before the season opener. It was a home game, and the arena would be packed. The coaches had already told me I was sitting it out, so I was frustrated. What if the guy filling in on my line had a great game? If the chemistry clicked with Deek and Oppy and they scored a couple of times, Coach might not want to break them up. Maybe they'd think I was fragile now, likely to get injured again.

Fitch nudged me away from the blender, where I'd been stabbing the pulse button over and over. "Stop worrying."

"I can't. You guys are playing tomorrow and I'm not." I'd been allowed a short skate at practice yesterday, but watching the game was going to drive me nuts.

"It's a long, brutal season. You know this. You don't want to be nursing an injury from day one. Having some extra rest will help you. You need your speed, and you don't have that when you're injured."

"If I stop thinking about hockey, then I try to figure out what to do with Katie."

Fitch poured out my smoothie. "Combine them."

I stared at him. "What?"

"You're going to the game tomorrow, right?"

I nodded. "I could be in a box, but I'd rather sit closer to the ice."

"Then get two seats and ask Katie to go with you."

Why didn't I think of that? Katie used to go to some of my games. Most people I met wanted to see the Blaze playing at the arena. And this was the season opener. Tickets were expensive, so she wouldn't go on her own. Not that she was likely to go without someone asking her. "Yeah. That could work. I could take her with us to Top Shelf after." First game of the season? We'd all be there.

Fitch smirked. "Sure. You could be her wingman."

I pointed at Fitch. "I'm not going to be her wingman. None of those fuckers better flirt with her."

Instead, I could introduce her to some of the women—wives, girlfriends, sisters. Most of them would be out tomorrow night, and Katie would have math stuff in common with Cooper's girlfriend and JJ's sister. Maybe she could make friends with them. Make her comfortable in my world.

That hadn't happened in high school. Katie hadn't been close to any of my teammates or their girlfriends. This was something I could change for the better.

* * *

*K*ATIE

I WASN'T sure if I'd hear back from Josh after that truth bomb I'd dropped. Not that he'd ghost me. We had history and he was basically a nice guy, but he and his mother were close and that had been blunt. Honest, but blunt. All the things I'd bit my tongue about back in high school I just…let out.

I could picture it. He'd say something like *We'll have to get together sometime*, but nothing solid and eventually it would fizzle out. That would be disappointing, if I was honest with myself, but school was my priority, so being friends with a popular hockey player probably wasn't a good idea anyway.

But with Josh, expect the unexpected.

Can't play the opening game

knee

They let me practice, not play

lame

I'm gonna watch

Wanna come with? As friends?

He wasn't happy about being benched, obviously. I thought the coaching staff was being smart, even if he didn't. And it made sense that he didn't want to sit alone. He was a people person.

I hesitated over the message, not sure how I should respond. He wasn't pissed about what I'd said about his mother, apparently, but I'd just convinced myself it was better not to be his friend. I didn't think he'd want to see me again. Now that he did, I wondered if I should be the one to say we shouldn't hang out. But I didn't want to be mean. He'd brought me donairs.

"What has your phone done to you?"

Andrea and I were at the sandwich place again. This time I'd ordered a sub. I'd walked to school, so I'd earned it. Living with Madeline, the model of perfection, had made me a little self-conscious about my weight. Not that I wanted to be like her, but a bit of effort wouldn't hurt.

Andrea had settled down about my knowing one of the hockey players. I'd explained high school, the bad breakup, and the five years of silence, so she'd stopped asking if I'd heard from him. But this would set her off again. "You can't freak out."

She froze. "Is that from Ducky?"

I sighed. "Why does everyone call him that? Yes, it's from Josh. Can you keep your voice down?"

"I will, I promise. It's just, I've never met anyone who knew any of the players."

I hadn't appreciated exactly how popular Josh was. Which had been obtuse of me. He'd been a fan favorite in Halifax when he was there, so playing at the top levels would only make him more popular. I just had a hard time matching the guy I'd dated with the man people in Toronto idolized.

I read out the message. "Should I go? I helped him out with his car when he hurt his knee." Wasn't going to mention falling asleep there. "But I was maybe too honest about what I thought about his mother, and I wasn't sure he'd want to see me again."

"Give me a moment. You didn't tell me you'd—done what exactly?"

"When he hurt his knee, he needed someone to drive his car back from the practice facility to his place."

She gaped at me. "He called you to come and drive his car?"

"His teammates were headed out to Ottawa, and he didn't want to leave it at the arena."

"Did you go inside? See the locker room?" She pressed a hand to her chest. "Oh, did you meet any of the other players?"

"No, no and no. Please, could you just pretend this is a normal person I'm talking about?"

She squinched up her face but finally nodded. "Sure. We'll pretend your ex is Josh the insurance agent."

"Insurance agent?"

"I don't fangirl over insurance agents. Work with it. So, you were honest about the mother who wanted to break you up. Whatever you said couldn't have been that bad. Why not go?"

I had the evening free. As we got further into the semester that would probably be rarer—courses and my research project would make things pretty busy. So maybe I should take this chance while I could? "I convinced myself he wouldn't want to see me, so I'm a little confused."

"Okay, pretending this is still the insurance agent. Do you like hockey?"

I rocked my hand. The game was fast and exciting, especially in person. I didn't like the fights, and when your boyfriend was on the ice, the hits into the boards were pretty stressful. But for this game I wouldn't know anyone playing. Except maybe Daniel and I didn't really know him. "I like some of it. I've never been to an NHL game though."

"Ticket prices are astronomical. I'm envious that you get a chance to go. If you like hockey at all, it's definitely worth it. Bet he gets good seats. Maybe he's in a box."

"As an insurance agent?"

"Business expense. Taking a client."

She had a point. This could be my only chance. "It might be fun—to see what it's like."

"You're okay going with your ex? Is he good company at a game?"

I had no idea. "I never went to a game with him. Like, not to sit with him. He was always playing."

"You're making it really difficult to be objective about this. Trying to think insurance agent, but I would absolutely take your place if that was an option."

I was *not* going to pass on this invite to Andrea. This wasn't a couple of free tickets, it was sitting with Josh. He'd need to concentrate on the game, not have someone fangirl all over him and distract him.

"Maybe he just wants to thank me. And he trusts I'll let him focus on the game."

"Good point. If you're not going to get pissed if he's not paying attention to you, and you're comfortable with him after being exes, then why not go? Have you got something better to do?"

"Not really."

"What's the downside?"

I couldn't explain. It wasn't something logical, but emotional. I had hurt feelings that hadn't totally gone away. Some anger that was settling on my parents instead of him. And something warm and mushy when I thought about spending time with Josh. And that feeling worried me.

Why? He hadn't given off any vibes that he wanted to pick up where we'd left off. He was a wealthy hockey player now and had women wearing his jersey and probably vying to sleep with him. Thinking he wanted anything more with me was delusional.

And even if it wasn't, I wasn't making promises about anything if I went.

It was fine. All fine. Just going to a hockey game, maybe to thank me for helping him out the other day. I texted back *sure*.

But I wasn't.

CHAPTER 14
GOOD, CHEAP LOBSTER

KATIE

JOSH SAID he'd pick me up. His knee was healed enough that he could handle the clutch of his Mustang. I hoped he was being truthful, and not just reluctant to let me drive. Then, as if he thought I was worried about it, he said he could park in the players' lot, and we'd be able to skip the hassle of finding parking.

I was new to the city and used transit instead of driving, but traffic was crazy and I'd heard enough people complaining about parking downtown for his concern to make sense. I could have said I'd meet him at the arena, but then he might have to come get me at the front doors, since I didn't have a ticket. His knee might be better but probably better to skip unnecessary walking.

I was waiting just inside my condo building's doors when he pulled up in his bright yellow Mustang. I opened the door before he could get out—this wasn't a parking zone, and it was the start of rush hour. I'd agreed to dinner before the game, so it was a little early.

"Hey Katie!" He was grinning ear to ear.

"Hey, Josh."

I slid into the seat, and he pulled the car out into the street.

Josh drove with a lot more confidence than me. There wasn't any chance to see what the car could do because this was downtown Toronto where traffic was terrible, and we rarely got into even third gear. We took only three times as long as we should to get to the arena, and Josh flashed his ID to get into the players' lot. It was mostly full, everyone already here to play. Probably why we were so early. Did he need to talk to his teammates or coaches?

Josh heaved a sigh as he looked at the other cars but smiled again as he looked at me. "So, I thought we'd eat here at the arena so there's no rushing to get back before the game."

"That's fine." I didn't really care. I didn't eat out much on my budget, so since he'd insisted on paying, I'd eat wherever.

He led the way through the doors from the players' lot. "I won't take you to the locker room or anything. Guys are getting ready, and they might not be dressed. We could go down after if you want?"

"If you want. I only know Daniel, and I haven't followed the team, so…"

Josh looked disappointed, but then grabbed my hand and pulled me toward an elevator.

When he'd said we were eating at the arena, I'd imagined getting hotdogs and popcorn from one of the fast-food vendors in the building. But the floor we got out on had paneled walls and thick carpet—this wasn't where regular fans came to watch the game. There was a man in a suit at the doorway to a restaurant, and we were led to a table where glass windows overlooked the ice.

A black linen tablecloth, yellow napkins and red menus— the Blaze colors. There was a well-stocked bar at one end, the whole room filled with that hushed atmosphere expensive restaurants had.

I was guessing hot dogs were not on the menu.

I leaned over to Josh and hissed, "I thought we were picking up fast food."

He leaned over and whispered back. "If I went to one of those places in the concourse, well, fans would get kind of excited."

Right. I sat back and drew in a breath. Josh was famous here. He'd be mobbed if he was wandering around. This was not high school Josh anymore.

One look at the prices and I wanted to slam the menu shut and walk out. I looked up, frowning, meeting Josh's gaze.

"Katie, I make a lot of money. I couldn't do anything nice for you back in high school, but I can now. Let me make up for that."

I didn't want to be the kind of person who focused on money and prices. But it had been a long, long time since I'd had really good food in an expensive restaurant, and it wasn't like I was going to put out because Josh bought me dinner. He was looking at me like a puppy begging for someone to rub his belly. "Fine. I'm going to pretend I didn't see the prices."

He grinned. "Why don't I just tell you what they have, and you pick without seeing what it costs? Because otherwise you're going to pick the cheapest thing. Which is lobster, by the way."

I snorted and pressed a hand over my mouth. "Lobster is not the cheapest thing on this menu."

Josh used his quick reflexes to snag the menu from me. "Sorry, but it definitely is. How long since you've had some good, cheap lobster?"

"It's been a while."

Josh tucked my menu under his and kept them both out of my reach. "Hmmm. You have a point. Lobster is cheaper with one of these shitty steaks."

The waiter stopped behind Josh, a pained look on his face.

"Um, Josh, I think this man wants to take our order."

Josh jumped. He looked at the waiter with rounded eyes, but managed to order some wine, the cheap lobster and shitty steak, along with appetizers. The waiter was polite but cool.

As soon as he left, I dissolved into giggles. Josh reached over and poked me. "That's not polite, laughing at the servers."

I swallowed another laugh. "His face when you said shitty steak."

He shrugged. "I'm just a dumb jock."

That removed any desire to laugh. "That's not true."

"I barely finished high school. Never got more education."

"I'm at university now, Josh, and I guarantee you that a college degree does not equate to intelligence."

"Katie, you're nice, but we know I'm not smart."

This was one of the things that really rubbed me the wrong way. "You aren't a person who learns well from reading and sharing knowledge in standardized tests."

He rolled his eyes. "And how else do you figure out if someone is smart?"

I waved my hand over the table. "We're here, eating at an expens—" He opened his mouth to argue so I switched to, "At a restaurant that serves cheap lobster and shitty steaks. You make millions of dollars, according to the salary that's published, and I know you have some sponsorship deals too, right?"

He shrugged, cheeks slightly pink.

"You have your own place, take care of it and yourself. And you must be hockey smart or you wouldn't be playing in the NHL."

"It sounds a lot better when you say it."

I held up a finger. "Plus, you can carry on an intelligent conversation about *Star Wars* for hours, if someone is willing to listen."

"A lot of people don't think that *Star Wars* is important."

I leaned forward over the table. "People can be smart about popular, commercially viable things just as well as about Greek philosophers or classical music. You can also be stupid about Greek philosophers and classical music, or *Star Wars*."

Josh smiled at me, a warm smile that sent fizzy bubbles through my body. "You've always made me feel better about myself."

I liked that comment more than I should have. "You did the same for me. I thought I wasn't pretty, or interesting to boys."

He cocked his head. "I remember, but I told you, you were hot and a lot of fun. How did you put it back then? Big boobs do not equate to pretty or interesting."

I rolled my eyes. "In high school they did."

"Not for me." The sincerity was impossible to miss, and he was right. I had bigger boobs now than I did then, but he hadn't ever made me feel like I was lacking. Until that breakup text.

* * *

*J*OSH

. . .

IT WAS WORKING. Katie was warming up to me, and this felt more like a date than two friends hanging out over food. We talked without any awkward pauses, and she laughed, not at me but with me. The guys might wonder how I knew Katie was the right woman for me, but this just proved it.

She didn't think I was stupid, and she talked to me like I was a regular person—not a hockey kind-of star, but someone she liked being with. We didn't talk about hockey at all.

The waiter brought our bill just before the game. I'd sat with my back to the glass so that I wouldn't be distracted by warm-ups. It had been a while since I'd watched a game live, rather than being on the ice. I hoped she'd enjoy the game. She'd come to some of mine when we were dating, but we'd never watched together like this.

Once I'd paid for the meal, I led her out to the elevator. I pulled a cap from my back pocket and tugged it down over my face.

She grinned. "That's your disguise?"

I shrugged. If we could get to our seats before people started to take photos or ask me to sign things, I'd be happy.

Sometimes it was enough. I'd timed it well—they'd just started the national anthem when we got to our section. We had to wait till they finished *O Canada*, but then everyone's attention was focused on the ice, and we made our way to our seats before anyone recognized who I was.

We were two thirds of the way up in the lower bowl, center ice. I didn't want to be right on the glass—it was harder to follow the action from there, and center gave the best chance to see plays developing on both ends of the rink. It was also an expensive section, so the people with tickets here were less invasive. They weren't as impressed by us players, or they wanted to seem less impressed. It made it easier to be part of the crowd in either case.

I'd asked Katie if she wanted a drink or anything, but we'd just come from dinner so we both passed on anything more. I made sure she was settled in okay, nodded to a few people who were trying to catch my attention, and focused on the ice where the puck was about to drop.

I wanted to be out there, so badly. I could skate on my knee, and the team had approved me for regular practice tomorrow, so watching from the stands was extra frustrating when I knew I could help.

They sure as hell could have used me.

Just a few minutes in, it was obvious there was something wrong with the team. They'd moved Gerbs up to take my place on the first line, and he hadn't gelled with Deek and Oppy. He made a pass and it was intercepted, forcing the play back to our zone. Cooper was playing as well as he always did but he couldn't be on the ice all the time. Petey was peppered, and eventually something went in.

Deek and Oppy needed to adjust for Gerbs's more physical, less speedy style of play, and I could see they were trying, but it wasn't working. After the second goal, Coach switched things up, pulling Barnes up to play on the top line.

There was a disputed call, so while they checked the replay, everything paused. It took me a moment to blink back to where I was. *Right.* I was here with Katie, and I was ignoring her.

I turned my attention to her. "Sorry, I got a little caught up there."

She raised her brows. "What are you sorry for?"

"Well, I should be paying attention to you. Like, do you have questions, or did you want to talk about something else?"

She placed her hand on my arm. I ran hot so I was just

wearing a T-shirt, and the feel of her skin on mine had every part of my body sitting up and taking notice.

"This is your job, right?"

I looked down at the ice. "I'm not playing though."

"But you guys study game footage and things like that, I remember. So watching is homework for you. I'm fine. It's not my first hockey game, you know. I even understand what offside is."

I should have known she understood the game when she'd watched it before. She was really smart. "I ignored you and I didn't mean to do that."

"Josh, I knew it would be like this when I agreed to come. It's not like we went to a bar and you ignored me to watch a football game. This isn't your hobby. Why don't you tell me who's taking your place and doing a terrible job with it?"

"How do you know they're doing a terrible job?"

She pointed to the Jumbotron showing the score. "I know you're a forward and you score goals. No goals up there, so…"

I couldn't point out my usual linemates from up here when everyone was still gathered around the coach, waiting for play to resume. "I normally play with Deek and Oppy. When the game started, Gerbs was with them, but now Coach has Barnes playing. They don't play the same style as me, so they're missing passes, and the usual plays aren't working."

"How do you play?"

"I'm fast. I'm not the biggest, but I'm the fastest guy on the team. So Deek made a pass that I'd normally get, because I'm good at getting ahead for him, but Gerbs didn't get there in time."

"They aren't looking to make sure the other player is there?"

"They couldn't see past that big defenseman who was on

him. And the game goes fast. You stop to check on things and everyone's moved on, and you get stripped of the puck. That's just as bad."

Katie nudged me. "See, you're smart."

I was going to argue, say that it was just hockey, but I didn't. I wasn't math smart, but I was hockey smart. Maybe she was right that it counted for something.

* * *

THE GAME CONTINUED to be a gong show. It was frustrating, because I should be down there, helping out. I'd been worried the team would do well without me and I might lose my place. Well, that sure as hell wasn't the case. We'd played better than this in practice, but somehow with the game we fell apart. I could only imagine what Coach would say in the locker room after. And what practice would be like tomorrow.

The one fun part had been Cooper coming out in the second intermission to be on the kiss cam with his redhead. She looked a little shell-shocked, and I was pretty sure she'd never been to a hockey game before. I hoped she was ready for being known as Cooper's girlfriend.

I imagined Katie sitting there, with me coming out for the kiss cam. I shot her a glance. She looked curious, but not like she was putting herself in that scene. I had work to do.

Then the third period started, and it was more of the same.

It was a relief when it was over. The Blaze lost and the crowd was quiet as they left. A few people told me the team was missing me and it would be better when I was back, but I wasn't *that* good. Cooper had been great, and Fitch was fitting in well for a newbie. Petey had stopped a lot of shots, but the forwards and the rest of the D had been pretty bad.

We waited until most people left before we stood up. I didn't want more people telling me I would save the team, or offering their advice, or asking me to sign things when I felt like we'd let our fans down.

I led Katie down to the players' section of the arena. I got us through with my ID, and the car was in the lot, but maybe she didn't want to hang out after that loss. "You still up for going out with the team?"

She cocked her head. "Do you guys not like to go out after a loss?"

I rolled my eyes. "We definitely need to go out to forget what happened when we get skunked like that."

"Then let's go."

"Sure?"

"I know you want to see your teammates, and this is interesting."

"It is?"

She nodded. "You're much more confident when it comes to hockey than you are with other things."

Katie was perfect for me. She thought I was smart when I talked about hockey, and about other stuff too. I had to find a way for her to watch me play, since I was a lot better than I'd been when she last saw me in high school. I would use anything I had to impress her.

The team doing so badly had been a downer, but she made even that better.

CHAPTER 15
A SAD-EYED PUPPY

KATIE

I'D NEVER BEEN to the Top Shelf, the bar the players met at. I hadn't been a lot of places in Toronto yet, since my budget was tight and my time limited, but thanks to Madeline meeting Josh there, I'd heard of the place. There was a sign at the door, *No selfies, no autographs, or no service.* That probably explained why the hockey team went there.

There was a guy checking people out at the door, but Josh was waved in. I looked around in interest. This wasn't too far from Madeline's, and if it was decent, maybe I'd come again when I needed a break. It was nice—not a club with loud music and dancing; not the kind of place where you expected to catch something if you used the bathroom. The drinks wouldn't be cheap, but there were two levels, a big bar, and food service too.

Josh led the way to some tables at the back under the second floor. It provided a bit of privacy and they had *reserved* signs on them. All the tables around were occupied, but Josh ignored the sign and took a chair. It must be reserved for the players. I sat beside him and caught some envious glances.

A few people greeted Josh and commiserated with him about the game, but then we were left alone, and a server took our order for drinks. Josh had chosen a place in the middle of the tables. He obviously felt comfortable with his teammates and liked to be in the center of anything going on. That was vintage Josh.

Our server, a pretty brunette, cast appreciative eyes over him. I could see the question in her eyes when she checked me out. I found myself leaning a little closer to him, as if I was claiming him, glad I'd taken some effort in how I dressed and did my hair tonight. As if I needed to prove I deserved to be around Josh. *What the hell, Katie?* We were friends. It wasn't anything to do with me if Josh wanted to pick someone up, like he had with Madeline. And I shouldn't be strangling the beer glass in front of me when those thoughts pushed through.

It would be awkward getting home if he picked someone up. He'd driven us from the arena and parked in a nearby lot, but it wasn't too long a walk to where I was living. It would be good for me. Or I could call for a ride. I wasn't dependant on him to get home.

Transportation aside, what would I do if some puck bunny did get cozy with him? I didn't know anyone else, so that would be uncomfortable. This had been a bad decision. I should have gone straight home from the game. But before I got myself too worked up over this hypothetical situation, his teammates walked in, distracting my anxious thoughts.

The players attracted a lot of attention: some applause, comments, waves. Fans probably came on purpose to see the team, even if they couldn't take pictures. Would the atmosphere be different after a win? Because everyone seemed a little quiet tonight.

"Ducky!" a couple of the guys called. That was new since high school. His nickname had been Middy then, short for Middleton.

Josh stood and they did some manly greetings involving slaps and fist bumps. I recognized Cooper, since he was on a billboard in the subway in nothing but a pair of briefs. He was with the redhead he'd kissed on the kiss cam between the second and third periods.

Josh waved at me. "Hey guys, this is Katie." He didn't say *my friend Katie.* Would they think something else was going on? "She's a math major, so you have something in common with her, Callie!" He directed that at the redhead.

"Ah, hi." Was Callie a math student? She was older than us by several years, best I could tell.

Callie frowned at Josh. "I'm a tax attorney, Ducky. Not the same thing." My expression felt stiff. She turned my way. "Where are you studying?"

"U of T."

She smiled then, making her more approachable. "I'm a U of T alum. But it's a big school. You finding your way okay?"

I nodded. Then Cooper grabbed her hand and took her to a different table. I let out a breath.

"Sorry," Josh said. Then he yelled out again. "Jessica!"

A woman who'd come in with the players looked at Josh, and approached when he waved her over. She was a pretty brunette, looking nice and unthreatening in jeans and a non-Blaze shirt. I wasn't sure which guy she was with.

"Jess, you do math stuff, right?"

She raised her brows. "I'm a financial advisor, so yes?"

"Katie's getting her master's in math. You guys have something in common."

Jess looked at me and rolled her eyes. I shrugged. Josh

was like a sugared-up toddler trying to put people together. But she sat down beside me, asking someone named Justin to get her a glass of wine. Ah, she was with him.

"You don't have to—"

"No, it's good. I don't come out very often, so I don't know everyone that well anyway. I'm happy to chat with you and not have to talk hockey. You're okay with that, aren't you?"

"That would be great. I'm only here because I know Josh, so…"

She nodded. "I'm not one of the WAGs, just Justin's sister. If that matters."

I let out a relieved breath. "I'm not a WAG either, just Josh's friend."

Her brows raised, but someone—Justin?—passed her a glass of wine. There was a resemblance between them, though not enough to make their relationship obvious. He tilted his head and she shook hers. He walked to the far table and sat near Cooper.

I looked back at her. "You sure you want to sit here?"

"Definitely."

"Do you know who everyone is? Because, true confession, I'm not a big hockey fan."

"I don't know them that well. I've dealt with Justin being a hockey prodigy all my life, so I've had to build up my own identity and friends away from hockey. Otherwise people want to use me to get to him."

That reminded me of Andrea. Not that she'd used me, but as soon as she heard I knew Josh, hockey was all she thought about for a moment.

"But Justin's played with the team for five years, so I at least know all the names."

My muscles, which had tensed when my brain got stuck on the puck bunny track, started to relax. A woman who wasn't a big hockey fan and wasn't dating or married to a player? This was someone I could relate to.

I took another sip of my beer as I looked around. The table was filled with large men I was pretty confident were all hockey players. "My friend is going to be so jealous."

"Hockey fan?"

"Both she and her girlfriend are. I wasn't sure if I should come tonight, but she encouraged me to."

"What did you think of the game?"

I paused.

She laughed. "They played like crap. Justin was moping all the way over."

"Well, I haven't watched hockey since high school, but the score was kind of a giveaway. As well as Josh's responses. Lots of groaning."

"So how do you know Ducky?"

I was going to have to ask him about that nickname. "Josh and I went out in high school. We ran into each other a couple of weeks ago. I helped him get his car home from the arena when his knee was injured, so he invited me to the game."

"But you're not dating again?"

I shook my head, and checked that Josh was deep into a conversation with someone on his other side. The guy had a loud voice, and no one was paying attention to us. "We're supposed to be trying the friends thing."

She studied me, as if testing my sincerity. "Ducky is a nice guy, so that shouldn't be difficult. You must be from down east, right?"

I nodded.

"You've been in touch since you broke up?"

"Oh, no. It was not a good breakup. I hadn't spoken to him for five years."

"That bad, eh? If that's the case, how did you run into him again?"

I felt my cheeks get hot. "It's embarrassing."

She leaned in. "It can't be as embarrassing as some of my stories. Like the last time I brought a guy home to the condo Justin and I share. The guy and I had been dating for a couple of weeks. I hadn't told him who my brother is because this is such a hockey town—thank goodness Johnson is a common name. Anyway, the guy stayed over for the first time, and when I got up in the morning he wasn't in bed with me. He was in the kitchen with Justin, asking for an autograph."

I giggled. "That sounds…"

Jess rolled her eyes. "Really bad. It was the end of that relationship, obviously, and a new rule that I don't bring guys home until I know they aren't hockey fans."

I checked on Josh again. "Okay, I can do one better. I had to leave my housing situation and moved into a new place about a month ago. Two weeks later, I'm in the living room watching a show on my laptop. It's about eleven p.m., and my roommate comes in making out with a guy."

Jessica's jaw dropped. "No way."

"Yep. I'm trying to break for my room, but then Josh recognized me, and well, we ended up rehashing our breakup and…"

"Did they hook up?"

I shook my head. "We, Madeline and I, kind of ganged up on him. I told her that he broke up by text."

"That is *so* high school. And not cool."

"Exactly."

She looked over at Josh, hands waving as he discussed something hockey connected with the guy beside him. "Then how did you get from that to here?"

"He showed up on my doorstep with donairs, apologized,

explained that our parents worked on him, and well…he's hard to say no to."

Her brows raised.

"No, not like that. Like a sad-eyed puppy."

She looked around me again. The movement caught Josh's attention.

"Oh, sorry. I got caught up in talking—"

"It's fine, Josh. Jessica and I are talking about non-hockey stuff, so do your thing."

He grinned. "Want another beer?" I hesitated. He nudged me with his elbow. "I'm not having any more, and I'll drive you home. Have more if you want."

"Sure. Another Keith's, then."

Josh waved for our server, and I looked at Jessica.

She lifted her hands. "Yeah, I get it. Puppy eyes is right."

An hour later, everyone was ready for another round. Two women in tight-fitting hockey shirts came over. They were very pretty, well made up, and they looked around the table like this was the real menu.

"Can we buy you a drink?" one of the guys asked.

Before long, three more women had joined us. I saw gazes moving between me and Josh, assessing whether we were together. I wasn't sure how to act. What did he want me to do? Scoot away? Was I supposed to be a buffer? A big part of me wanted to wrap an arm around his just to see how they reacted.

And that was a problem. This was definitely becoming *let's hook up* hour, and I wasn't playing that game. I pulled out my phone to check the time, and all of the things I had to do tomorrow crowded into my head.

"I need to head out now. Classes in the morning."

Jess frowned at her own phone. "I should get Justin and head home too."

Josh had been talking to…possibly Crash? But he noticed what I was doing. "Time to go?" he asked.

"I don't want to break up the party. I have to leave, but you should stay. I can call a ride."

Josh pushed back his chair. "We gotta go, guys. See you in the morning."

I stood up beside him. Leaning close to his ear, I whispered, "You don't have to—"

He took my hand, short-circuiting the rest of that sentence, and pulled me after him as he made his way around the table.

There was a chorus of "Bye, Ducky" and "Nice to meet you, Katie" as we left them behind. Jess put her hand to her head in the *call me* gesture and I nodded. We'd already exchanged numbers.

"You sure about this?" I double-checked with Josh.

"Yeah. We came together, we leave together. I can shoot the shit with those guys tomorrow."

What about hooking up? Did he want to do that? I wasn't brave enough to ask.

My phone buzzed as we hit the entry doors. There was a foyer between the outside doors and the inside ones, keeping the worst of the wind from sneaking into the bar. The buzz was the particular tone I'd set up for work messages.

"Can you give me just a sec? This is work, and it might be a schedule change for tomorrow." The prof had been complaining of a scratchy throat, and if he was taking a sick day and I had to fill in, I wanted all the notice I could get.

"Sure." Josh was always agreeable. He leaned against the wall as I took a step away, putting a finger in my free ear while I listened to the message.

Nothing from the prof. Just a change in a lab session location. While I was listening, the door from outside opened and a woman entered. Like the women who'd joined the table earlier, she was gorgeous and dressed for attention. She had blonde hair—not natural, I decided. Perfect makeup. I'd put on blush and mascara and lipstick, but the lipstick and blush were probably gone by now, and the mascara flaking under my eyes. She was wearing boots with a four-inch heel over tight, very tight jeans. I honestly wondered if her shirt might rip, unable to contain her generous boobs in such a tight space. The Blaze logo was so stretched out it was almost unrecognizable.

"Hey, Ducky." Her voice was low, husky, seductive. "I was hoping to see you tonight. How's your knee?" She touched his chest with one perfect, blood-red fingernail, running it down toward his jeans and what the actual fuck?

Josh stepped back. "Um, it's fine."

Something changed, like the place was lit differently. The man standing there was no longer the teenager I'd known in high school. He had the same shaggy brown hair, but there was a shadow on his jaw, like he needed to shave again. The jawline was sharper, and his face more angular, less round. He wasn't that much bigger, but he had a presence about him he'd never had in high school. He wasn't a hockey wannabe; he'd made it. He was successful, admired, and had the world at his feet.

He wasn't surprised or flustered that this woman was after him. This happened to him often. She was going to suggest a "workout" for his knee, and I was just not having that. For all my talk about letting it happen? *Nope.* I took the two steps necessary to get to his side and slid my hand into his. He jerked his head toward me in surprise.

"We've been keeping it iced, and now it's all good again." I tried to give him a sexy smile as I looked up at him. "You put those ice packs back in the freezer, right?"

He nodded slowly, still looking shocked.

I turned back to the bunny. Her eyes ran down my body

and back up. I didn't have the curves she did. Mine were the "too many snacks and not enough exercise" kind. My idea of a workout was walking to and from class instead of taking the subway, and the weather had not been accommodating lately. None of my curves spilled over my bra, fighting to get free the way hers did. I'd dressed to stay warm in an arena and be comfortable. The tatty pair of Uggs, well worn jeans, and a puffy jacket kept me warm but didn't do shit for my figure.

Maybe she didn't mean to look like she couldn't believe we were together. But her skepticism showed, and hey, I'd actually dated the guy for almost two years.

I blamed it on my pride and some vanity when I pushed up toward Josh and kissed him.

CHAPTER 16

I'M SORRY. I'M NOT

JOSH

KATIE WAS KISSING ME. It took a moment to catch on. She started to pull away and I thought *Hell no* and wrapped my arm around her back, bringing her closer. She relaxed into me, the way she used to. I wasn't sure why she'd launched herself at me, but I was on board. Totally on board. Had we moved past friends just like that?

I wove my other hand into her hair, tilting her face enough that we could make the most of the kiss. I used my tongue on her lower lip and she opened, letting me into her mouth. *Yes.* Kissing Katie wasn't like kissing anyone else. We'd learned with each other, and it still did something to me no other kisses had. They made me feel warm and welcome and *home.*

My hand moved down to her ass. She had more flesh there than before and I wanted to explore. But that was too much for her. She pulled back and I let her go reluctantly. She was breathing fast and I knew she'd felt my hard dick against her. She looked around, but no one was paying any attention to us. The woman who'd come in while Katie was listening to her message was long gone.

She closed her eyes, her cheeks flushed. "I'm sorry."

"I'm not."

She laughed and opened her eyes. "I just…that woman."

"The puck bunny?"

"The way she felt entitled to touch you. It got to me."

That was disappointing. She'd just kissed me to scare off a jersey chaser? Was that all the kiss had been about?

"Then I grabbed your hand, which now that I think about it is just as bad as what she was doing and she looked at me like you couldn't possibly be with me and well, you had, and I wanted to prove a point."

She hadn't been overcome with an urge to kiss me because I was wearing my lucky jeans that made my ass look good. But there were a couple of things I needed to straighten out with her. "Just to be clear, you have permission to touch me anytime you want. I don't like it when strangers do that, but I like it when you do."

She blinked at me.

"And of course I could be with you. You're amazing. You were back in high school, and you are now. I mean, I'm glad you kissed me, but you didn't have to."

She wasn't holding my hand anymore. She was chewing on her bottom lip though, so she was worried. I wanted to grab her again, kiss her until she didn't worry anymore, but Katie was a thinker while I was more impulsive.

"The bunny is gone. Do you want to go now?"

The nod Katie gave me was relieved, so I held the door open for her. I wouldn't push. But she'd definitely been into that kiss, which made me more optimistic.

This was a good step on the Get Katie Back plan.

The air was cool after the bar, a sure sign winter was

coming. Katie tucked her jacket tight to her with crossed arms. I considered putting an arm around her, just to keep her warm, but figured that would upset her. I'd gotten a kiss tonight. Not a brief meeting of lips, but a real, arousing, tongue-in-mouth kiss, so I'd settle for that. For now.

"Any problems?" I asked as I pointed the car in the right direction to take her home.

"Problems?"

"The phone call."

"Oh, no. Just a change in location for a lab." She started chewing on her lip again, so I let the conversation lapse.

With no traffic, it was only five minutes later when I stopped in front of Katie's building. She stretched out her hand to open the door.

"You know, if you ever want to go to another game, I'm happy to get a ticket for you. Or tickets, if you want to bring a friend."

She cocked her head. "That's a nice offer, but I'm not sure who I'd go with."

"Maybe Jessica?"

She smiled. "Jess doesn't go to a lot of games. But thanks, I enjoyed talking to her. I think we're going to meet up again."

Excellent. I wanted her to be comfortable with the women who hung around with my teammates. I was a little annoyed at Cooper pulling Callie away before she'd had a chance to talk to Katie, but tonight had been a big night for them, with the public outing. If that had been me and Katie, I wouldn't have felt like sharing her attention with anyone either. Next time.

"The offer stands. Just let me know."

"Thanks. I had a surprisingly nice time tonight."

"Surprisingly?" I was a little offended, but at least she did have a nice time. I just wished she liked it enough to go again, because hockey was the biggest part of my life.

"I haven't watched a game in years." Since high school, maybe? "And I wasn't sure what it would be like, meeting your teammates."

"They're nice guys." Mostly.

"I'm glad you have them, Josh. You need friends, and they seem like good ones."

"You too."

She frowned. "Me too?"

"You're a friend too." A smile crossed her face, and I had to consciously stop myself from leaning over to kiss it.

"Yeah, I'm a friend too."

Then she did open the door and head into her building. I watched until the elevator doors closed behind her.

We were friends. And that kiss showed we had chemistry.

How did I earn enough trust back that she'd combine those two, so we'd be together again?

* * *

KATIE

JOSH DROPPED me off and didn't say anything more about the kiss. I was grateful, because I was thrown by it. The condo was quiet when I let myself inside, since Madeline was on the road. No distractions for my thoughts.

What the hell had come over me? Jealousy? Possessiveness? Dog in the manger-ness?

I needed to work this out, so I sent a quick text to Nora. With the time difference, she was probably asleep, but just in case…

My phone rang. "Nora? You're awake?"

"The joy of being pregnant again. Leg cramps. Every time I lie down in bed they start up, and I don't want to keep Arlo awake. What's up, sis?"

Not a rousing vote for pregnancy. I dropped into a chair and tried to pin down what exactly was bothering me, and came up with "Josh."

"Josh? Hockey player Josh? Ex-boyfriend Josh?"

"Yep."

"Ah. He plays in Toronto now. Did you run into him?"

I gave her an edited update, not mentioning exactly how I ran into him. "He brought over some donairs and said he wanted to be friends. He apologized for how things happened in high school. And he told me Mom and Dad convinced him that breaking up with me was the right thing to do."

Nora gasped. "They did? What? Give me a moment. Stupid cramps." I heard sounds of her moving around. "Okay. I'm trying to remember what was happening then. That was around the time I told them I was pregnant, wasn't it. I'm sorry, I didn't have a lot of bandwidth to help you then. You went to Grandma's, right?"

And after Josh had broken up with me, I hadn't been helping her either. "Yeah. They suggested it, since I refused to go back to school. But now…well, now I'm wondering if they just wanted to make sure we didn't get back together."

"Was that a possibility?"

After kissing him tonight? More of a possibility than I realized. "I don't know. I was pissed and heartbroken when he broke up with me, but I really loved him. Still, breaking up by text was pretty bad."

"By text? He sent you a text? I hope you hunted him down and shoved his text up his ass."

"Not exactly."

"What did you do?"

I fell back in the chair. "Nothing."

"You didn't ask him why?"

"No," I said, voice quiet.

"Why didn't you? If you loved him that much."

I let out a long breath, releasing something I hadn't admitted before. "Because I thought I knew why."

"You did?"

"He was this big hockey prospect, and I was just the math nerd."

"Aww, sis. Insecurities, right?"

"Yeah. Why would he want to be with me?"

Nora huffed. "I do get that Mom and Dad were freaking out about me back then, but still…they shouldn't have interfered. And if you've thought you just weren't enough for him all these years, well, that would have an effect on you. Have you talked to them about it?"

"Not yet. I've been trying to figure out how upset I am, and how angry it's okay for me to feel."

"Katie, I love you, but you need to speak up. When you were in high school, that was difficult to do, but you're an adult now. You have to stand up for yourself. In your relationships, in your work—everything."

That reminded me too much of my wishy-washy behavior with my advisor, and I steered the conversation elsewhere. "I did tell Josh off. But with Mom and Dad, it's hard. They only do what they think is right for us."

Nora let out a long breath. "I hear you. They love us and support us and want us to reach our goals, but that does come with some heavy expectations."

So heavy. "I don't want to disappoint them."

"Like I did, you mean?"

My mouth dropped open. "That… I mean…"

"You can say it, you know. Mom and Dad did."

That shocked me. "What?"

"They even offered to raise the baby so I could stay in school."

Something else I hadn't known. "You didn't want that?"

A long pause. "Honestly, no. Getting pregnant threw me for a loop. It upset all my plans and freaked me out. But it also forced me to think. I'd been busy and focused on med school, becoming a doctor. Total tunnel vision. Honestly, I was lucky Arlo was willing to put up with my schedule and priorities. And then, when I saw those lines on the pregnancy test, he was a rock."

Nora's partner was great.

"But having to make those decisions forced me to look at what I wanted. Really wanted. Getting away from the hamster wheel for a few days while I worked things out made me realize I didn't want to do med school and residency and put life on hold for years. I had a great partner, we were expecting a baby and…that was good."

I swallowed. Back then, after the breakup with Josh, I'd been focused on my own misery. I'd stayed with Grandma and been removed from what was going on with my sister. I'd missed what she'd gone through. "I never knew all that. So, you're not upset that your plans changed? You're happy?"

"I am. I *so* am. It was hard for Mom and Dad, since they'd had such big plans. But I needed to live my life for me. And what you're saying about how they manipulated Josh—I'm sure they thought it was for the best, but that's not cool. Remember, it's your life. Figure out what you want."

"Right now, I just want to figure out what to do about Josh."

"Ooooh." Nora's voice was teasing. "Sounds like there's more going on than donairs. Ugh. Now I'm getting a craving for those."

"Josh said he wanted to be friends. After I heard what

Mom and Dad and his mother did, I thought I could do that. But then tonight I kissed him."

"Katie! Details!"

I told her. Not just about the puck bunny, but about how the kiss had been so good, and Josh saying I could kiss him anytime.

Nora laughed. "I'm so glad I'm done with dating. To me, sounds like he wants to pick things up again. What do you want?"

I slid down in the chair, staring at the ceiling. "Hell if I know."

"You don't want him hooking up with puck bunnies, apparently."

"Yeah. That confused me."

I heard Nora mutter something. She must have covered up the phone.

"I gotta go. Sorry, sis. Pipsqueak needs his mom. But quick advice, since you called. Seems like you still have some feelings for Josh. You should tell him, and maybe you two could see where it goes. Deciding to go out with him, or whatever, doesn't mean a lifelong commitment. If something is still there between you after five years, maybe it's worth exploring."

"Maybe it's just nostalgia."

"One way to find out."

"But he's famous here. I mean, people ask him for photos and autographs. I really don't understand why he'd want to be with me, a math nerd."

"Enough of those insecurities. There's more to him than hockey and more to you than math. Just don't be afraid to try something. I never thought about being a mom, and it turns out I love it. But I really have to go now. Love you."

"Love you too." And she was gone.

I set my phone on my chest and kept staring at the ceiling.

Nora and I hadn't been that close growing up. Three years between us had been a lot, and I'd always felt like I was losing a competition with her. Our parents might not have intended to foster that, but they had.

I'd never known that she was happy about getting pregnant five years ago. That she'd given up med school because she thought it was her best choice, not because of obligation. The way Mom and Dad had. Or at least, made us believe.

I'd had my life mapped out—Bachelor's degree, master's and then a PhD. Become a professor and live a life among my numbers.

Was that what I wanted, or was that what was safe, for me and my parents?

CHAPTER 17

DID SHE ASK TO SEE YOUR LIGHTSABER?

JOSH

THAT KISS from Katie stuck with me all night, and I went into practice with a big smile on my face.

Didn't last. Coach was pissed about the game, and he worked us hard. The trainers had told me that I should stop if I felt anything with my knee, but I didn't take the out. Hockey was a team sport, so I did the suicides with the others. I just hoped I could make a difference when we got on the ice for a game.

Before dismissing us, Coach had us gather around. More than a few of us were leaning on our sticks for support.

"I don't know what happened last night. I hope it was just a reaction after last season. But you're fucking better than that, and I want to see that next game. Instead of freaking out over losing the goddamn Cup, you can think about sweating your balls off in practice if you screw the pooch like that again."

I wasn't sure if that was really motivating us the way he

hoped, but he dismissed us so we hurried off the ice quickly before he changed his mind.

"Knee good, Ducky?" Cooper asked.

"No worse than the rest of me." I pulled off my practice jersey and tossed it toward the laundry carts.

JJ stopped by on his way to the showers. "My sister liked your girl. Said she was nice."

The grin that the kiss had started came back. "Thanks. I appreciate your sister talking to her."

"So, *is* she your girl now?"

With my skates off, I started working on my pads. "Hope so. She kissed me last night."

The guys who were around me oohed and whistled. I threw my socks at them, but I didn't really mind.

"Just a kiss?" asked Oppy.

"It was a great kiss."

Guys started chirping. JJ leaned down. "Better to take it slow and get it right than rush and mess it up."

I nodded and he left. Conversation moved on to muscles sore from practice, plans for the night, and I started to worry. JJ might have thought I was taking it slow, but really I was letting Katie drive. And I had no idea what speed she wanted. That kiss hadn't been just a test drive, had it?

When I came back from the shower, I finally found a message from Katie.

Glad to be back on the ice?

I stared at those seven words. What exactly was Katie thinking? Did the kiss tie into that somehow? I'd had a few incidents of misinterpreting texts, so I had to be sure to get this right.

Cooper paused on the way to his stall, towel around his hips. "You okay there, Ducky?"

I sighed and shoved the phone in his face. "What does that mean?"

Cooper took the phone from me and held it back a few inches. "This is from Katie?"

"Yeah."

"She knows you're playing again?"

"Yeah."

"Then I think she's asking how your first practice back went." He passed the phone back to me.

"I was hoping there was subtext there. Like, maybe she wanted to see me in person to know how I was doing."

Cooper shrugged. "I don't know her well enough to guess on that. Tell her how practice went. We're leaving tomorrow for a couple of games in New York. Keep things light and friendly till we get back. See how it goes."

I could do that. I started to text.

Felt good to be back. Leaving tomorrow for a couple of away games.

* * *

KATIE DIDN'T REPLY that day. I was nervous about that as we headed to Pearson Airport to fly out. Fitch drove, and my leg kept bouncing as I watched the city as we headed west. It must have bothered him.

"Do you have to bounce around like that?"

"What?"

"Your leg. It's almost moving the car."

"Sorry, man. I'm a little on edge."

"Why?"

"I convinced Katie we should be friends. I was ready to take it slow. But that kiss was different. Maybe she hated it and now she doesn't even want to be friends."

"Didn't you talk about it?"

"I was afraid to. In case she said it was a mistake."

"Not great on communication, you two."

He had a point. That had done us in last time. "I told her she could kiss me anytime she wanted, so this is definitely up to her now."

"Maybe she needs time to figure out what she wants."

I chewed on my thumbnail. "What if she doesn't want to see me again?"

Fitch shot me a glance. "Not possible. You've got your own special charm."

That sounded like I was a weirdo. "What does that mean?"

"It means she was crazy about you before. She's afraid of being hurt again. Before she goes all in, she needs to make sure you're not going to do something stupid this time."

"I would never."

He frowned at me before focusing back on the road. "If I'd asked you back in high school if you'd hurt her, what would you say?"

I sagged in the seat. "Fuck. You're right. But I've learned and I'd never do it again."

"It's going to take time to show her. You can't expect to just tell her, and she'll believe it."

"I guess. But I don't want to lose her. Not again."

We pulled off the 427 to get into the airport. The team had a private jet when we traveled so we didn't have to go through the main terminals. It was nice, because I'd traveled the regular way and the waiting, the lines—it was all exhausting.

New York was a short trip, so we got there in good time to do a light practice and hit up the hotel for our game day rituals. I still hadn't heard from Katie, so I didn't get my usual pregame nap the way I liked. I spent too much time trying to figure out what she was thinking, but I wouldn't know till I heard from her. Maybe I should just ask her what was going on.

I'd give her another day. So I wasn't pressing her, but I

wasn't going to ignore her either. Two days should be enough.

Soon, it was back to the arena for warm-ups, and then, the game.

The game was a shit show. Again. We were *bad.* Just like the last game when I'd watched with Katie. I scored a goal and assisted on one with Cooper, but that was all we got. Meanwhile, New York scored *seven* times. We couldn't make a pass to save our lives, and we spent what felt like half the game a man down while someone was in the sin bin for stupid penalties. Petey was peppered, and he couldn't stop them all.

We trudged back to the locker room, everyone feeling like shit, with a lecture from Coach to come. I pulled off my jersey and pads, figuring I might as well be comfortable for the rundown coming. I checked my phone and there it was. A message from Katie.

Good luck with the game tonight.

That ship had sailed, and sunk in the New York harbor by now, but reading that message put a smile on my face.

"Are we interrupting, Middleton?"

Shit, that was Coach. I dropped the phone. "Sorry, Coach."

"What the fuck are you smiling about after that game?"

Oops. Still glad to hear from Katie, but this was not the time for it. "Um, just a friend."

"Did your friend watch the game?"

I shrugged. "Dunno, but the text was from before it."

Coach crossed his arms. "Because since the puck dropped, there's been nothing to smile about from where I was watching."

And he was off.

There was something wrong with us and it was Coach's job to figure it out and find a solution, but hell if I knew what it was. We did good in practice, but when the game started, when it counted, we fell apart. It obviously related back to last season, when we'd totally fucked up the overtime in that last important game. But how to fix it? No idea.

Normally practice the morning after a game with a back-to-back happening was optional. Tomorrow it was not. Coach couldn't work us too hard with another game to play, but he was pissed, so we were skating in the morning.

* * *

ONCE COACH HAD FINISHED RIPPING us a new one, Cooper made everyone go out for something to eat. Most of us wanted to crawl back to the hotel and forget the game as soon as possible, but when our captain said we had to meet up, we did.

He'd found an Italian place not too far away and ordered massive quantities of food and beer for us. Once we'd all gathered around some pushed-together tables, he stood. "When these pitchers are empty, it's water for everyone. Don't overeat or coach will kill us at practice in the morning. And that is the last we're mentioning hockey tonight. Anyone who does is paying the tab."

So, we were team building.

It wasn't easy to get the conversation going, not when we couldn't talk about our jobs, which were hockey, or our favorite sport, which was hockey, or what we were doing tomorrow, because, again, hockey.

"Ducky—what were you smiling about to get Coach pissed off?"

I swallowed the mouthful of pasta I'd been chewing. "I wasn't the reason Coach was pissed." That rant had definitely been earned by the whole team.

"Warning, Ducky."

I nodded at Cooper. That was getting close to having to pony up for the food. "Katie sent me a message." I looked over at our captain. "But I can't say what it was about."

Crash elbowed me in the ribs. "Dirty stuff? Or just the thing that cannot be named?"

"Not dirty stuff." Though that would have been nice. At least the text meant she wasn't ghosting me.

"But it was still good?"

My mouth twisted as I considered. Not being ghosted was good. But that text was baseline good. Something more friend-y, like asking about getting together when I was back, would have been better. Talking about kissing again would have been excellent.

I shrugged. "Better than nothing."

Then I felt bad. *Anything* Katie was good. I was lucky she was giving me a chance to be friends again.

"What's better than nothing?" someone asked from down the table.

"Ducky's girl. But we can't say what it is because we can't talk about it."

"Ducky's girl is better than nothing? You can do better, Duckman."

I couldn't let that go. "Katie is *way* better than nothing. That's not what we were talking about! She sent me a message, and we were just figuring out what it meant."

"Did she ask to see your lightsaber?" Oppy asked.

I glared at him. That had been embarrassing. Both times. And was why I didn't trust my interpretation of texts.

"No!"

"Remember that time the woman got his number and asked that?"

"No. What happened?"

I dropped my head into my hands.

"Ducky was thrilled and asked her over. He invited her to

his bedroom, where he has all his *Star Wars* stuff. She headed straight for his pants."

Yeah, she'd been using *lightsaber* to mean something else. But how was I supposed to know?

"So you hooked up instead?"

I lifted my head. "No! Not when she pulled out a red condom."

The table exploded in laughter. And yeah, that was funny, until a few weeks later someone I met asked to see my lightsaber again. I thought I knew what she meant, but when I started to drop my pants, she covered her eyes. She'd wanted to see my actual *Star Wars* memorabilia, not my dick.

"So what did your girl really say?"

"I can't tell you."

"Was it dirty?"

Crash answered for me. "No, it was about what we can't talk about. Right, Ducky?"

I nodded, but the conversation had taken off on its own. "What are we not allowed to talk about? Threesomes when it's two guys?"

"Are we not allowed to talk about that?"

"Some people still freak out about the gay thing."

"Ducky and his girl had a threesome with a guy?"

I said *no*, but no one was listening to me. They went off the rails talking about threesomes and how to describe if the two same-gendered people got with each other or not, and I actually learned some things. That led to the guys talking about vacations and where the best places to go were in the offseason, and suddenly the meal was over.

We'd managed to get through it without anyone getting more than a warning about mentioning the banned topic. Cooper had let everyone off, so he put down his card to pay for the meal.

"Good job, Ducky," he said when I paused to thank him for the food.

"Me? I thought we couldn't talk about…you know."

He shook his head. "Once you got everyone talking about sex, we managed the meal without anyone obsessing over the game."

I snorted. "I guess you can say it since you're paying."

He took back the card from the waitstaff, signing on to what I was pretty sure was a very generous tip.

"I can say it because I'm making up the rules." He slipped the receipt into his wallet and grinned. "Now, let's get back for curfew and a good night's sleep."

CHAPTER 18
MY PATH TO ACADEMIC GLORY

KATIE

JOSH DIDN'T ANSWER my text right away, which made sense. He was playing a game, and he couldn't have the phone on the bench or the ice with him. I could only imagine the number of phones that would be destroyed if they did that.

Actually, I could probably work out a formula. Say, so many guys on the team, with one phone per person…

My phone ringing distracted me while I was still working on variables, like how often a puck might hit a player, perhaps when they were blocking shots, or a check against the boards and the force that would have. They didn't have pockets in those uniforms, did they?

For a moment, something very much like anticipation sparked at the idea of Josh calling me. The call wasn't Josh though. It was my parents. And unlike usual, my first response was anger.

I loved my parents. They were great. Supportive and loving. But what they'd done in high school—that was wrong. Even if I understood their reasoning. There was a weight of expectations they had for us, and once Nora decided to keep her baby, all those expectations landed on me. And they'd decided breaking my heart was worth it to ensure I didn't get sidetracked.

I was ambitious and wanted to do something with my life, but I was doing it for my parents and sister as well as for myself and…that was a big part of the reason I'd left home to come to Toronto. To get some space. Something even more important now that I knew what had happened five years ago.

I couldn't not answer. And I should clear up this last bit of the past since what had happened then affected my future. I curled up on the couch and accepted the call.

"Katie! Are you okay?"

I blinked. Mom sounded worried, which made no sense. It derailed my plans for this conversation. Everything was going fine. I mean, a couple of my students were being pains in the ass, and my advisor was a total misogynist, but that was part of life as a TA and not anything my parents would know about. Not something I wanted to share.

"I'm good, Mom. How are you?"

"You sure everything is fine, Katie-bug?" Dad's nickname for me, once I became an adult, was a little much, but I knew it came from a place of love. At least no one was here to hear him.

"Sure I'm sure. Doing the TA thing, stretching my brain in class, and my roommate is really nice." Maybe they were worried about Madeline.

"We heard you ran into Josh." Mom's voice was still a little panicky.

What the— "Where did you hear that?" Nora wouldn't have told them, would she? Fuck, this would be bad.

"Josh's mother dropped by work to mention it." My

mother's voice was tight. She was not a fan of Mrs. Middleton. And as far as I knew, they didn't run across each other. Probably on purpose.

I still thought of her as Mrs. Middleton. She'd never asked me to call her by her first name, the way my parents did with Josh and all my friends.

"She told you I saw Josh." Josh said he'd figured out his mother didn't like me after he'd talked to her, but why would she go out of her way to tell my parents?

"You remember what happened with Josh last time."

Of course I remember, Mom. And now I could get to the angry part of this conversation. "You mean when you two and Mrs. Middleton convinced Josh to break up with me so that I didn't give up on school?"

Silence. They hadn't expected me to know. I didn't say anything else, waiting for them to figure out how to spin it.

"We wanted what was best for you," Dad said. Josh's excuse for the breakup as well.

"And you knew better than me what that was?" I was holding back my anger by a thread. They always praised my intelligence, but they didn't really believe it, did they?

Mom spoke. "You were so young, and emotions are intense when you're that age."

That was the excuse they were going with? "Why did everyone think I was so stupid for Josh that I wouldn't do what was right for me? Seriously. I understand Mrs. Middleton. She's always been possessive. But I expected better of *my* parents."

Another silence. I wasn't making this easy on them. I still had issues from that breakup, and that wasn't all on Josh.

"Your sister—" Dad began.

I cut them off. "I'm not Nora, and the fact that you thought you had to scare off my boyfriend because Nora got pregnant? Is not fair. You assumed I couldn't use my brain to make the right decision for me. That somehow, because I was female, I would be run by my emotions. So you manipulated Josh to break up with me."

Dad countered. "Your sister is also smart, but she's now at home with a kid, after dropping out of med school. And she's pregnant again so who knows if she'll ever finish her nursing degree? She had plans, and they're gone. We didn't want the same for you."

But manipulating my life instead of talking to me? Not cool. "We'll never know what might have happened if everyone had left us to figure things out for ourselves, will we? But I've got my degree now, so crisis averted!"

Dad asked, "But you're still going to get your master's, right?"

I pulled the phone away for a minute and yelled into a pillow.

"Katie?"

I lifted my face from the pillow. "Yes, I'm still working on my master's. Do I need to send you my grades to prove it? Maybe the papers from my work as a TA?"

They'd better not say yes because no way in hell was I reporting back to them like that. I was twenty-three years old, not thirteen.

Dad realized he'd pushed me as far as he could. "We don't mean to upset you, Katie-bug. We're just worried."

I drew in a long breath. "What are you worried about?"

"You and Josh were very…involved."

What the actual fuck? "So you're afraid if I see him again, I'm going to give up my academic career and ask him to give me babies?"

"No, of course not, just…you wouldn't do that, would you?" Mom questioned.

I was going to destroy this phone as badly as any hockey player on the ice might. "I'm an adult. I'm following the goals

I set a long time ago. I am smart enough to make my own decisions and decide what is best for my future on my own. And whether that's to get my PhD or to drop out and get a job selling burgers, that's my call."

"Oh, Katie-bug. No. You're so smart. Don't waste that."

Did they think I was intelligent or not? "Just not smart enough to make my own decisions?"

"I think we're getting a little off topic here." I wasn't sure what topic my dad thought we were on. "We wanted to be sure you weren't getting involved with Joshua again."

They really did think I couldn't think in Josh's presence. Or they had no faith in me.

"Again, that's my decision. You have no say over who I do or do not date. But do you not realize he's a big fu—fudging deal here? He's one of the top players in the NHL. He's making more money in a year than I'm likely to in a lifetime. Why would he want to entice me off my path to academic glory?"

Another silence. Mom sighed. "You're right. It's not like you're back in high school or have anything in common. We didn't mean to upset you—his mother made it sound like you two were together and we worried."

That didn't make it right. My hands were shaking, and I was in danger of saying something I couldn't take back. If I ever saw Mrs. Middleton again...

"Moving on—how is Nora doing?" Since Nora hadn't spilled the beans about my kissing Josh, better for them to think she and I hadn't talked recently.

My folks might not be happy that she threw away being a doctor for being a mom, but they loved their grandson. I managed to keep the topic off my possible love life for the rest of the call and hung up before they could get back around to it again. After all, I had an academic career taking up my time, so I needed to work.

I was still vibrating with anger an hour after that. Josh's mother, interfering, trying to break me and Josh up before we could get together. Assuming I'd forget everything that had happened. And my parents—their opinion of my common sense that low...

Well, last time they'd managed to write the script for Josh and me. This time, I was going to make my own decisions. If I wanted to keep seeing Josh as a friend, they could just live with it. Before I could second-guess myself, I sent another text to Josh.

Want to get together when you're back in town?

* * *

JOSH

THE ANSWER WAS OBVIOUSLY YES. But getting a time worked out was more difficult.

We had a couple of evening games once we were back, and I didn't want to have a rushed get-together after I got out of the arena. The way we were losing, we weren't feeling good after our games.

The next couple of nights that I was free, she had an evening class. Then Cooper had everyone over for a team social event. I was not allowed to bail. I'd asked Katie if she wanted to come, but she said we should talk first.

I spent way too much time trying to work out what that meant. What did she want to talk about, and was that good or bad?

Finally, a week and a half later, I had a night with no game, no team commitments, and she didn't have anything either. Her roommate was out, so she invited me over. I picked up Thai on the way.

Katie was quiet when she opened the door. "Come on in. Thanks for getting dinner."

I smiled at her, wanting her to be comfortable. She shouldn't ever feel bad around me. Whatever she said, I wasn't going to be angry. Disappointed maybe, but not angry.

I followed her to the kitchen. She had plates and utensils out on the island, so I set the food down and started to pull out the containers.

"Want a beer?"

"Sure. Whatcha got?"

That got a grin out of her. "Keith's. Madeline also has a couple of craft beers and some wine if you'd rather."

"Keith's for sure. Cooper had some of that expensive shit at his place the other night, but why pay more for something that's only half as good?"

"Exactly. Madeline says I'm brainwashed."

"The guys tell me the same thing. Too bad—they're the ones losing out."

Katie set my beer in front of me and settled on a stool. For a minute, we were busy sharing the food.

She took a bite and moaned. "That's so good."

I nodded. "I know a lot of good places around—I can give you recs if you want."

That got our conversation going. I told her about a couple of takeout places I knew that weren't too expensive, and then we talked about restaurants we liked back home. And then it was us. Just talking, telling stories... It was easy with Katie. Easy, and comfortable, and just made me happy.

I wanted more of this. I wanted it all the time.

When we'd finished all we could eat, I helped her pack the leftovers in the fridge. We had another road trip coming up, so I convinced her to keep them. She put the dishes in the dishwasher and grabbed us each another beer before leading me into the living room.

I sat on the couch, hoping she'd sit with me, but she curled up in a chair. She was looking nervous again, so it seemed like the talk part was now. And maybe this wasn't going to go the way I wanted.

"My parents called."

Something twisted around my guts, clenching them tightly. Katie's family was close, and they hadn't liked us together before. I hadn't understood that, so now, even though I didn't think I was any kind of a problem for her education goals, I couldn't trust that they were happy about us hanging out.

"Your mom told them we were spending time together, and they were worried. It made me angry, but I talked to them about what happened."

"I'm sorry Mom did that." I was beginning to understand how much Mom didn't want me with Katie.

"And I talked to Nora. And as pissed as I was—am—about how everyone was so manipulative back in high school, I was at fault too."

"Wait, what? You didn't do anything wrong." Everyone else had made decisions for her, but what did she think she'd done?

"I didn't ask you why. I didn't fight back, for us. I just accepted it and hid away at my grandmother's."

That wasn't something I'd even considered. "Oh. So, maybe we could have talked, figured out what to do together?" A smile flickered across my face, and my guts relaxed.

"I could have insisted that we talk, maybe found out what was going on."

"Yeah, our parents wouldn't have been able to manipulate you like they did me." Katie had seen things about my mom that I'd missed. I'd been too quick to accept what was on the surface.

"Don't be so hard on yourself. They played on your vulnerability. And mine."

"What?" *Katie felt vulnerable?*

"You know why I didn't ask anything when you sent that text?"

I obviously hadn't given this much thought. "Because of Rhonda?"

She twisted the beer bottle in her hands. "That didn't help. But even right after. I figured, yeah, it was inevitable."

"But why?" What problems had she seen in what we had together that I'd missed?

Her eyes dropped. "Because I'm just me. A math nerd. Smart about that, but not as pretty and—"

I sat up. "What the hell are you talking about? You're pretty. No, you're beautiful. I like the way you look."

Her gaze flickered up. "Thanks. But the closer you were getting to being drafted, well, more people wanted to be with you. Hang out with you, go out with you."

I frowned. "I never cheated, Katie. I never wanted to."

"I'm not suggesting you did or would. I was insecure. Being smart was always the priority in my family, and once you were done with math classes, what did you need me for?"

I shoved myself out of my chair. "What the—do you think I was using you? Just being with you because you were helping me with math? Because I could have found another tutor. Probably one who would have done the assignments for me and not made me work."

"Josh, I'm not accusing you of anything. I'm talking about how I felt. Could you just listen?"

I wanted to move. To do something with this jittering

frustration I felt. But Katie was biting her lip. I pulled in a deep breath.

I was worked up because if she thought those things, I must have done something to make her feel like that. But maybe I was wrong. I sat down. "Okay, keep talking."

She watched me for a moment, then continued. "I get it. It was a shitty thing to think about you, and it was all based on my own insecurities. I know you wouldn't do that. But, somewhere deep inside, I expected that one day you'd look around and see that you could do so much better." Her gaze fell to the floor. "I don't have a lot of confidence in my attractiveness."

My mouth opened to argue but she continued.

"Just like you don't have a lot of confidence in your intelligence."

"But *I*—"

She held up her hand. "It's not true about you. I know, you had a rough time in school, and I've told you that doesn't mean you're stupid."

I rubbed my hands through my hair. Katie thought I'd find someone I liked better. Someone more attractive. I didn't get that, but I always thought she'd find me stupid and maybe get tired of me. My thinking that was because of how I felt about me. Not what she'd done.

So her feelings weren't because of me messing up. *Right?*

"Can we make a rule that if I can't say I'm stupid, you can't say you're not pretty? Not beautiful?"

Her nose squinched up, but then she nodded. "Anyway, I apologize for letting my insecurities contribute to what happened back then. I can't blame it all on you because I could have talked to you and didn't."

I dropped back in the chair. "So you're not pissed anymore?"

A corner of her mouth quirked up. "I'm still pissed about

the text thing, but I'm angry with our parents about why it happened, not you."

That all seemed good. "So that's what you wanted to talk about?" We could still be friends, and I could work on getting us to more if that was the case.

I'd push for more until she said no. That was how I got to be in the league even though I was one of the shortest players. I was fast, and I was pushy.

"Yeah. We can be friends with a clear slate."

Tension eased out of my body. And determination filled it up instead.

CHAPTER 19
AM I GOING TO LOOK STUPID?

JOSH

I WAS PRETTY STOKED about that chat, till I wondered if part of it was her making sure we were *just* friends. The friends thing was good, but could we never move past it?

I sent her some memes and "how are you doing" texts when we were on the road. Friends could do that. I wanted to move on to spending quality time together. But if I made it too date-like, she might say no. If she told me it wasn't happening, I'd have to respect that, but I wanted as much time to woo her as I could before she had a chance to shut the door on us.

Figuring out when we were both free was also a thing. I played on average three nights a week. Half our games were away, so unless we played our crosstown rivals we were on the road. Katie had a couple of evening classes. She wasn't the professor, but kind of was so she had to be there.

I had to come up with something we could do together that wasn't too datey and then find an opportunity when we were both available to do it. I spent a lot of time trying to solve that problem.

Even at practice. Which wasn't like me. I normally didn't think of anything else while I was on the ice, but Katie was important. I didn't get distracted while I was actually doing drills, and definitely not when I was playing. But times like now, when Coach was working with the third line, I sat on the boards, watching with part of my brain while I weighed ideas.

Asking her to dinner would definitely be a date activity. I'd gotten away with it when we were going to the season opener, but that was kind of thanking her for keeping me company at the game. And giving her tickets to watch with someone else when we were playing this badly? Didn't seem smart. I needed to be sneaky until she remembered how good we were together.

Maybe a group activity. Or something two people did with other people around. The guys I hung out with were my teammates, and did I want them in on it? Not unless Jess was there, so Katie had someone she could relate to. I didn't know any of Katie's friends here in Toronto.

If there was a Tolkien film coming out, I could book an advance screening since I was a hockey player and we had fans. But there wasn't one. There were a few things I could get preferential treatment for, but which of those things would she like? We'd gone to a driving range with Cooper and Callie in the summer, but Katie wasn't into golf.

"Middleton!" I jerked my mind back to practice and dropped off the boards.

"Yes, Coach."

"Enough daydreaming. Is that what's wrong with this team? Got something more important to think about?"

"No, sir." Didn't need to give the man more reason to be pissed. It was too late though. We were still losing games, playing like shit, and he was frustrated. I'd given him a chance to vent that, and that was on me. I definitely had to deal with the Katie thing so it didn't impact my play.

I stopped for the trainers to check out my knee after we got off the ice. Everything was fine, no pain to report. Guys were coming out of the showers by the time I was stripping down.

"What was that?" Oppy asked, flicking me with a towel.

"Sorry." Coach had kept us an extra half hour after my slipup.

"It's not like you to flake out like that," Deek, my other linemate, said.

"I know. It's a personal thing, and I'll keep it off the ice, I swear."

Barnes passed by. "Still that girl?"

"Oh, right. That's why he's not focusing on his game?"

"I'm focusing just fine, fuck you very much." I currently had more points than anyone else. Sure, we were just a few weeks in, but…

"What's the problem?" Oppy leaned against his locker, watching me closely.

"It's not a problem," I argued.

"Well, you were distracted and Coach got pissed. You're normally his golden boy."

I huffed. "I'm trying to think of a way to hang out with her, as friends."

"I thought you wanted to date her."

"I do, but she's not ready yet. I need something fun we can do together that isn't too much like a date. And then after we spend a lot of time together, we can be more than friends." Everyone frowned. "It worked in high school. She was my tutor first. Then we started hanging out and pretty soon dating, for almost two years."

Royster slapped my shoulder. "Okay, we have to help

Ducky find some way to impress his 'friend' so they can move into having sex again."

I glared at him, because it wasn't just about sex, but if they could think of something I hadn't, it would help.

"A nice restaurant?"

"That's boring, and also, definitely a date." I'd come up with that idea on my own.

"But if he can use his reputation to get into someplace expensive with a long wait list…"

Bongo turned to me. "Does she like that? When you use your hockey influence?"

I shook my head. "Not really. If she did, she'd have asked me for stuff, right?"

Everyone nodded. We all got hit up for favors and gifts.

"We need something not boring, and not too much of a date. Something friends can do." Oppy frowned, like it hurt his brain to think that hard.

"You said she's smart, right?" Mitch asked.

I nodded. "She's here doing her master's. In math." Yeah, I was bragging.

"And you think she'd date down to you?" Bongo teased.

That was a good question. "I hope so." But maybe she was out of my league now.

"Ducky, that was a joke."

"Maybe it's not. I mean, hockey doesn't last forever, and then she'd be stuck with me?" Right now, I had money and was known to some people, but she hadn't been jumping over the chance to be with me, had she?

Mitch spoke up. "I've got it." He was tapping on his phone, looking things up. "Yeah, this will work. Find out when she's free."

"What is it?"

He grinned at me. "An escape room at Castle Loma. She gets to use her brain, and you can have dinner after."

I frowned. "Am I going to look stupid?"

"She's in STEM, right?"

"STEM?" Oppy was frowning again.

Mitch explained. "Science, tech, engineering, math. Those are traditionally male-dominated fields. She's probably had to prove herself over and over again."

Had she? I should ask her about that. I'd never considered that, because she'd always been so brilliant at math that it was a given. "Okay, so still want to know why I should do something I won't do well at."

"You are going to go and let her shine. Let her use her brain, and instead of competing with her, you support her. That's going to win you major points."

Approving murmurs came from around the room. That sounded good. Really good. I was never going to fool Katie with how smart I was. She'd been my tutor, so she knew. But I could definitely support her when she showed how smart *she* was.

An escape room. That wasn't a super romantic thing. But if she felt good about me after… "Yeah. Let's go with that."

"We can go with you, make sure everything goes smoothly," Royster added.

"Oh, hell no."

"Ah, come on Ducky. We wanna hang out with her too."

I shook my head, recognizing disaster when it was right in front of me. The guys began to argue about whether or not they should be on this non-date. Then Fitch nudged me.

"Yeah?"

"How important is it that this really not look like a date?"

"Kinda?"

"Then maybe take a few of the guys along. Maybe Jess— JJ's sister. They seemed to get along when we were all out at the Top Shelf."

He had a good point.

I stood up. "Hey, assholes." The conversation dropped. "A few of you can come along. A *few*. Like, JJ if he brings his sister." I considered. "And Cooper with his girlfriend."

JJ turned around from where he'd been dressing. "What?"

"Bring your sister and come along to the escape room."

Mitch, who was dressed and ready to leave, explained to JJ. JJ turned to me with his rare smile. "Oh, this sounds like fun. We'll be there."

"I'll check with Callie," Cooper said.

Good. Two math people along, and JJ and Cooper were guys I could trust not to embarrass me. Not too badly, anyway.

"Do Jayna and I get to come?" Mitch asked.

I nodded. He'd thought up the idea after all. That was eight people—big enough to not be a date.

"It can't all be couples," Royster pointed out. He was right, but JJ and his sister weren't a couple.

Unfortunately, I'd lost control by then.

* * *

*K*ATIE

I HADN'T SEEN Josh for a week and I was second-guessing myself. I'd been pissed at my parents and wanted to prove to them that I could see Josh and not get sidelined. But they had a valid point. Getting involved with him again, even if we kept it to the friend zone, was complicated. And friend zone was all I could do. I was still thinking about my conversations with Nora and my parents and not completely settled in my program at school, thanks to my misogynistic *maybe something less taxing* advisor. I did not need more complications.

I'd dithered over whether I'd done the right thing asking to see Josh again, and then whether I should actually see him again. I'd worried that the kiss might have made him think I wanted to date again. Turned out, I didn't need to worry. When we were finally able to find a time we were both free, he'd suggested an escape room at Casa Loma, which was fun and not too intense for two people who were walking a line between friends and more. Unless he thought we'd be going back to his place or mine after. I got to fret about that until he picked me up with Daniel and JJ and Jess in the back seat. We were definitely staying on the friend side of that line. *Good. Very good.*

So why the hell did I feel…disappointed?

The only free seat was the front, so I let myself in without debating it. Twisting my head around I said. "Hi, Jess. Nice to see you again."

She smiled at me. "Couldn't let this be too hockey player heavy. Did you officially meet my brother, Justin?"

"I don't think so."

He nodded his head. "Nice to meet you officially, Katie."

"Shouldn't I be in the back seat? I mean, I'm not that big." The guys didn't look comfortable back there. They shook their heads, so I scooched my seat up as far as it would go.

I checked the three hockey players. The Blaze had lost two more games on the road, so they had to be feeling bad about the start to their season. But they seemed okay, heckling Josh about his driving and joking around about how quickly they could do this escape room, since they had Jess and I as secret weapons. That was healthy, right? They could put hockey aside for a night out.

When we got there, the place was certainly impressive enough, lit up against the night sky. I'd looked it up when Josh suggested we do this. Casa Loma was the self-indulgent and massive castle built by Canada's version of a robber baron. It had stone turrets and chimneys and included an underground tunnel to the stables as well as secret passageways, according to the internet. It looked like an interesting place, and was open to the public, but we were just going to a small part of it to participate in an escape room. They had a few.

Josh paid for parking, and we piled out of the car and headed around the side to where the escape rooms were. Tonight wasn't the time, but I'd definitely be interested in coming back and seeing the rest of the place. Who could resist a secret passage?

Almost immediately, we were joined by more of the hockey team. Cooper, of underwear fame, was with the same redheaded woman Josh had introduced as Callie the other night, the woman he'd kissed on the arena kiss cam. That clip had been played over and over. Based on how he stayed beside her, holding her hand, and the looks he was giving her? Yeah, he was taken.

There was one other woman in the group, Jayna. She was dating Mitch, the backup goalie. Since Josh didn't immediately share her math qualifications, I assumed she was not a numbers person. The rest of the guys were introduced by nicknames, of which I only remembered a couple. Crash and Bongo, because, well, those were unusual. There were three other guys, one a dark and broody Russian who I think they called Pete.

"Are we ready?" Cooper asked.

The group seemed a little unsure. "Are we going to look stupid here?" someone asked, maybe Bongo?

"Don't worry about it. We have our secret weapons." Josh wrapped an arm around my shoulders. "Katie is getting her master's in math, remember?"

Had he talked about me?

"And Callie is a tax attorney. So let's go beat this thing."

Josh sounded totally confident. Were they expecting tax or legal questions?

The hockey players had booked the whole room for themselves. A group was normally ten to fifteen people. Based on how many other escapers wanted to talk to the players while we were waiting, even though they'd signed up for the other rooms, having the place to ourselves would give the guys the chance to do this without fans interrupting.

So this was not a date, but a team bonding thing. I was here to solve math problems and that was good. No disappointment, not at all.

It was eye-opening to see how people reacted to the hockey players, and not just in a fan hangout like the Top Shelf. I had mostly avoided hockey after Josh and I split up. And when I saw the players reacting like regular people with Josh, they seemed normal because he was just a normal person to me.

But they weren't, not in this city. My concern that maybe Josh wanted to be more than friends? Was just a delusion.

He came back from the check-in and grabbed my hand. "They're ready for us."

Daniel rounded up the others and we headed into the room for the first puzzle, Josh still holding me. But that wasn't something I did with my friends. Now I wondered if that idea of him wanting more was really a delusion. I was so confused.

* * *

WE DID NOT ESCAPE in time. This was a challenging task, and honestly, the guys weren't much help. They were stupidly competitive, and they might work together on the ice, but here they tried to do too much individually. Callie was focused, and she and Cooper solved some of the puzzles, but the group had been split into sections for the different problems, and Royster, Crash and one of the other guys spent more time dishing on the others than trying to solve anything.

Jess and I worked on puzzles together, with JJ and Josh hanging around us but mostly letting us do the work. I liked Jess. She was friendly, and like me, was with the players but not *with* a player. We hadn't been able to meet up yet, since she had a regular nine-to-five job and my hours were all over the place, but I had to make that happen. I needed friends in this city.

After not escaping from the room, to groans and catcalls, all within our group, we were released and everyone headed to the parking lot. By some kind of mutual agreement, we went out for a meal after. Cooper and Callie took off on their own, but the rest of us had burgers and beers at a high-end burger place.

Despite failing the escape room, I had a good time. I sat between Jess and Josh. Unlike the guys, I wasn't a competitive person, so I didn't really care if we solved the room or not—I was having fun. Daniel frowned at his teammates when they did something stupid, but maybe they needed some time to not worry about hockey. We hardly mentioned the subject at dinner either, though people did come up to the table to ask for selfies, autographs and answers to questions.

When we piled into the car again, I got shotgun without calling it. JJ and Jess shared a condo not far from the building Josh and Daniel were in, but Josh dropped Daniel and the twins off first.

"Do we have something else planned?" I asked.

Josh was still parked in front of his condo building after Daniel disappeared inside. "I just wanted to maybe talk for a bit?"

"Okay." I wasn't sure what about.

Despite saying he wanted to talk, he was quiet on the way over to my place. I was happy to relax in the comfortable seat and watch the city moving past us. Josh was a competent driver and familiar with the city streets.

Madeline's place wasn't far, so he soon pulled into a parking space on a side street. During the daytime the parking spots were limited and always occupied, but not at this time of night. I twisted in the car to see his face.

He was watching me with his worried puppy expression. "Did you have fun tonight? The guys weren't too much?"

Was that what he was worried about? "It was a lot of fun. Your teammates are easy to get along with. You're the only hockey player I know, so I wasn't sure what they'd be like."

He shrugged. "They're just people."

"You're right. And since I knew you back in high school, you seem like a normal person. But others don't think you are." People like Andrea. "You guys are kinda famous around here." I was happy he had found his dream. Despite our high school history, he was a nice guy.

"We play a sport. Not a big deal."

It actually was, based on what I'd heard about hockey player salaries. "I'm glad you haven't got a big head about it anyway."

"So, um, would you like to do something like this again?"

"An escape room?"

"Not sure about that. But hanging out. Friends."

Right. Friends. He was an outgoing guy—the hand-holding thing was probably just to make me feel included. And more of this? I'd had fun. I didn't know a lot of people in the city, and sometimes it was lonely. So far, I'd only done free-time things with my roommate, who traveled half the time, and Andrea, who had a partner and was busy on her own. Now, I had Jess and Josh to hang out with as well. He was busy during the season with games and practice and traveling—it didn't have to be complicated. "Yeah, that would be nice."

"Even if we just hung out, watched a movie or something?" His brow furrowed, like he was worried I might not like that.

"Honestly, some days that's all I have the energy for."

"I'd like to watch that *Lord of the Rings* show with you."

"Didn't you watch it?"

"Yeah, but you know more about it. I'd like to hear what you think of it."

That sounded...great. Easy, comfortable, low stress. Friendly. "Let's do that."

There was a big smile on his face. "When are you free?"

CHAPTER 20
SUBTLE

JOSH

THE TEAM finally notched its first win at home. The game was tied at the end of regulation, so went into overtime and then a shootout. Which wasn't great, but at least we could score when it was one guy against the goalie. Petey held up his end—he was the only one of us playing well in games right now.

Coach didn't let up in practice. We were at the bottom of the Eastern standings. The crowds at home were quiet, and there was a different air, both in the home arena and on the road.

Everyone expected us to lose. And we were going on a road trip, which only made it harder to win.

I didn't know what all went into making our schedule—there were a lot of teams, and some shared their arena with basketball teams or other groups, so fitting things in had to be difficult. Katie probably knew how to use math to make it all work. This trip we were playing the California teams and

Seattle. The time changes were brutal—it felt like we were playing after our normal game would have ended. Our internal clocks were messed up.

It was nice to hit Cali later in the season when the change from the cold in Toronto was a relief, but we were arriving at the beginning of November. Pretty sure we were hitting Edmonton and Calgary in February when it would be fucking freezing.

"Hello?"

I blinked up at Fitch. We were carpooling to the airport again, and were ready to leave. "Yeah?"

"I asked if you wanted to take some coffee with us."

"Sure. Sounds good."

He filled up a thermal cup for me, adding the creamer I liked. "Tired this morning?"

I shrugged. "We don't have to get up this early most days."

He held up his hand. "We'd better go."

The sooner we left, the sooner we'd be back and I could spend time with Katie again.

* * *

I TEXTED Katie a picture of the Space Needle once we got to Seattle. She sent back a photo of the pile of papers she had to grade. After this trip I could finally work out some time for us to spend together now that I didn't have to worry about doing something more exciting than watching TV together. I wanted to see her, hear her voice, not just letters she'd typed. But it was coming. We were officially friends, and with some time, I'd convince her we could be more. That this time I'd do things right.

I was in a great mood as we settled into the hotel. We had a good skate at their new arena in Seattle, and I napped before we headed back for the game. After doing well in practice and warm-up, I told the guys this was it, we had it now. We were going to turn our season around on this road trip. I just knew it.

I knew shit.

The puck dropped and we couldn't play.

I did okay. I didn't draw any penalties, but if anyone picked up my passes, it was a player from Seattle. Petey had been our rock, but tonight he let in three in the first period, and first intermission our locker room was despondent. I wanted to tell them we could get this back, but I'd tried that kind of thing before the game. My good feelings from working things out with Katie didn't translate to the team.

By the end of the second, we were down 5-0, and we were lucky it wasn't worse. We'd killed a couple of penalties but couldn't stop them scoring five-on-five. Coach put Mitchell in for the third, and you could say it was an improvement—he only let in two. Royster and I managed to score a goal together to mess up Seattle's shutout, but that was the only good news from that game.

I asked if anyone wanted to go out after, but no one did. I didn't either, just thought maybe someone needed to hit up a bar or club to cheer them up.

We were quiet on the flight to California.

We pulled off a win in San Jose. Not a pretty one, but they were struggling this year, and some kind of shit was going on with their team. They took stupid penalties. We got two power play goals and only gave up one, so we finally got another W.

That cheered us up until we played Anaheim. And then LA. We got a point in LA since we didn't lose until overtime, but three points out of a possible eight wasn't anything to celebrate.

* * *

ONCE WE DRAGGED our sorry asses back to Toronto, it was a relief when Katie and I could finally find a night to watch the *Ring* series. An evening without any hockey to think about was almost as good as spending time with Katie.

I asked her to come to my place. Where she was living looked a lot nicer, but my place was more comfortable, and I still felt a little awkward about Katie's roommate. My mom had added some stuff to make the condo look nice, but I didn't have time to fuss with things that weren't essential.

A super comfy couch and a kick-ass TV *were* essential. I always had Keith's on hand, so beverages were covered, but I also made sure we had the red licorice Katie liked, and her favorite flavor of chips.

"Sure you don't want me to leave?" Fitch asked while I was pacing around, suddenly wishing I'd gotten more of those decorative things Mom had talked about. Not like Katie hadn't already been here, but...

"Not this time. Maybe after she's comfortable. But if it's too much like a date she might not come again."

And I definitely wanted this to continue. My strategy wasn't complicated. Back in high school, we'd gotten together for tutoring. Started talking and hanging out to watch TV and then we were dating. It worked before, so it would again. Maybe.

The desk called to say my visitor was here. I'd made sure they knew she was welcome anytime. I headed for the door, so I could meet her in the hallway.

"She was here before, right?"

"So?"

"So she knows her way."

I turned. "Yeah. If I look too eager, it's pushing that date line."

Fitch rolled his eyes. "You could just ask her out on an actual date."

I shook my head. "Not yet. It's going to take a while for her to forget what I did back in high school. I can be patient."

There was a knock and I jumped before walking at a normal pace to the door. I heard Fitch snicker.

I opened it and there she was. Similar to when we'd been going out in high school, but different too. The blonde streaks in her hair looked good. She'd pulled her hair up in a ponytail and was wearing a jean jacket over a T-shirt with the ring from LOTR and the script inside it on the front. She could read that writing, not me, but I knew what it was and didn't try to decipher it. If I looked too closely, I'd be appreciating the changes in the curves she had, and this was not the time. "Hey. Nice shirt."

She grinned. "Hey Josh, nice shirt."

I looked down, as if I'd forgotten what I was wearing. I couldn't, because it had taken me fifteen minutes to decide. Anything hockey would be trying too hard to impress her with my career. Anything related to *Lord of the Rings* would be trying too hard to do the same with the books she loved. So I finally settled on an old Keith's Pale Ale T-shirt. It was soft and maybe a little snug, showing off the muscles I'd worked hard for. Subtle, I thought.

Her eyes drifted over my chest. *Yes!*

"I've got beer in the fridge, ready to go."

She held up a bag she'd been holding. "I brought some too."

I stood there, grinning at her, so happy she was there.

"Can I come in?"

"Oh, sorry. Sure."

I stepped back, and she heeled off her Vans before following me into the TV room.

"Hi, Daniel."

Fitch had settled in an easy chair. There was another recliner, but it didn't have as good a view to watch the screen as the couch, so Katie and I would share that. It might have seemed a little obvious, but the couch was big enough for at least five people. Not especially cozy.

"Katie. How are you doing?" He nodded at her.

I took her six-pack and headed to the fridge with it.

"Okay. Glad the weather has cooled down."

"How's school?"

I was back with three bottles of beer in time to see her curl into a corner of the couch and roll her eyes. "Let's just say I want to talk about that as much as you want to discuss your job."

Fitch tilted his head. "Good point. Josh tells me you're an expert on this *Lord of the Rings* stuff."

I handed him a beer and put the other two on the coffee table in front of the couch. I picked up the remote and turned on the TV.

"I'm a fan. I've read the books—"

"Multiple times," I interrupted.

"And watched the movies and the show."

"Multiple times."

Katie ignored my interruptions. "Have you read them?"

"No." Fitch swallowed some beer and made a face. I scrolled through the menu to find the first episode. "I moved to the US from Sweden when I was ten and people told me I should read them, but they were a little too challenging for my English back then."

"And he's never seen the show, so it's all new to him. I told him you could answer any questions he had." He owed me after that freaky dragon tattoo movie, and I was collecting.

Fitch looked a little nervous.

Katie laughed. "I'll only answer if you ask. I know not everyone is as keen as I am."

He looked over at me. I sat on the couch, not too close too

Katie, but not as far away as I could be. "I won't quiz you on it either."

Katie smiled at me. "Josh only watched the movies. He wasn't a big reader. And no"—her smile turned to a frown—"it's not because you weren't smart enough. A lot of people find those books challenging."

I could feel my cheeks heating up, so I asked "Ready?" and hit play.

* * *

FITCH HAD questions for Katie after the first episode, and she was excited to talk about it, her eyes shining.

"The biggest difference is Finrod's story, but since they didn't have the rights to the *Silmarillion*—" Katie stopped herself. "Sorry, I can get carried away."

Fitch shrugged. "I asked."

"And I over-answered."

"No problem. But I have some things to deal with, so I'll let you two watch the next episode. Good night, Katie. Catch a ride in the morning, Ducky?"

"Sure."

Katie frowned as he walked away. "Did I bore him that much?"

I was pretty sure he was trying to help me, but I couldn't tell her that. "He's dealing with a divorce and she's on the West Coast, so it might be that."

"Oh, I'm sorry."

"Yeah. It happens, but it's never fun."

She dragged her teeth over her lip. "Did you ever get serious—sorry, that's not really my business."

"I don't mind you asking. I never got serious about anyone, so I don't have anything like that in the past. Do you?" *Shit.* She wasn't seeing anyone, was she? I'd never thought to ask.

She shook her head. *Phew.* "No, it's been school for the past five years. No one serious."

But there had been nonserious guys? That idea chewed at me, but I had no ground to stand on. I'd had a lot of nonserious women. I'd been trying to find another Katie, but there was only one.

The one and only was looking at me with furrows in her brow. "Can I ask you something?"

"Of course." She could ask me anything.

"Why do your teammates call you Ducky? Back home they called you Middy."

I dropped my head on the back of the couch. People were so used to the name Ducky that they didn't ask anymore. But back in juniors, Middleton had become Middy. Or sometimes Midster. "You're going to laugh."

She sat up. "Your teammates call you a name that mocks you? Seriously?"

She sounded upset on my behalf, and that at least felt good. "No, nothing like that. It goes back to after I was drafted, and I don't think these guys even know why. Like, I have no idea where Fitch came from."

"His last name isn't Fitcher or something? I don't remember what he told me."

"No, it's Astrom."

She rolled her eyes. "Hockey players are weird. So, how did you get your weird name?"

"I was drafted by Nashville, remember?" She nodded. "They flew me in for prospects camp. We were there for a couple of weeks."

"I'm sure you did great."

"Not that great. They told me I was going to play on their

farm team that year. But at camp, my roommate was a fan of that TV show, *Friends.*"

She tilted her head. "You watched it?"

I snorted. "I didn't have a choice. He had it on *all* the time. And the two guys who were living together on that show had a duck and a chicken as pets."

"So what, you were Ducky and he was Chicky?"

"No, but after, I was sharing a house with another guy from the farm team. When I told him about the show and the animals, he thought it would be cool to have a pet duck, but he wouldn't have a chicken because he didn't want to feel guilty about eating chicken."

She laughed. "He didn't eat duck?"

"I guess not. But it sounded like fun. I found a guy who let me buy a duckling. Cutest thing ever. We called him Donald."

Katie covered her mouth, but I heard that laugh.

I sighed. "A few months later, I got called up when one of the team's wingers was injured. I asked, but the team was going to put me up in a hotel till they knew if they were keeping me, so I couldn't bring Donald."

"I guess most places aren't really prepared to deal with pet ducks."

"Donald had to stay with Smitty. Anyway, I'd call up to ask how Donald was doing. My teammates heard me asking about the duck, so I was the duck guy, and that became Ducky."

"They call you Ducky because years ago you were on the phone asking about your duck." I shrugged. "How is Donald now?"

"You really want to know?" She nodded, a little smile on her face. I pulled out my phone. "Here's the latest pictures. Turns out Donald is actually a girl, but anyway, she's doing well. Those were the ducklings she had last summer."

Donald was a white duck, with a slew of little yellow ducklings around her.

"You never wanted to get her back?"

I shook my head. "She's happy and has lots of room. And I'm traveling all the time—not good for a pet."

She considered me, mouth pursed. "Do you like being Ducky? Could you ask the guys to call you Middy again instead?"

"I'm used to it now." And I really didn't care.

"Is it okay if I still call you Josh? I'm not sure I can manage Ducky."

"You can call me Josh. I like it."

She dropped her eyes to her lap, twiddling with a piece of licorice. "So, should we watch another episode?"

I hit the play button to move forward to episode two, reminding myself we were just friends for now.

CHAPTER 21

MAYBE YOU SHOULD LISTEN TO HER

JOSH

OUR NEXT HOME GAME, the fans were subdued. Coach came into the locker room before we went out, reminded us that this was our place and we could win this game. Cooper promised a reward for whoever scored the winning goal, or for Petey and Mitch, our goalies, if we got a shutout. Knowing Cooper, it would be something good.

We didn't go out there bursting with confidence, but we were determined. Like when we didn't want to get up for an early practice but powered through it so we could have a nap. Or something.

We scored two in the first, Montreal scoring one, and the mood was shifting in the arena and the locker room. Second period, they tied it up but we managed a goal at the beginning of the third. With two minutes left, it looked like we'd hold on to a win, but they scored on a breakaway a minute before the buzzer.

Overtime, we were a mess and they won.

Coach came in, looked at us and just shrugged before he turned and left.

"What the fuck?" Royster asked.

I shrugged. "What fuck are you asking about? That game? Coach? Us?"

"All of it. What the fuck is our problem? We're better than this. We know it because most of us were here last year, and we almost won it all. We can do it in practice, but this season? Make it a game and we fuck up all the fucking time."

He was right.

Cooper scrubbed a hand over his face. "Management wants all of us to talk to some sports psychologists they're bringing in."

Royster protested. "They had us do that after last season."

He shrugged. "The problem has to be in our heads. You're right—we have the skill, we can play in practice, and we killed it on the ice last season. So it's in our heads."

"Sorry." Mitchell hadn't played but he looked as defeated as any of us on the ice.

"No way, Mitch. That wasn't all on you."

Players chimed in, the ones who'd been on the ice that last shift, taking the blame. We all felt it. Like, if just one of the shots I'd missed had gone in…

Mitchell still was carrying that burden. So was Cooper. And Crash, JJ and Petey—we all would give our left nut to get that game as a do-over. But that wasn't how life went.

I hadn't scored or assisted in the game tonight, so I missed the press interviews. I felt sorry for the guys who did —it was more a punishment than anything else with the way this season was going. I was glad Cooper had found someone to be serious about over the summer because he carried most of the burden as captain, and he needed something to go right for him. His girl knew nothing about hockey, so it was probably a relief to leave it all at the rink.

And me, I got to see Katie now, when our schedules synced up. I didn't know how I'd lucked out finding her again, but she was my happy place, since hockey was majorly sucking.

* * *

I wasn't excited about seeing a shrink, but I figured it wouldn't hurt. When my appointment came up, I went in to practice early and knocked on the door of the office they'd given the doc.

A middle-aged Black woman sat across the desk and invited me to sit down. There was no couch to lie on, since this was a spare office and kind of pokey. Just the desk, her on one side, and an empty chair on the other.

"Good morning. I'm Dr. Rogers."

I sat in the chair. "Uh, hi. I'm Josh Middleton."

She glanced down at the paper in front of her. "Thank you for coming in, Josh. You know why you're here?"

"Because we suck." Her eyebrows lifted. "I mean, we're not playing well."

A faint smile crossed her face. "I understood what you meant. You believe I'm here to help the team play better?"

I shrugged. "Honestly, yeah. They didn't have anyone come in last year when we were playing good."

She rested her forearms on the desk. "There's a difference in play this season?"

"You must know that."

She tilted her head. "The team record is different, but are you playing differently?"

I frowned. The difference in our play was the reason for the difference in the results. "It's almost all the same players, but we're playing like sh—crap. We're okay in practice, but we're terrible in a game."

"Why do you think that is?"

"We're spooked, after last season. The last game."

She nodded. "You've heard of the yips?"

"Yeah, it's like that." Perfect way to describe us.

"So do you believe the issue is more mental or physical?"

"Mental. Obviously." She didn't respond, so I kept going. "We can play in practice, so we have the skills, we're in condition, we know what we need to do. We just can't execute when we're in a game."

She stared at me for a moment and I fidgeted. "Do you feel responsible?"

I splayed out my hands. "For last season, or this one?" She waited again. "We all feel responsible for both. Except for Fitch, and probably Petey."

"Who are they?"

"Oh, Fitch was traded in over the summer. He had nothing to do with last season and he's playing solidly. Petey is our goalie. He wasn't in net when we lost last year. He's playing well this season, but he's not getting a lot of support."

"How are you responsible for last season?"

Hockey was a team sport, but it did depend on everyone doing their best. "I didn't score. Like, if I'd scored in regulation in that last game, we wouldn't have gone to overtime, JJ wouldn't have slid into Petey, and Crash and Mitch wouldn't have been on for that last shift."

"Hmmm. Could all the players have that same concern, that they should have scored in regulation?"

"Maybe? Not the goalies, obviously. Some of the guys don't score a lot, but any of us could have put the biscuit in the basket and that would have been it."

She scribbled something down. "And your responsibility for this season?"

I chewed on my lip. "I dunno. I mean, I started out okay,

but now I don't know if I'm getting worse, or if it just seems like that since nothing is working?"

"Like the yips are catching?"

I considered. "Hockey is a team sport. You need the other guys for a team to succeed. So, I guess it could."

"Is there someone who could have started this cycle?"

"I'm not blaming anyone!"

She shook her head. "It's not a matter of blame. But if one person was affected, it could have spread. So, similarly, maybe there's one person who could get over that insecurity, and it would expand to everyone else."

"I suppose." I looked over her shoulder at a blank wall. Could it be that easy? If so, I wasn't the person who could do it. I'd been sure, back in Seattle. "I don't think it's one person. I think it's most of us. Maybe all of us. We were a really tight group. The way teams are when they're playing well. I think it's all of us or none of us."

"That's an interesting perspective, Josh. Thank you for sharing it."

I focused on her again. "Hey, I don't really know. I'm just saying stuff."

"You don't have a lot of confidence in yourself?"

"I can play hockey, and I know that. But this other stuff, the stuff that's in our heads? I don't know that."

"Do you think your teammates would understand that better?"

I shrugged. "Probably."

"Why is that?"

"Some of them are really smart. I didn't even go to college. I needed a tutor to get through high school math."

She nodded slowly. "There are different kinds of intelligence, Josh. Not all are measured on standardized tests."

"You sound like my tutor."

"Would you say your tutor was smart?"

"Oh yeah. She's brilliant."

"Maybe you should listen to her."

* * *

KATIE

JOSH'S TEAM was not doing well. I sympathized, because I was also struggling with my research project. I was so frustrated with my advisor.

He nitpicked at my proposal, but when I asked for ways to improve he was vague and told me that it was my job to figure it out. Some of my peers were getting into their research projects, and I couldn't even get approval on my topic. He was dismissive, and though there wasn't anything I could clearly identify, I definitely felt he'd be happier with a male student.

I dreamed of a scenario where I had a guy present the same project just to see what kind of response he would get, but it was complicated and not something I knew how to do.

He also had an attitude I was becoming too familiar with. Pure mathematics, that was the ultimate. Applied math, like the finance stuff my project dealt with? Next best. Math education? Only for those who couldn't handle the other two. I felt myself getting further behind and it was so frustrating.

Mom and Dad had diverted money from Nora's education account to mine, since Nora was only going part-time now and I was on the PhD track. They wanted us to be free to concentrate on our studies instead of working, so the only job I'd ever had was tutoring. It was great experience for teaching and helping the students I was responsible for now, but if I dragged out this program, the money would be gone and I'd have to take loans or get a job or both. I wasn't sure there were enough steady tutoring gigs.

I frowned at my laptop, email open. I could make an official complaint. I'd drafted a letter detailing all the problems I'd encountered. I just had to add the address for the chair of the department. But could I really do that? What repercussions might follow? Was it even possible for me to graduate with the way he was behaving?

Maybe I shouldn't be here. Nora dropped out when she had a eureka moment after getting pregnant—was this my moment of truth?

"Ms. Baker?"

I slammed my laptop shut as I looked up to the third-year student who was standing in front of my desk.

I shared this space with the other math TAs but had my own desk. We spent some office hours here, but normally I worked at the condo.

"How can I help you?"

Norman was one of the keener students, so I didn't have a problem remembering his name. He showed up for every lecture and every lab, happy to ask and answer questions. He loved my math T-shirts, so that was a sign of good taste.

He was wearing a faded hoodie and khakis, backpack on his shoulder. His hair was falling down over his glasses and he fidgeted, looking over my shoulder then down at my desk, never quite settling.

"Are you okay?"

He nodded, jerkily. "I heard that you know one of the hockey players? On the Blaze?"

I blinked. Not what I'd been expecting. "Yeah, I went to high school with Josh Middleton."

"Ducky."

I waited. Was this some kind of test, where I was supposed to prove I knew him? I wasn't playing that game. It didn't matter to our TA/student relationship if I was or not, and I had no desire to share my personal life.

"So, like, do you ever see him?"

"Norman, that's not really any of your business."

"I just wanted to get his autograph. I've got his jersey and hoped maybe if you knew him, you could do that?"

I liked Norman. But I didn't owe him any favors. I didn't need to start a precedent with students coming to me to get autographs or pictures or any of the other things people asked Josh for. And I had no intention of taking advantage of my friendship. Did people do that? Maybe there was a reason Josh wanted me as a friend.

"Norman, I'm your TA. I'm happy to help you with anything you need in your coursework. However, my private life and my friends are not open to exploitation."

His cheeks flushed. "Sorry. I just thought, if you did know him, you wouldn't mind helping out. I'd do you a favor too."

"I appreciate the offer, but no."

He turned away but stopped in the doorway. "But you do know him, right? Any chance he might come by?"

Not if I had anything to do with it. *Jeepers.* "I wouldn't announce if any of my friends were coming to visit. Especially not if I felt people would take advantage of them."

He almost bumped into my advisor, standing in the doorway. "What has that young man in such a tizzy?"

"He wanted me to do a favor for him."

"An extension?"

Was there a way I could avoid explaining the details? "No."

He stood, waiting.

I caved. "I know one of the hockey players in the city, and he wanted an autograph."

There it was. The knowing look in his eyes. Like of course I was only here to connect with a hockey player.

"A close friend?"

"Not that close." But my cheeks felt warm, and he was drawing his own conclusions. Taking this as confirmation of his own bias.

"I'm tied up in meetings tomorrow, so we'll have to reschedule our get-together."

Why couldn't he have just emailed me? Then he wouldn't have overheard Norman. "Fine," I gritted out.

"Let me know anytime you're ready."

My hands were fisted in my lap. I'd been ready. I'd hoped he would finally approve my project.

He wandered off again.

I opened my laptop. I reread my email to the chair.

I didn't want to be a complainer. People had to deal with adversity and learn to work through it. Sending this would say I couldn't do it on my own. How would I explain that to my parents?

I left it in drafts. I'd just work harder.

CHAPTER 22
WAG ADJACENT

JOSH

AFTER ANOTHER LOSS IN DALLAS, we spent the night in a hotel before flying back north. I think we were all happy to get some rest and postpone returning to our disappointed fans in Toronto.

I was up early in the morning, thanks to the time zone changes, and went out to get coffee. It was nice to stretch my legs a bit before the flight, and the weather here was great. Some places we went, there were a lot of hockey fans, but not in Dallas. There were fans, sure, but basketball and football were the most popular sports here, and both of those teams' seasons were underway. The local billboards had way more b-ball adverts than for our sport. Hockey was better, obviously, but not as good a fit down here.

My phone beeped while I was in the lineup for my drink and I pulled it out, hoping maybe Katie had decided to call. We'd texted, but I liked hearing her voice. Sadly, it wasn't her but my agent, Allen.

I declined the call and texted I'd call him back. Hockey might not be as popular here, but I wasn't talking to my agent where someone might overhear and leak whatever I said. I left the coffee shop to find a quiet corner. Allen was a good guy, but he didn't call to shoot the shit. He usually emailed, since I couldn't respond when I was working out or practicing or playing or even traveling. A call meant something was up.

"Hey, Allen."

"Give me three teams you'd like to play for."

I was confused and hadn't had my coffee yet. "Uh, Team Canada in the Olympics, the Toronto Blaze and…" Could I pick one of those dynasty teams from the past? Allen didn't normally ask weird what-if questions. Maybe it was for an interview?

"Josh, I'm not joking around. Three NHL teams that aren't the Blaze."

"What do you mean?"

He sighed. "The Blaze are struggling."

"Yeah." Hockey was less of a happy place this season. Not that I hadn't been on teams that lost—well, not many. But that was part of sports. This season was frustrating because we had the talent. We'd done so well last season that expectations were high. Something wasn't gelling, and none of us knew how to fix it.

"Management has to shake something up. They can't let things ride. Too many talented players on the team, too many big contracts. They haven't completely given up yet, but they're starting to look at options."

Options. A sinking feeling settled in my belly. Allen asking where I'd like to play meant I was one of those options.

When I'd been traded to the Blaze, I'd had one year left on my contract. Nashville hadn't made the playoffs for a couple of years, so going to a competitive team had been exciting. I'd gladly signed another contract with the Blaze. If I had a choice, I'd rather be with a team that was in the playoffs and in the hunt for the Cup than one looking for a high draft pick.

I hadn't been eligible for a no-trade clause. At that point, I had no ties to the city anyway. Katie wasn't there then.

Now, maybe, that no-trade clause would be nice, if I'd been twenty-seven and old enough to get one. Except management could usually make things uncomfortable enough to make a player willing to move. If some other team was offering a lot for me, draft picks to help the Blaze in future, if they didn't think the team could win now...

"They want to trade me?"

"No, they want this team to turn around and play up to their potential. But if that doesn't happen soon, someone's moving."

"And it's me?"

"I don't have anything definite yet. Just someone dropping hints, so I'm looking out for my clients. They don't want to lose you, Josh, definitely not. You're one of the few guys doing well this season."

That was good to hear, or was it?

"They can't move Cooper. He's the face of the franchise, with a big contract, and if he left, the city would riot. They wouldn't get much for Petrov—he's at the end of his career. Still playing well, but he's up there for a goalie. Even though he isn't a big cap hit, I don't think they're ready to give his backup the starting role yet."

Losing De Vries last season after the trade deadline had been a shock. Mitchell had done pretty well until that overtime goal in the playoffs, but that was a big one.

"You're young and playing well, so you're one of the players they could get a lot of return for. I could see offers for Johnson and Crash but they won't get as much for them as they will for you."

That lead feeling was getting heavier. "So if they decide to break up the team, it's probably me."

"Depending on what they're offered, and if they want to rebuild or tweak for next year. That's out of our hands. You think about where you'd like to go, and I'll put out some feelers, see if I can find out what might go down."

I swallowed. "Thanks, Allen."

Sometimes players found out they'd been traded on TSN or ESPN. Allen was a well-connected agent, and he usually got a heads-up, even when things moved fast. I knew he was looking out for me.

"Don't say anything to anyone. This is mostly speculation, but I need to know what you want in advance so that we come out ahead of this."

I liked Toronto and I liked this team, but getting traded was a fact of life for athletes. And if things were different, I'd be excited about another opportunity to be on a competitive team. I wanted to hoist the Cup at least once. That had been my dream for most of my life.

But things were different now. Katie and I were friends and I hoped things were progressing to more, but there was nothing concrete yet. Nothing that would stand up to my being traded to another city.

She'd said, that first night when I went home with her roommate, that back in high school, when we'd been together almost two years, she might have broken up with me depending on where she'd been offered a scholarship and where I'd been drafted. She wasn't going to give up her master's program or transfer to where I might be. Not for a friend.

She'd also said we could have tried long-distance, but that was then. Would she be willing to do that now? I was trying to earn her trust again. If I had to leave Toronto, I was pretty sure that was the end of me and Katie.

I promised Allen I'd think it over and give him some options, but when I got back to my room I searched for the best math programs in the US and Canada, not the best teams.

Even if she decided tomorrow that she'd be with me, there was no time to make the relationship strong enough to handle a major separation. It was tough, when one partner was away so much. I'd had teammates go through breakups with girlfriends and wives. If I was traded and I wanted any chance with her, my best play was to ask her to give long-distance a chance for the rest of this season, and then hope there was a math program good enough wherever I went to tempt her to join me. I didn't have a lot of confidence in that.

Fuck. I needed the team to start clicking. If we didn't get it together—I could up my game, but if we all didn't gel—it would just make a better case for the team to trade me. Should I try to mess up instead? I shuddered. Not sure I could do that. Even if I could—it might make the team trade me anyway.

I wanted to win. I'd wanted that from the first shift I played in a hockey game, but it had always been something I left on the ice. Now, my off-ice life depended on how we did as a team on the ice. I needed to find a way to get this fixed, ASAP.

I went back to the coffee shop to get caffeine. I wasn't going to solve the team's problem without waking up my brain.

* * *

Katie

· · ·

I GOT A MESSAGE FROM CALLIE, asking if I'd like to do brunch with her and Jayna. I'd met up with Jess a couple of times since the escape room, when the team was out of town, but I'd only talked to Callie once or twice. Still, I needed to clear my head. I'd spent more than enough time reviewing my project proposal and grading papers and dealing with my own assignments. I wanted some non-math time. Callie never talked much about her job, and Jayna was a former hockey player who now did PR work so it would be a nice break.

Winter was definitely on its way. I'd put on my puffy jacket with a hat and scarf since I'd decided to walk. This far into November, even if we didn't have snow yet, it was cold, the air crisp. Storefronts were decorated for Christmas and the streets were full of people. The city felt alive. Like I'd been missing out, absorbed in my own little academic world.

I was smiling when I pushed open the door to the diner, glad I hadn't turned Callie down. It took me a minute to find her and Jayna. They'd grabbed a table in a corner, and I wove my way over to them through the chatter of voices filling the room. The place was packed, the smell of decadent food promising a good meal.

"Hey, Jayna and Callie. Thanks for inviting me. I needed this." I pulled out a chair and sat, unwinding my scarf and opening up my jacket.

"Thanks for coming to the inaugural meeting of the anti-WAG club." Jayna announced.

Callie shook her head. "That name needs work."

I blinked. *What?* But a server came by with menus and a pot of coffee and I quickly flipped my cup over for a fill.

"I'm having eggs benny." Jayna dropped her menu on the table.

Callie was still frowning at the list of options. She finally huffed a breath. "I'll have the same."

"I'm definitely having pancakes." I had a sweet tooth, which was why I had more curves than I had in high school, and I wasn't going to deny myself to fit the mold of some model. Life was too short.

I closed my menu. The server, obviously experienced, swooped by for our orders and left with the menus after refills on our coffee.

I dumped sugar and creamer in my cup and stirred it with the spoon. "So, what's the anti-WAG club?"

"You know what WAG stands for, right?" Jayna cocked her eyebrows.

"Wives and girlfriends, yeah. But you two *are* girlfriends, right? Where does the anti come in?"

Jayna grimaced. "Technically I am, but… Sorry, I'm a little touchy about that, family issues. Nothing against the group of women who are happy to be players' wives or whatever. But I *was* a hockey player. I still think of myself as one. Not so much as a girlfriend. I have my own separate identity, my business, and that's my baby right now."

"I have a high-pressure job too," Callie said. "I'm not giving it up. I have issues too, but the bottom line is, Cooper knows and isn't asking me to."

It was nice that they had that support. Was it uncommon?

"Braydon gets it." A fond smile crossed Jayna's lips. "He's told me I have to support us once he's done with hockey."

"Does he think that's soon?" Even if he wasn't a superstar player, he'd be making good money as long as he was playing.

"After the playoffs last season, he's a little spooked. Plus, he had a whole thing planned out in case he didn't make it to the NHL, so he's just making sure he doesn't jinx himself."

That was smart of him. I thought I'd figured it out. "So, this anti-WAG thing is about being a nontraditional WAG?"

Jayna nodded. "Exactly but try to make that into a catchy phrase."

NTWAG. Yeah, that wasn't going to work. "But why am I here? I have no talent for catchphrases."

The two women exchanged glances. "You're a grad student, right? So you're nontraditional too."

I dropped my hands to my lap. "But I'm not a WAG. Not a wife or a girlfriend," I clarified.

"But you and Josh—"

I shook my head. "We dated in high school, but we're just friends now."

"Really?" Jayna flinched as she spoke. "Sorry, of course you know what you are, but Ducky has been spending so much time with you—we assumed you guys were dating. I apologize if we overstepped. It can be a little overwhelming when you start dating a professional athlete, and since you're a student, we thought we should reach out and offer our support."

These women were nice. I'd like to be in a group with them. But I couldn't claim to be dating Josh just to get friends. "If you were running some other kind of club, I'd definitely want to be part of it. I promise. But I'm more like Jess. Sort of WAG adjacent. She's a sister, I'm a friend."

Callie narrowed her eyes, staring at Jayna, then jerked her head in a nod. "Let's do that."

Jayna was also confused. "What do you mean?"

"If we're going to be anti-WAGS, then being a wife or girlfriend shouldn't be a requirement. I like Jess. Let's add her to the group."

I looked between the two of them. "You're making a nontraditional player-adjacent club?"

Jayna grinned. "You're right. This is even better. You in, Katie?"

"Absolutely. Where do I sign up?"

CHAPTER 23

DO YOUR MAGIC

JOSH

TOMORROW WE WERE PLAYING MINNESOTA. Here, in Toronto. Just like the last game of the playoffs. We were all trying to pretend we weren't freaking out, but we were. We'd talked to the shrink, but despite that, our play hadn't improved and we were on edge. Even Coach. He was extra critical at practice and made Coach Salo keep working with Mitchell after the rest of us were done.

The locker room was tense. Obviously our struggles this season were mostly mental, and obviously it was because of how last season ended. But if you didn't know that? The tension in this room would have proved it.

I'd showered and was getting dressed when Mitchell came off the ice, jaw set and sweat dripping down his face and neck. The guy had worked on his going-down-early issue that led to the final goal over the summer, and I swear no one had been able to fool him into doing it again. But we all remembered. And worried. Guys were watching Petey

197

like he might collapse at his stall. Like repeating that last game was the worst thing that could happen.

And really? It was a game. We wanted to win. But look at De Vries—done playing because of cancer. Or Fitch, getting divorced. Someone had lost his dad last season. So what if we did lose to Minnesota again? Maybe if that was done we could forget that one fucking goal.

"Cooper!" I hollered.

Coop had gone to check on Mitchell. After I yelled, he gave Mitch a pat on his pads and came over to me. "Yeah, Ducky."

"We should play Mitchell tomorrow."

Oops. Guess I'd said that a little too loud. The locker room turned dead silent except for the sound of showers in the background.

"What the fuck?" Royster asked.

Oh well. In for a penny...

"We're all walking around on eggshells here, like the worst thing in the world would be if Petey got hurt and Mitchell was in and we lost. Well, guess what? It's not. There are things out there, so much bigger, like cancer and babies and family and shit. We're already losing games. So let's put Mitchell in, play Minnesota, and get it fucking done with."

Everyone stared at me but no one said anything.

Cooper was staring in my direction, but he didn't really see me. His brain was going at top speed. I could almost hear it. "Why not?"

Voices started to murmur, then question.

"Why the fuck not?" he said loudly and everyone stopped. "Ducky is right. We're fucking petrified. Losing like that sucked, but guess what? Half of the teams that make the finals lose. That's hockey. Mitchell is a hell of a good goalie, but that stupid goal is an albatross on his neck. On all of our necks." He turned to Petrov. "You okay with that?"

Petrov, naked as usual, shrugged. "If it helps the team."

Cooper nodded. "I'm going to talk to Coach." He turned and left, still wearing his compression gear.

Barnes shook his head. "Well, Ducky. You're either the smartest motherfucker on the team, or everyone is going to hate you."

If this team didn't start winning, it wouldn't matter if they hated me, since I'd be traded. I guess we'd find out.

Cooper didn't get back to the locker room before I left. I wasn't sure I wanted to know what was happening with my idea. In the moment, it'd made a lot of sense, but right now I was pretty sure it was the dumbest thing I'd ever come up with.

Katie came over that evening to watch TV. She noticed how I was fidgeting. She picked up the remote and hit pause. "Is this about the game tomorrow?"

I dropped my head on the back of the couch. "We're all worked up about it, and I may have done the stupidest thing yet."

She jabbed me with her elbow. "Did you break up with the team by text?"

I froze, remembering that I could be breaking up with the team. Not my choice, but someone might hear of it by text...

"Too soon?" I blinked at her. "Josh? I'm sorry, I didn't mean to—"

I sat up. "It's not that. But there's something that might happen and I should tell you about it."

I didn't want to. I'd been hoping to get past this without telling her anything. But in high school, I'd decided things for her. And she needed to know, if I asked her to move past friends, just what might happen.

Katie curled up her legs, facing me. "Something bad?"

I ran a hand through my hair. "My agent called, when we

were in Dallas. The team isn't playing well, so they might trade someone."

Her eyes widened. She was smart and saw where this was going.

"They're going to trade you?"

"He heard some rumors. Wanted to give me a heads-up."

"You don't want to go."

No. And I wanted her to want me to stay, but I wasn't brave enough to ask that. "I want to stay in Toronto. But I might have suggested something stupid at practice and—"

She pressed her hand on my mouth, and I stilled, heart pounding.

"Don't call yourself stupid. What did you say?"

She dropped her hand, and I wanted to say *stupid* again to get her hand on me. Instead, I swallowed. "I suggested we play Mitch against Minnesota tomorrow night."

She cocked her head. "Trying to break the jinx?"

"Maybe? It just seems like we're scared, and there are bigger problems." Like being traded away from the woman you loved and were finally getting a replay with.

"Are they going to do that?"

"Coop went to talk to Coach, but I don't know."

"If the team wins, maybe they'll play better and you won't be traded?" Did she sound hopeful or was I hearing things because I wanted it so much?

"I hope so. We've got a good group. We came so close..." Damn, that still hurt.

Katie bit her lip. "It's going to be hard to concentrate in class tomorrow night when this game is so important."

I wanted to ask if this changed anything. If she would consider giving me another chance. But if she said no, it would hurt as badly as being traded, so I chickened out.

* * *

The locker room was tense.

Normally at morning skate we knew who was starting in goal by the way the coaches had them practice. This time, it was definitely weird. Fewer drills with someone in net, and both Mitch and Petey were sent off at the same time.

I stopped by Cooper. "So, what's up?"

He watched where the two had just left the ice. "Coach said he'd think about it." He jerked his head at the exit. "It took a lot of convincing for him to even consider it, but obviously he is. He didn't tell me what he was going to do."

"If he starts Mitch and we're a disaster, he's gonna be pissed."

"If he starts Mitch and we're a disaster, his head is on the block."

"Shit. Didn't think about that." I'd thought my neck was the only one at risk.

Cooper tapped my shin pad with his stick. "If he doesn't start Mitch and we're a disaster, his head is still on the block."

Not just his. If Allen was right, and he usually was, the team was going to have to trade someone. Maybe several people. But I would be one of the ones to go.

Coach blew his whistle. "We're done. Get some rest."

That was not going to be easy to do.

* * *

Putting on my gear before warm-ups, I kept an eye on Mitch and Petey. Their stalls were at the end of the room, together, a little wider since their gear was bigger too. Mitch was doing his usual routine—everything had to be done just so since he was superstitious as fuck. Petey? Petey did his meditation and got dressed, same as always. Cyborg. Had Coach told them who was starting? It was impossible to tell.

We skated out for warm-ups and that was when we knew.

Coach was rolling the dice on my idea. I didn't get nervous before games—a little excited, sure, but this was what I liked about being a skater instead of a goalie. I was on a line with two other guys, and we had four lines of forwards. Everything wasn't on me. If I had a bad day, someone else could pick up the slack. It kept my nerves in check.

Today, I was nervous. Because this idea was mine.

When we tromped back to the locker room, the whole place was vibrating with tension. It hadn't been like this since the last game last season. *Fuck.* What had I done?

Coach walked in. Most of us were on our feet, too antsy to sit. Mitchell sat with his head in his hands. He looked a little green. He didn't usually puke before a game but I wouldn't bet against it now.

"I can tell you this is just another game. One of eighty-two. What happens out there won't matter."

We looked at each other. No one was buying that.

"But the way you're feeling now, the way I'm feeling, that's not true. We've had a monkey on our backs since last June. Let's do this and get it over with. A win would be good, but if we lose and you start fucking playing again, I can live with that." He paused but we were all shocked silent at that speech.

He shook his head and left.

"We're not waiting for this game to be over," Cooper said. "We're fucking playing NOW!"

That got cheers from everyone. Petey reached down to say something to Mitch. I hoped it was helpful—Petey's idea of support was sometimes a little odd.

In any case, Mitch stood up, hit the floor three times with his stick, and followed us out.

The arena was tense. Quieter than usual. When the starters were introduced, there was a noticeable pause when Braydon Mitchell was announced, and a few boos.

Someone started to chant *Petrov, Petrov*. To his credit, Petey chopped his hand in front of his throat, and the chant died away.

Coach hadn't just started Mitchell; he'd moved Crash up to play with Cooper, and JJ down to the second D line. So, for the first face-off, we had the same six guys on the ice as when that goal went in and ended our playoff hopes.

I twisted my mouth guard back and forth. This could be the stupidest idea I'd ever had.

Then the puck dropped, and all I could focus on was hockey.

* * *

MINNESOTA DIDN'T SCORE on the first play, but they did within the first five minutes. It wasn't a breakaway and Mitchell didn't drop too early, but there was a scramble around the net and the puck slipped through his five hole.

Fuck.

The look in Mitchell's eyes? Killing me. I skated up to Deek, our first line center. "We're getting that one back."

"We are, huh?"

I waved toward our goal. "Mitch is all in his head. Let's give him a chance."

Deek tapped me with his stick. "I'll get you the puck. You do your magic and get that goal."

And I fucking did. Minnesota was feeling the pressure too, and they had relaxed after that first goal. I was one of the fastest skaters in the league, and tonight I was faster than anyone coming after me. Deek won the face-off, and I slipped around those fuckheads like they were standing still. I faked the goalie and slid the puck just inside the net after he'd gone down. And that red goal light? The best thing I'd seen in weeks.

My teammates crowded me and the arena was rocking. Yes. *This* was how we did it.

By unspoken agreement, it was on. This wasn't just another game for us, or for Minnesota. Three penalties were called in the rest of that first period. I couldn't move my skate without someone being right in my face, and Mitch got to stop fifteen shots before the first intermission. The score was still tied, 1-1.

As we took a much-needed break in the locker room, Cooper stood up.

"I'm proud of how you all played in that period. And maybe I should tell you it's a long season and not to give everything to one game, but fuck. Our season's been a shit show, and there's a good chance we're not in the playoffs this year. So let's make this game count." He tapped his stick on the floor. "This, right now, is our playoffs. Show them what we can really do."

We all banged our sticks on the ground, even Mitch.

"And whoever scores the game winner gets a bonus from me."

More banging. And cheering. Then, we went out and did it.

It wasn't an easy game. Minnesota scored, and then we'd even it up. Lots of penalties, shoving. Crash even got in a fight, and I hadn't seen that before. But when we'd tied things up 4-4 with only a couple of minutes to play in the final period, Cooper got a breakaway and fucking nailed it. He went down under a pile of crazed Blaze bodies.

I pulled him up since we still had forty seconds on the clock to hang on to our lead. "Didn't want to pay anyone else?"

He smirked. "If you wanted it, Ducky, you knew how to get it."

"Next time."

Minnesota played all-out for thirty-five seconds, till JJ managed to clear the puck into the neutral zone and the final buzzer went before they could regroup. The crowd was roaring, I'm pretty sure Mitch was blinking back tears, and every one of us was ready to collapse from exhaustion. We'd given everything.

Cooper got first star. He'd been voted that mostly for the game winner, but we knew. He deserved it for more than that goal. He'd led us to that win. Whether that would spill over to the rest of our games, who fucking knew, but the Minnesota monkey was off our back.

Inside, I was cheering for another reason. This should stop trade rumors for a day or two as well.

After maybe five minutes of yelling and rehashing the game, Coach came into the room. "That was an impressive performance, men. How's the lip, Crash?"

Crash shrugged. It wasn't bleeding, but with the adrenaline waning, it was going to hurt.

Coach looked around the room, eyes landing on every one of us. "When Cooper told me his idea, I thought he was joking."

"Actually, Coach, it was Ducky's idea."

Coach turned to me, but I was staring at Cooper. He shrugged. He'd been willing to take the blame if it went pear-shaped but gave me the credit when it went well. Hell of a captain.

Coach shook his head. "Hell, if I'd known it was Ducky's plan, I'd have never considered it."

Everyone laughed, including me.

"Whoever dreamed it up, it went well. Good job, Mitchell. I know that wasn't easy, but your teammates had your back. Practice tomorrow is optional, but I expect to see that kind of heart on the ice for our next game. Right?"

"Right," we echoed.

Coach left, and we all dragged our asses to cooldown and showers. Katie wasn't coming to the Top Shelf after the game because of school stuff and it was a relief. Right now, I just wanted to sleep. For about twenty-four hours.

But then we needed to talk. We, the team, had been carrying the Minnesota monkey on our backs. But I'd also had one when it came to Katie, from back in high school. It was time to get that one gone as well.

No more giving in to fear.

CHAPTER 24
IT WAS ALL COMING BACK TO ME NOW

KATIE

I'D BEEN CLOSELY WATCHING the results of the game throughout my evening class. Pretty sure I wasn't the only one, based on how many of the students had their eyes glued to their laps. I couldn't call them out on it, since I was just as guilty.

We were all relieved when the Blaze pulled out a win. I texted Josh immediately.

Great game!!!

It deserved the exclamation mark. I knew how worried he'd been.

Josh responded later.

Thanks. When can we get together?

We'd been hanging out a lot and were near the end of our co-watch of the last season of *The Mandalorian*. I'd been expecting he'd want to wrap that up soon.

I'm free tomorrow night.

Can I come to your place?

Most of the time we'd met at Josh's, because it was still a little weird that Madeline had brought Josh home. Right now she was traveling again, so I agreed. I even said I'd cook. My parents might not have let us take regular student jobs, but they'd made sure we were perfectly capable around the house. Unlike Josh's mom. But I pushed that thought aside.

I went with a simple pasta sauce and salad. Not too much to go wrong there, and I'd made it frequently enough that I felt confident. I made sure there was lots of beef in the sauce, because I was feeding a hockey player. I was cooking extra pasta too.

Even though it wasn't a complicated meal, I was surprisingly nervous.

My nerves weren't about the food. Josh had never been a picky guy, and despite that expensive restaurant we went to before the hockey game, he hadn't seemed to be any kind of a food snob now.

But talking to Jayna and Callie had made me self-conscious about being with Josh. They'd thought we were dating. Was that a problem? Was Josh not hooking up with anyone? Not in the city, because I knew what he was doing here, but on the road? Was that why they'd thought we must be together?

I didn't like thinking about that. Something else to brush aside.

The buzzer announcing Josh took me out of my thoughts. No one was making Josh spend time with me. He was here because he wanted to be. And it wasn't my business what he was doing when we weren't spending friend time together.

When I opened the door, it was amped-up Josh who was waiting on the other side. He was almost vibrating. His hands clenched and unclenched on the handle of the bag he was carrying, and he was bouncing on the balls of his feet. Probably because of last night's game.

"Hey Katie."

I stepped back. "Come on in. Still excited about beating Minnesota?"

"Oh yeah. I—oh, that smells good."

"Thanks."

"I brought a bottle of wine. I hope it's a good one."

I rolled my eyes. Like either of us were wine snobs. "I'm sure it's fine. And congrats on the game again. I know you were worried about that one."

He nodded jerkily. "Especially because they did play Mitch like I'd suggested."

Josh sat on a stool to tell me about the game. It was nice, sharing his thoughts. I opened the bottle of wine and poured some into two of Madeline's wineglasses. The less expensive-looking ones.

"That is amazing. See, you are smart. You figured out what the team was hung up on, and your idea got them over it."

His cheeks turned pink. "I know hockey pretty well."

"All the guys in the league must know hockey. But you thought of that idea because you know people as well."

"Thanks. I'm feeling really good about that."

"You should. Hungry?" His hand was tapping on the island, and I knew his feet probably were moving too.

"Yeah, but there's something I need to ask you first."

"Oookay."

His mouth twitched as he watched me. I started to fidget too, like it was contagious. His gaze was intense. It didn't feel like he wanted to ask a question about a TV show we watched, or if I'd come to another hockey game.

He cleared his throat. "Can I kiss you?"

My eyes blinked, but nothing else was moving. Had he really asked if he could kiss me? Josh wanted to kiss me?

I'd kissed him last month. And he'd said I could kiss him

anytime, but that had just been a joke, right? Because we'd gone into friend mode after that and—

"Katie?"

My mouth finally moved, dropping open, then closing again so I could swallow and speak. "You want to kiss me?"

He nodded. He wasn't moving any longer, still and waiting. Like he was waiting for the puck to drop.

"Why?" I didn't understand and my brain didn't seem to be operating.

"Because I want to." He paused, but yeah, my brain had skipped out. "I like being friends with you, but I want more. I have since I saw you again, but I thought I should show you that you could trust me again before I pushed you. But all this time, I've wanted more, and I need to know if that's ever going to happen."

"Really?" That came out in a squeak. *Josh* wanted more? This new, improved, more confident and successful version of my high school boyfriend was interested in the not-much-changed math nerd that was me?

Not sure what was showing on my face, but he stepped around the counter, moving with slow steps till he was standing in front of me.

"I want you in my life. As a friend, if nothing else. But yeah, I really want more."

I had a long list of reasons why this was a bad idea, focusing on school, his popularity, my own insecurities. The fact that he could get traded. But the way he was looking at me silenced them all.

I lunged at him. I wrapped my arms around his neck and kissed him. He was right there with me, pulling me close with those strong arms and meeting my lips. My brain might have been struggling to understand but my body was fully on board.

Kissing Josh was both familiar and strange. I knew what

he liked, the sounds he made, the way he moved his hands over me as he kissed me. But he'd changed—bigger, stronger and more confident.

And my response was familiar and strange too. He'd always been able to light me up and tempt me to more, always more. But now there was nothing in the back of my brain on alert for sounds of someone like my parents breaking in on us. Everything was swamped by that kiss, and I didn't care if Madeline walked through the door or Norman asked for an autograph.

I finally pushed back, needing air. I was panting, my skin sparking like I'd been electrocuted, only in a good way.

Josh watched me like there was no one and nothing else around us. That laser focus on me, just me, was almost as arousing as the kiss. He leaned forward, and reluctantly I leaned back.

"Katie?"

"The stove is on. I'm going to burn something." Something other than me because I felt hot and lit up, like I hadn't in too long.

He dropped his head, taking a long breath. "Okay, if you want to eat now—"

"Not a chance." I stepped away from him and turned off the burners. "Can you wait for dinner?"

A slow smile crossed his face. "And do what instead?"

"Get me off."

"Absolutely."

* * *

Josh

. . .

KATIE GRABBED my hand and pulled me down the hall to the bedrooms. Her door was open, and I paused in the doorway to see what her space was like now. I needed a moment to get some control back or this was going to end too soon.

Lots of books. She'd always loved books. She still favored blue too, since her bed had a blue duvet. There were some clothes piled on the desk chair, like she hadn't expected this to happen tonight. She grabbed the clothes and threw them in her closet.

I stepped in, so I was in front of her when she turned around. "Don't worry about that. I want to take off everything you're wearing and throw it across the room anyway."

She shivered, then looked down at herself. "Go ahead."

"I might make a mess."

"Don't care."

"Good to know." I reached for the hem of her sweater and pulled. She raised her hands. I lifted it up, getting to see Katie's skin for the first time in five years. A quick tug over her head and there she was, in a blue bra. Yep, she still liked blue.

Her tits were bigger, and she had a few freckles scattered over her skin that I didn't remember. I lifted a finger to trace over her collarbone, where her chest was falling and rising as she breathed.

I wanted to take a picture, but I didn't think I'd forget this anyway.

"You now." Her voice rasped.

I quickly grabbed my long-sleeved T-shirt and raised it over my head, throwing it on the floor somewhere. Her breath caught. I looked down, wondering what she thought.

I was broader now. More hair on my chest. I wasn't one of those guys who shaved or waxed. Was she okay with that? Then she ran her fingers through my chest hair and I groaned. Her hands felt so good. She paused, then moved to

212

my nipples. Yeah, those were still sensitive. She remembered. She circled, then ran her fingers over them, and like there was a nerve between those and my dick, it got harder, pressing against the zipper of my jeans.

"My turn," I growled.

I reached around her back and traced over her bra till I found where it opened. I brushed the straps down, and then finally got to see her boobs. Pale red nipples, already tight and waiting for my fingers. I echoed her movements, circling them then brushing across them. She shivered, her fingers curling on my chest. A knot inside me relaxed. I hadn't been sure I'd remember how to please her, but it was all coming back to me now.

It wasn't enough though. I grabbed her waist and carried her to the bed, dropping her on it. She laughed, but stopped when I opened my jeans and shoved them and my boxers off my legs. She pushed up on her elbows and stared at my dick.

I looked down, making sure there wasn't anything weird going on there. If I'd been with the team in the locker room at a game, someone might have put some dye in my underwear or something, but it looked normal. Hard, but normal for that. And not too much different from when I was last with Katie, I didn't think.

I watched her looking at me, her eyes focused right there, and her tongue moved across her bottom lip. My dick throbbed. She got up on her hands and knees and crawled over to where I stood at the side of the bed.

"I've missed you." She wrapped her hand around my cock and squeezed.

Something like a whimper escaped me. "He missed you too," I whispered because fuck if I could think when she had her hand wrapped around me. She swiped her tongue up the underside and my knees almost buckled.

I put a hand on her cheek, pulling her back. I climbed

onto the bed and stretched out across the bottom, legs hanging off the side.

"Comfy?" She raised an eyebrow.

"If you're going to put your mouth on me, my knees aren't holding me up much longer." A big smile crossed her face, but I wasn't saying it to make her feel good. It was the truth.

"You're stable now?"

"Yes, ma'am."

"Hang on."

I did. I gripped her duvet with both hands as she demonstrated that her oral skills had only improved while we'd been apart. Or maybe it was just because it was Katie. Her mouth, her lips, her tongue, her hands—pleasure shot through my veins and I couldn't keep quiet.

"Stop, please," I finally said, sure I was going to come if she didn't give me a moment. And I refused to do that before I was inside her. That was where I needed to be.

She pulled off my dick, her lips making a popping sound, and that alone almost shoved me over the edge. I squeezed the base of my dick and tried to get my brain back online. She sat up on the bed, naked from the waist up. I had to change that, because I needed to taste her pussy again.

I pushed up, grinning proudly as she stared at my abs. I'd worked a lot on my body over the past five years. "You're overdressed, Katie."

She leaned back. "Then do something about it."

Exactly what I wanted to hear. I twisted so I could reach her jeans. First, the belt, then the button and zipper. I tapped her hip. "Lift up." She shivered and raised her ass. I was tired of waiting and pulled off the jeans and her underwear together, tugging them down quickly and getting them caught around her knees. She laughed again.

Such a familiar sound. We'd laughed a lot as we'd learned

sex together. We'd had to make do with stolen moments and whatever locations we could find, so there'd been a lot of fumbles and a lot of mistakes along the way. But that had been okay, because we'd been together.

When her clothes were off, I took a moment to look at her. All of her. She'd had her turn to admire me, and there were a lot of things I needed to see with her. I wanted to know what changes the five years had done to her. Her laughter died as she lay there, hair spread around her, arms to her sides, her legs stretched out beside me.

She wasn't as thin as she'd been, but I liked the way she looked now. Curvier, older, better.

I must have spent too long staring because she brought her legs together, hiding her pussy and asking, voice tentative, "Josh?"

I couldn't let her think there was anything wrong. There wasn't. I ran a hand along each calf, gently easing her legs apart again. "Just enjoying the view."

She shook her head. "I'm sure you've seen bet—"

"Shhh." I ran my hand up her legs, moving between them, eyes on her pussy. "Never seen anything better."

I dropped my chest to the bed, gently pushing her thighs up and apart. Yeah, that was what I wanted. That pretty pussy, looking wet for me.

That wasn't all I wanted though. I moved forward, till my face was right there.

"Josh?" she asked again, so I licked up from her pussy to her clit. She moaned and shivered. But she didn't ask any more questions.

I took my time, getting reacquainted. Remembering her smell and taste and the things that made her noisy. I could tell she had her mouth covered, the way she'd had to back then when we couldn't let anyone know what we were doing.

I lifted my face. She had her fist shoved in her mouth.

"You said your roommate was away?"

She nodded.

"Then be as loud as you want. I like it." She slowly pulled her hand down. I grinned. "Lets me know I'm doing something right."

She shuddered and I got back to work. Though calling it work wasn't fair. This was flat-out a pleasure.

Not sure how long I spent using my mouth to make her squirm…and she did get loud. I kept that noise going as long as I could until she pushed me away.

"Katie?"

"Inside me. Now."

I sat up because being coachable was a virtue of mine.

CHAPTER 25
WITCHY MAGIC

KATIE

MY CHEEKS WERE hot with embarrassment, because I couldn't remember ever being that noisy during sex before. Josh hadn't forgotten anything—every touch, every kiss, every lick that made my pussy go wild. But I was close enough to orgasming now that I could come with him inside me, and I wanted that. I wanted him wrapped around me when I fell apart.

He pushed up and I was able to twist over to open my bedside drawer for a condom. When I turned back, Josh was on his knees, cock jutting out in front of him, hand stretched for the package. I passed it over, admiring the show as he opened it and rolled it down over his cock.

He'd always been fit, and I'd been self-conscious because I was not. He'd only gotten fitter, grooved muscles making his body a work of art, and I was softer than I'd been before. Softer, rounder, could he really want that?

His eyes glowed warm as he stared at me, so I pushed

those thoughts aside. He reached for a pillow and shoved it under my hips. This was new, but he could do what he wanted if he'd just get inside me. He grabbed the base of his cock, and with an unexpectedly endearing look of concentration, pushed the tip in.

I was more than wet and feeling that nudge of heat was so good. He dropped onto his hands, leaning to kiss my neck as his hips surged forward and filled me. Not sure whose moan was louder, but it was so good. Every nerve in my body had come to life and little zaps of pleasure raced through my veins. He pulled out, most of the way, and I lifted my legs to grip his waist. That put him at the perfect angle when he thrust back in, and I shouted.

He gripped my shoulder in his teeth and pumped his hips, rubbing against me perfectly with every thrust, and my arousal climbed as I raked my hands down his back. Thank heaven for athlete stamina. My voice grew louder and louder, and when I finally came, I screamed, tightening my body around his as I shuddered and finally collapsed.

"Oh, Katie." He moaned as he pressed harder and faster until he shouted my name again as he came, his cock twitching inside, and then collapsed on top of me.

We were slick with sweat and our breathing was fast and shaky. There were still tremors running through me, or that might have been him. Finally, as our breathing calmed down and the chill of the ambient room temperature started to cool us off, Josh lifted up and pulled out, holding on to the condom.

I flapped a hand to the side of the bed. "There's a garbage pail there."

He dealt with that then returned to cuddle beside me, wrapping a hand over my waist. "You okay?" His breath whispered against my neck, sending a shiver through me.

"I'm boneless. Might not be able to get up for a while. Hope you weren't too hungry."

"I'm good." I felt his smile against my shoulder. "We've still got it."

I nodded, but my brain clicked in.

I'd just had sex with Josh. How the hell had that happened? I'd hated him since we broke up, sure I could never forgive him for that pain and humiliation. And now I'd invited him in, to my home and my body. What kind of witchy magic did this guy have?

"Hey, what's wrong?"

My body was tense, no longer loose and comfortable. "I never thought this would happen again."

Now his body tensed. "Are you sorry it did?"

I didn't want to say yes and hurt him, and I couldn't honestly say I was sorry for an orgasm like that. I shook my head. It wasn't regret, just a massive shift in my mindset of the past five years. "Not sorry. Just adjusting."

His hand smoothed over my hip. "I don't want you to feel bad about this. I didn't want to push you."

"You didn't. I was totally on board. Just…trying to wrap my head around it."

"You change your mind? Regret it?"

I shook my head again. "That felt too good to regret. But just a few weeks ago, you were like Darth Vader to me." Might as well use a simile in Josh's wheelhouse.

He frowned. "I hope you're not saying you're Luke Skywalker."

We both said "Eeewww" together.

"Let's pretend I was Leia."

"Not any better."

"Sorry, my brain isn't working right."

Josh grinned at me. "I sexed your brain too hard."

I slapped at him with one hand. "That's not a thing."

He cuddled up against me. "Is too."

"Dork."

He wrapped an arm around me. "Is it okay to snuggle?"

We hadn't had much chance to do that in high school. "Of course. Why wouldn't it be?"

He shrugged. "I don't want anything to spoil this. It was pretty good."

"Just pretty good?" I made my voice teasing, but for me, that had been something extra. Was it just another fuck for him?

He leaned up on one arm to meet my gaze, hair ruffled, lips still slightly swollen, eyes warm and serious. "I don't want you to freak, but it was…it was incredible. Except for the Darth Vader incest talk."

I shoved him. "I admit, that was a mistake. Let it go before I have to bleach my brain."

He grinned, then leaned forward and kissed me. I melted into the mattress, my body willing to try another round. "I can distract you. Make sure your brain doesn't need bleaching."

I moved my hand down his side, noticing the twitch that told me he was still ticklish there. I slid my hand to his back, pulling him against me.

"Distract me."

* * *

Josh

When I woke up in the morning it took a minute to figure out where I was. Not my own bed. Not a hotel. This was someone's room—then I felt Katie in the bed behind me and a big smile crossed my face.

Yes. I had Katie again.

After round two, we'd gone back to the kitchen to salvage dinner. Fortunately, she'd turned off the stove so nothing was burned or on fire. We ate food that was probably good, but I didn't care what I was eating. Just that she was sitting across from me and smiling at me while her hair was messed up from our time together. Having sex.

I'd wanted a repeat. But first, food.

We'd talked about everything and nothing while we ate. Then we went back to her room and did it again, till we fell asleep together.

Things were looking up. The team had beaten Minnesota, which meant there was no need for a trade, and Katie and I were us again.

I checked the time. I should get going, since I had practice. I lingered, watching her sleep. I hadn't been able to do that before, back in high school. Unlike when she fell asleep in the chair at my place, she looked comfortable. Relaxed. Her hair trailed over the pillow behind her head, one hand under her cheek as she lay on her side, turned toward me. The covers were pulled tightly up to her neck, but I knew she was naked underneath.

My dick wanted to do something about that, but we'd been up late, and I wasn't sure when she had to be at class. I didn't want to disturb her if she needed the sleep. I slid out of bed, half hoping she'd wake up, but she just sighed and snuggled farther into the covers.

The room was a little cold, so I pulled on my clothes as quickly and quietly as I could. I glanced back at her one more time before opening the door and slipping out. I sent her a quick message, wishing her a good morning and telling her I'd had a fantastic time. Then I got back to my car and drove to my place on the mostly empty streets.

Practice was drastically different from anything we'd

been through for the past month or so. Coach was smiling, for one thing. There was more conversation in the locker room, and a more relaxed air on the ice as the coaches gave us a lighter workout.

At the end of practice, we circled around Coach.

"That was good, what you did last night. I was proud of how you played."

The relief was palpable.

"Good understanding of the team dynamic, Ducky."

My face went hot as all the attention turned to me. "Yeah, well, if it hadn't worked…"

Coach shook his head. "Let's not go there. It did. We're heading out tomorrow, and I expect that kind of play on this road trip. Enough slacking off."

We hadn't been, any of us, but we got the idea. It was time to play up to our potential, and now we believed we could.

Back in the locker room, I checked my phone. Katie had sent me a picture of the kitchen. We hadn't cleaned up last night, too focused on each other. There was a pile of dirty dishes.

Sorry. Want me to come and wash those now?

I got it. Just wanted you to feel guilty.

I do. So guilty, I'll take you out for dinner tonight.

There was a pause, and I stood, still in my sweaty gear, waiting for the response. I thought we were properly dating now. In a relationship where we spent time together and went on dates.

Fuck. Fitch had said things had to be different. We should have talked about this, not jumped to sex.

Finally my phone buzzed.

I don't get home till seven. Is that too late?

I didn't care if we ate at midnight, as long as we did it together.

Pick you up at 7:30?

222

Great.

I tossed my phone down and started to pull off my gear. Now I just had to find a great place to take her.

* * *

KATIE

So, that was it. I was dating Josh again.

I wasn't as naïve as I'd been last time. He wasn't perfect, and neither was I. He was a big hockey star, while I was a student. Our chances of lasting beyond a few weeks were small. Right now, I was the one who got away—was given away, or something like that. But I suspected when he remembered how ordinary I was, he'd get bored and move on.

In the meantime, we were always good in bed, so that would be fun. And as long as I didn't expect too much, I'd be okay. I had to control my expectations or I'd be hurt again.

Tonight, we went out to a restaurant. Josh wanted to call some expensive place that had a waiting list, get in using his star power, but I was tired after a long day of classes and study and wanted something easy.

Josh immediately changed plans and promised we'd do easy. Easy was a steakhouse, with prices that made me blink, but the guy was making bank so maybe that was another perk of dating him for a while.

"Order anything you want. This isn't like when we went to Tony's."

I laughed, remembering our most extravagant date from high school. "Right. You only had an appetizer because everything was so expensive. You didn't need to take me there, you know."

"It was our anniversary. I wanted to treat you."

"It was sweet."

Josh's smile was blinding. "Sweet is good, right?"

I nodded. Sweet, funny, considerate—he was all of that. Even though Josh had money and fans—here came another one to get his picture or autograph—being with him was easy. There were no tense silences, no effort to keep the conversation challenging or interesting.

We both ordered steaks, and Josh insisted on an appetizer to share. I agreed to split a bottle of wine, and we joked around, making up stupid descriptions for the expensive wines.

"Bouquet of dirty socks with a note of cheese."

"Elements of goldenrod and ragweed, inspiring memories of allergy season."

The waiter sniffed when he heard us, but Josh ordered one of the expensive wines and he left with our orders.

"He wasn't impressed by our wine descriptions." Every waiter in the city was going to hate us.

Josh shrugged. "I ignore that stuff. I'm never going to impress anyone with my brains, but I play the sport I love and make a shit ton of money at it, so I don't worry about what other people think."

I cocked my head. "Josh, you need to get over that. You are not stupid. But do you really not care what people think, or do you just try not to?"

A corner of his mouth quirked up. "It's more true than it used to be."

"Good. Ignore those people who judge you."

"You never did. And I always liked that."

"Why would I judge you?"

"You're really smart."

I reached across and covered his hand with mine. "Josh,

school is not the only measure of intelligence. I told you that."

He twisted his hand so ours were twined together. "I try not to be down on myself, really. But repeating a grade in elementary school didn't help. And until I got good at hockey, I was the short, stupid kid with the bad clothes."

"That left a mark, I get that. But look at what you've accomplished. You finished high school."

"With your help."

"But you did the work. I didn't take your tests or do your homework. I helped, but that was because mainstream classes didn't work for you. And now you're playing hockey professionally—so many people want to do that and can't. You're doing it and you're one of the best." I thought back to my conversation with Nora. I wasn't sure I was that smart outside of books. "I know how to study and take tests. You may notice that there's not a lot of jobs outside of school where someone does that. In fact, most people are no longer affected by school at all. It doesn't matter if school was a challenge for you. When it comes to life, you're winning."

"Yeah, but—"

"No buts."

His cheeks turned pink. "Coach complimented me today."

"I'm not shocked, just so you know. What for?"

"For the idea of starting Mitch in goal. Cooper told him it was me."

"See?" I squeezed his hand. "You're not just a good player. You get the game. You were the guy who figured that out."

The waiter came back with our drinks. I reluctantly pulled my hand away. There was something comforting about being close to Josh. He and the waiter did that tasting thing, and then the waiter poured the wine. I took a sip and sighed.

"Good?" Josh was watching me.

"Very good. Thank you."

He took a sip of his own wine and set it down. "I want to ask you something." He looked serious.

"Okay?"

"We're together now, right? Boyfriend, girlfriend, exclusive? We didn't say that last night, and I want everything clear."

Any walls around my heart that were still up crumbled. *This guy...* "Yes, if that's what you want."

"Thanks for giving me a chance, in spite of how things happened in high school."

"It was partly my fault, and mostly our parents. Why don't we just agree that it's the past and done?"

Our waiter returned with our appetizer, deep fried calamari. I reached for a ring. It was hot, shockingly. I dropped it on my plate and shook my fingers.

"Impatient."

"Hungry."

Josh used a fork to pass some more rings to my plate. "Give them a minute to cool off."

"I'll try. Why don't you tell me what it's like, achieving your dream and doing exactly what you always wanted to do."

Josh looked down for a moment. "Sometimes I can't believe this is really my life."

I listened as he told me a couple of stories. It wasn't just training and playing games, and even if I wasn't the biggest hockey fan ever, it was fascinating.

I was finally able to handle the calamari and dipped it in sauce before dropping it in my mouth. *Mhmmm. Good.* "How does Nashville compare to Toronto?"

Josh served himself some calamari. "It's different. In some ways, Nashville is more like Halifax than Toronto—smaller. But hockey isn't as big there. They like football best."

A man stopped at our table, just after our steaks arrived. "Are you Josh Middleton?"

Josh smiled and agreed, taking a selfie with the guy while his food grew cold. When the guy moved on, I asked, "You didn't have all these people approaching you at dinner in Nashville?"

His brow creased. "Is it bothering you?"

"Not really. I like seeing how much people admire you. You worked hard for this, and you deserve it. But your food is getting cold."

"Next time I can take you somewhere that won't happen."

I reached out for his hand again, reassuring him. "I don't mind. I just hope for your sake that you can eat your steak before it's too cold."

"Cold food isn't the worst thing. It's people like this who make it possible for me to play for a living, so I'm okay with it."

Another patron slowed as he walked toward the restrooms, and I glared at him so he kept walking. Fortunately, after that, no one bothered Josh until his meal was done and we were pondering dessert.

"You want something?" Josh asked after signing a napkin for a couple of kids who raced back to their own table. "The chocolate cake looks good."

I licked my lips. Some of the desserts sounded really good, especially the cake. But I was already full from the calamari and the steak. I had ideas for how to end this evening, and a bloated stomach didn't play a part in that.

"I don't think I want anything more to eat. I'll just fall into a food coma, and that will be the end of this date."

Josh's eyes shot up to mine. "Oh yeah?"

I nodded. "Want to come back to my place instead?"

CHAPTER 26
WORK BEHIND THE NET

JOSH

KATIE WAS GIVING ME A CHANCE. For the whole evening, there'd been something like a hovercraft under me. Not that I wasn't touching the ground, but I felt a little floaty. This time I wasn't going to mess things up. This time I'd be the best boyfriend anyone could be.

This time I wasn't going to listen to everyone else. I'd told her everything, and we were okay.

When we got to her place and she hung up her coat, I wanted to wrap my arms around her and taste her mouth. And then taste other parts of her body. All of it. But while I didn't want to get advice from people which could mess us up, I had to listen to Katie.

We'd had dinner and she'd invited me back, but that didn't mean sex. Not necessarily.

"So, I was wondering…" How did I say this?

She turned and looked at me. We were almost close enough to touch. "You were wondering?"

"Why did you ask me back here? I don't want to assume anything."

"I want orgasms, Josh. Can you help with that?"

My heart stopped and my dick twitched. "Definitely."

I dropped my head to kiss her. She tilted her face up and wrapped her arms around my neck as our lips met. Kissing Katie was just so good. She tasted a little bit of the wine we'd had, a little of the cool air we'd walked through, and a lot that was just her.

I tilted my head and she opened her mouth and I could stroke her tongue with mine. That hovercraft feeling was stronger, like I might drift away if I let go of her. But that was the last thing I was going to do.

I hadn't known, back when we were in high school, that not all kisses would be like kisses with Katie. How do you know how good something is when you've had nothing to compare it to? Over the past five years I'd discovered it wasn't easy to find what we had. Chemistry or pheromones or what the hell ever—everything we did was just so good. I knew now that was a gift, not something you found often. Maybe only once.

She pulled back, and I moved forward to keep our connection. She pressed her hands against my chest.

"Bedroom." Her voice was husky and she was breathing hard.

So was I, even though I was in pretty good physical condition. "Absolutely." I still had my arms around her waist so I lifted her up. She squeaked, then laughed, wrapping her legs around my waist and hanging on tightly with her arms. I remembered the way to her room and kept my lips busy on her neck and ears as I shuffled us to her bed, relishing every shiver that went through her body and every muffled moan I heard.

I tripped over something on her floor, but we were close

enough to her bed that we landed safely.

"What was that move?" She laughed.

I looked back. "You left some shoes on the floor."

"Sure." I leaned up, ready to prove it to her, but she tightened her arms around me. "Do you really care what's on the floor? I don't."

She had a point, but I wanted to make one too. I tugged us both closer to the edge of the bed and then slid down. I landed on my knees and moved her legs to surround me. She propped herself up on her elbows. "Are you interested in what's on the floor now?"

She slapped my shoulder. "Seriously?"

"Do you want me to move?"

"Only if moving gets you closer to going down on me."

And suddenly I didn't care about the floor argument either. I shoved her skirt up her legs, exposing lacy panties. "Nice." My voice was almost a growl as I traced her folds through the sheer black material with one finger.

"I planned ahead."

I leaned down and ran my nose up and down her pussy, breathing her in, scenting her arousal. Me, it was easy to tell —my dick made my interest known. But women...that was trickier. And knowing I was doing it to her, that our kisses had turned her on, made me bigger, prouder—my chest expanding—and relieved.

I stuck out my tongue and ran it over the lace, over her. Getting a faint taste. I heard her mutter "Fuck" and then her body shifted as she fell back. I ran a finger over the panties again. Taking them off meant moving her, and I didn't want to do that. But working on her with them on would limit my scope. Ripping them off would probably piss her off.

Despite being one of the shorter guys playing hockey, I could still work behind the net. So, tight space it was. I slid a finger under her lace, ran it up and down, then shoved the fabric aside and used my mouth.

There wasn't a lot of room for my fingers along with my lips and tongue, but I did my best. She whimpered, and twisted, and then her hands locked into my hair, pulling my head close. As if I was going anywhere. I managed to get two fingers inside her channel, moisture slicking my way, and licked up to her clit and sucked on that.

"Nghgghh." She pulled more on my hair and I repeated the maneuver, sucking a little harder. She squirmed and moaned, and then she clenched on my fingers and almost yelled a long "Aaaahhhhh" as she came.

She wasn't faking or being polite. With Katie and me it was just good.

I gave her another lick and slowly pulled out my fingers, cleaning them off in my mouth. I couldn't see her face, just her breasts, still in her sweater, rising and falling, her hands now spread on her duvet. I pushed back up on my feet and looked down at her.

What an incredible sight. Even though none of the good stuff was bare. Her panties were wet and, I realized, pretty twisted. Her skirt was around her waist and her face was flushed, hair mussed up on her bed.

Her eyes fluttered open. A smile crossed her face. "Okay, I do care about what's on the floor. When it's you doing that."

I crawled onto the bed, leaning down to kiss her neck. She wrapped her hands around my face, pulling me down for a long kiss, not caring that I tasted like her.

Her hands slid down to my chest and pushed up, then shoved me onto my back. I went willingly, ready for anything she wanted. She straddled my waist, my hard dick pushing against her ass.

Her eyes were sparkling as she looked down at me, cheeks flushed, biting her lip. Her hands moved over my pecs, and even with both of us clothed, this was great sex. The difference was the person, not the activity. I had to make sure I never lost this person again.

"So…" She paused, and my hands moved up her thighs. "I'm trying to decide on our next steps. Would you prefer me to ride you, like this, or a blow job?"

My dick got impossibly harder and my hips jerked, my whole body reacting to her words. My mouth opened, but I couldn't make words. Her lips on my dick, or her pussy wrapped around it? How was I supposed to choose?

She ground onto my erection, grinning at my moan.

"If you can't decide, I guess…"

I swallowed, trying to form words because I definitely wanted one of those.

"It'll have to be both."

Both? What—but she reached her hands down to pull off her sweater and I didn't care. Anything she wanted to do was what I wanted.

She bared her top half. Then she inched back, sliding her hands under my T-shirt. I lifted my body to give her room to pull it off, and her eyes locked on my abs. *Hours in the gym for the win.*

She shook her head and tugged the garment off. She ran her hands over my pecs, through the hair on my chest, and I shuddered. Then she moved back, ass sliding over my thighs as she unbuckled my belt and pulled down the zipper of my jeans.

My dick almost ripped through my boxers. She ran her hand over it and I closed my eyes as I fought for control. She slid back, pulling down pants and underwear. Her weight left my body when she hit the edge of the bed, and I opened my eyes again to see her pull my socks off with the rest.

She moved her hands to her own waistline and unbuttoned her skirt. Eyes fixed on mine, she slid the skirt down,

232

letting it fall. She pulled down the panties, let them drop to the floor, and waited.

"You're fucking beautiful, Katie."

A small smile lifted her lips, and then she put a knee on the bed, leaning forward on her hands. "I think we'll start with a blow job. But you can't come. Not till you're inside me."

"If you keep talking like that, I can't promise."

She reached out a hand for my dick, giving it a soft stroke. "You're a professional athlete. I'm counting on your stamina." Giving me an evil grin, she reached down and slid her mouth over me.

I was loud. No way I could hold back when Katie sucked me in. It was hot and tight and heaven. I fisted my hands in the cover on her bed, holding on and desperately trying to ignore the way my balls pulled up and sparks shot up my spine.

"Katie, fuck, your mouth…nrghh."

I finally reached for her because she had to stop if she didn't want me coming right fucking now.

She sat up, face flushed. "Ready for option two?"

I nodded, body shuddering. Seeing her like this was pushing me to the edge.

She leaned over, running her tongue over my abs and up my chest. I lifted my hands to her sides, smoothing over her ribs and landing on her waist. She gripped my nipple in her teeth and gave a tug.

"Katie!" She was killing me.

She grinned and slid far enough up to kiss me. Our tongues met, twisted, and I was lost in the taste and feel of her.

Then I realized the wiggling wasn't just about the kiss as the head of my dick started to slide into her tight pussy. She groaned, or I did, or we both did. It felt incredible, beyond anything I'd experienced. Something flickered in the back of my brain, but it was lost as she slid down until my dick was completely inside her.

"Fuck, Katie."

She pushed herself up till she was straddling my hips. Every move stimulated those nerves, and I battled to keep from coming. She wanted this, and I didn't want to end the fun early.

She drew a shaky breath. "Ready?" Her voice was raspy, the turned-on version of her that I'd jerked off to so many times.

I nodded and gripped her hips.

She braced her hands on my chest and lifted up. I hated the loss of her heat, but then she dropped down, deeper, and I moaned. She twisted her hips and shuddered.

I wasn't going to last long. I couldn't, not after going down on her and having her mouth on me. I didn't want to leave her hanging, so I moved my fingers to her clit and gently rubbed.

"Josh!" She lifted and dropped again, and I pressed on her.

We repeated, each time her body shaking harder.

"Josh, I'm gonna...gonna."

I pressed and shoved my hips up and then got to watch my favorite thing—Katie coming. Her head tossed back, her eyes closed, her mouth open as she shouted my name. Her pussy clenched on me and I was done. My own eyes closed, and I shouted her name as I shot inside her, every cell in my body climaxing.

Katie dropped on my chest. Her panting breath brushed my shoulder, and her sweaty skin slicked against mine. My dick softened, and slid out of her, with my come.

"Shit!" That's what my brain had been trying to tell me. Katie blinked at me. "We didn't use a condom."

Her eyes went big, the orgasm high leaving them. "Shit," she repeated.

"I'm sorry, Katie. So sorry."

She shook her head. "I'm the one who slid onto you without waiting. It was like…"

"Yeah." It was like old times. Back in high school. We'd been each other's firsts, and once she was on birth control, we didn't always use the condom.

Her forehead was frowning again, and I hated doing that to her. "Um, we get tested, by the team, and I was negative the last time. And I haven't been with anyone since."

Normally I would have. If I hadn't tried to hook up with her roommate, and then, once I'd seen Katie again, no one else interested me.

Her eyes scanned my face. "I had a complete physical before school started. There's been no one. I'm on birth control."

"So, you're okay?" I couldn't believe I might have risked her future, or her health. Thank fuck I was always careful—except around Katie.

She nodded.

"I'm sorry. I won't do that again."

Her forehead smoothed. "Actually, I hope you do a lot of that again. But we should use condoms. What with my family history and all."

I nodded. She had plans and dreams and I didn't want to interfere with them. Her family would freak and hate me forever. And depriving Katie of what she wanted wasn't happening.

Condoms were a smart idea. We'd been fine in high school, but I wouldn't risk her. Not ever.

CHAPTER 27

ONE STEP CLOSER TO LEAVING

KATIE

I TOLD Josh I needed to clean up and escaped to the bathroom. Before starting the water, I stared at the woman in the mirror.

Who was she?

I *never* had sex without a condom. Not since Josh.

Nora had sworn they used protection when she got pregnant. I couldn't swear my parents had, because that was not a discussion we had, but in case I inherited some super eggs which could get pregnant at will, I was careful. Very careful.

Josh was the only one I'd gone bare with before, and tonight I hadn't considered STIs or pregnancy or anything rational. It had been like high school, when we'd gambled with stakes we couldn't afford. We'd been lucky then.

Or maybe not lucky. Maybe the super-egg genes had passed me by, and we were fine. I was on the pill. I trusted him enough to not worry about STIs if he told me he was negative.

236

I turned on the tap and wet a washcloth.

Things were moving fast. Not just the sex, but the feel-ings. All the pain from high school, all those vows I'd made to never let him hurt me again had been wiped away and the good feelings rushed back. I wasn't going to say I loved him, not this soon, but I could see it happening.

Josh was right there with me. Neither of us were putting on the brakes.

I went back to the bedroom with the cloth, still not sure if I was doing the right thing with him. Josh was lying on the bed, hands crossed behind his head, incredible body displayed on my duvet. He smiled at me as I came to the bed and leaned down to clean him up.

"Thanks." His voice was soft, and his eyes watched me closely.

I threw the cloth into my laundry basket.

"You okay?" he asked.

I stretched out beside him and he wrapped his arm around me. "I think so."

"I thought you might be freaking out. I really am sorry about the condom."

I shook my head against his chest. "That was on me. And yeah, freaking out a bit, but not about the condom. It's just… we're going fast."

I felt him nod. "I know we are, and honestly, I'm good with that. It feels to me more like we're just starting from where we left off, you know? But if you need some time to figure out if this is what you want, I'll try to pull back. Just don't ghost me, okay?" He swallowed, and I knew I could hurt him. Badly.

I pressed a kiss to his chest. "I probably should think it over a bit. I forgot how you dive into things, no waiting."

"Do you want me to go now?"

I shook my head. Right now, I wanted to enjoy the

hormones rushing through my body. Tomorrow was enough time to worry. "We should get under the duvet though. It's cold."

Josh threw his arm back and found the edge of the covers. He pulled them down and rolled us over. With some twisting and laughing we found ourselves snuggled up under the duvet. His body was warm, wrapped around mine. He pressed a kiss to my forehead.

"Even if you decide we have to go back to friends, this has been everything, Katie."

He might not be book smart, but he knew exactly how to get to me. It wasn't manipulative, just honest.

I was in so much trouble.

I floated into sleep, deep and uninterrupted.

Josh woke up before me. He kissed my head, said something about practice and used his phone light to find his clothes. I tried to remember where I'd thrown them, but sleep pulled me back under and when I woke up, I was alone. I checked the time on my phone and found a text from Josh.

Hope you have a great day! XXOO

I grinned. I sent a *You too* back to him and pulled on a robe to go out and find coffee. I needed to get to school.

* * *

JOSH

I DIDN'T WANT to leave Katie, not when we were finally on the same page about a relationship. I'd offered to back off, but she hadn't asked me to. I wanted to spend every minute with her that I could.

So heading out on the road was suckier than usual. We all got tired of hotels and airplanes. Crowds in the arenas who booed us. Playing at home was better. On the other hand, that cloud that had been hanging over our heads was gone and we were finally playing the way we should. We'd gotten the Minnesota monkey off our back and won four of five games on the road. I had an additional monkey off my back, because with the team playing like this we still had a good chance of making the playoffs, so there was no need for management to shake things up with a trade.

We'd gotten back late last night and then had to come in for practice without a chance for me to see Katie. As we stripped down in the locker room, there was a lot of talk about Christmas, just a couple of weeks away. What people were doing, what they were getting their friends and family for Christmas.

I had to get Katie something, but I didn't know what. We were new enough with this replay on our relationship that I should probably show some restraint. I wanted to get her a car, so she could get around, but I shut that idea down. Maintaining a car was expensive, and I didn't know if there was parking available in her building. Not something I could slip into a conversation without her noticing. Plus, a car itself was expensive, and even though I'd be happy to pay for the insurance and gas, I didn't want to spook her. She might consider that going too far, but damn, gifts were hard. You couldn't ask about them in advance.

I'd love to get her a ring, but that would be even spookier. I was going to do that, I had no doubts, but I'd wait. Maybe till she was done with school, or at least done with her master's, so her parents didn't think she was giving up her dream.

What else? Prepaid transit here in Toronto? That wasn't very romantic. A flight to Nova Scotia so she could see her family? But I'd miss her, and she had classes to work a trip around.

A new phone or laptop? Maybe?

My phone buzzed and I jerked to grab it. It wasn't Katie though. Allen. Probably just calling to tell me the trade was off. I answered and told him I'd take a minute to find a quiet spot.

Around the corner, I didn't see or hear anyone. "Allen."

"Josh. Ready to pack your bags?"

For a moment, the hallway swirled around me and I heard nothing but my blood pounding in my ears. I braced my free hand on the wall so I didn't fall over.

"Josh?"

"What are you talking about?"

"They've worked out the details of the trade. You're going to Seattle."

I dragged in some air. "No! We turned the corner. We beat Minnesota, we went on a winning streak. We can still make the playoffs."

"It's a business, kid. They're switching things up. Don't tell anyone yet, since they won't announce for a day or two, but you and Mitchell are heading west. It's a good team, young, currently in playoff position, and you'll still be on the top line."

I wanted to argue, or yell, do something to convince Allen this wasn't the right move. But it wasn't his decision. It was a team decision, and Mitchell and I had no power to say no. Not unless we gave up on hockey. I couldn't even tell Mitchell he was going, and this would have a big impact on him and Jayna.

Katie. What the hell would happen with Katie? Did they have a math program in Seattle? Would she be willing to transfer? Could she now, when it was a few months into her first year? I doubted it.

"The teams are arguing draft picks to round out the deal, so they're saying it's just in theory, but it would take something drastic to derail it now. They want it done before the Christmas freeze, so it won't be long."

My breathing was too fast, and I concentrated on slowing that down so I didn't pass out. My fists had clenched and I had to deliberately relax my fingers.

"I get that you don't want to move, but this is what hockey is. Seattle is eager to have you."

"Yeah." I couldn't conjure up more words. None that weren't curses.

"I shouldn't really have told you, but December is a tough time to move, and I wanted you to have some notice. I'll send you living options. You're from Halifax, so you can be by an ocean again."

I didn't give a fuck about the ocean. Not when it would cost me Katie.

He hung up, but I stood there, coming to terms with my new future. I wanted to go out tonight and play badly. So badly that no team would want me. So that Seattle would retract their deal, or ask for someone else.

But I couldn't do that to my team, not when things were finally turning around and they had a chance to make the playoffs, go all the way this year. *Fuck.* They'd be doing it without me. That was...not possible. We were really tight. I wanted to win the Cup with these guys.

I wasn't sure how long I stood there, but when I finally was in control of my body, I headed back to the locker room. I couldn't let anyone know there was a problem, since I couldn't explain what was going on. Thankfully, most of the guys were gone by then—heading for lunch or a nap. I was glad Fitch had brought his own vehicle today. I didn't want to pretend to be happy with anyone right now.

When I got out of the shower, there was finally a text from Katie. She had a class tonight, but wished me luck and asked if I wanted her to come over after.

I hesitated. I wasn't going to be good company. But I needed to talk to her. Trades were sometimes leaked, and I didn't want her to hear I was leaving from anyone else. I'd learned my lesson. We *would* talk about this. I didn't think we were at a relationship level where she'd go with me, but maybe I could convince her to do long-distance.

I messaged that I was looking forward to seeing her, and headed home. It might have been better if Allen hadn't told me. But this way I had time to get used to it, so when it happened I didn't punch something. Sometimes these things happened so quickly guys were on a plane without the chance to pack. I at least had an opportunity to talk to Katie and didn't have to leave without saying goodbye.

Damn it.

I didn't get any sleep before I had to get to the arena. I was quiet during warm-ups. Thinking too much about the trade. It wasn't final yet or they wouldn't have let me play tonight, but Allen was good. He knew things before other people did. He wouldn't have told me if he didn't think it was happening.

"You okay, Ducky?" Cooper stood in front of me. I was sitting in my stall, staring at the floor, waiting for the game to start.

I looked up at him. "Oh, sure."

"Problems with your girl?"

I shook my head. Not like he was thinking.

He tapped my pads with his stick. "Well, let's win this one. One step closer, right?"

I forced a grin. "Yep."

Except for me, it was one step closer to leaving.

We headed onto the ice, lights down, the spots on us as we spilled out, the crowd cheering. When they announced the starting lineup, I listened to the cheers for Josh

Middleton with my eyes closed, soaking it in, for what was probably the last time.

The fans in Toronto had been great. I'd give them a game to remember for when I was gone.

I skated to the line, waiting for the puck drop.

As soon as Deek had the puck, I raced forward and sideways, giving him a target for a pass. One of their defensemen headed for me, but I caught the puck and slipped past him, over the blue line, using my speed to miss the check he'd planned to hit me with. A pass to Oppy, and we'd scored on the first play of the game.

My teammates applauded us, but I didn't feel the excitement I normally did when I played well. So next shift, I pushed a little harder. Got a little too eager and was called for offsides. Still, I got a goal before they'd had a chance to even the score. That wasn't enough though.

Back on the bench, waiting for the tap to get back on the ice, Deek nudged me. "You okay?"

"Why wouldn't I be? We're killing them."

"No one is supposed to literally be killed. You just seem… more aggressive than usual."

Yeah, I'd checked one of the other forwards a little harder than normal. But this was a big game, important in ways Deek didn't know. "Just want to make sure we get the win."

Three minutes before the end of the first period, we were up three nothing. All three goals were when I was on the ice, and I had an assist and a goal. Maybe I could get a hat trick. That would be a way to go out. Hell, maybe it would convince management that I was worth keeping.

I jumped over the boards for what would probably be our last shift this period. The forward I'd hit chirped at me while we waited for the face-off.

"Kind of pushy there for a shrimp."

"Yeah, this shrimp is making you look like shit, asshole."

The puck dropped and I started moving.

After, I couldn't remember what happened in those next two minutes. I played them, and later watched the replays, but the next thing I was aware of after the puck drop was lying on the ice, my knee shooting pain up and down my leg.

I'd hurt before. Been bruised, broken a bone or two growing up, but this was different. The injury in the preseason had been minor, and I knew this wasn't. I curled up, trying to protect the joint that was sending throbbing waves of agony through my body. Someone was speaking to me, asking me something, but all I could focus on was the pain.

There was a stretcher. No, I couldn't be carried. I was a hockey player, and I'd get off on my own. But I couldn't stand, couldn't push up from the ice. I could do nothing but endure the agony and wait for something to stop it.

The jostling to get me on the stretcher was too much. Suddenly everything blacked out, and there was no pain, no crowd, nothing at all.

* * *

THE NEXT TIME I was conscious was in the hospital. I felt an IV stuck in my hand, but if it was a painkiller, it wasn't working. I blinked my eyes open to see what was going on. I was in a room by myself, and Coach was there. The game must be over. Who'd won? But before I could ask, pain shot up from my knee.

That part I remembered.

"Middleton. Josh. You've torn your knee, and you need surgery." Coach's bedside manner could use some work. His words sounded far away. "The doctor here is going to explain, okay?"

I slowly turned my head and noticed a woman in a white jacket standing near Coach. Had she been there all along?

Her mouth opened and words came out but they didn't make sense. Medical jargon, knee, surgery, rehab.

I opened my mouth, desperately tried to form words. What came out was more air than sounds, but I pushed. "How…long."

The doctor spoke, but Coach overrode her. He knew what I was really asking.

"Six months. Everything goes well, should be six months and you're back."

The doctor glared at him, but I couldn't worry about that. Six months? Even if the team went all the way, I'd just be back after the finals ended. Except I was being traded. Was I, now that I was injured?

If everything goes well. What the— What could happen that wouldn't go well? But I couldn't make more words, and another jolt from my knee had the world blacking out again.

CHAPTER 28
'I LIKE A CHALLENGE

KATIE

Supervising the night lab was mostly quiet. At this point in the semester, with exams nipping at their heels, students weren't goofing off. I'd given them some review questions and stood by to assist if they needed it. The more they did on their own, the better their chances once they were sitting in front of that upcoming exam.

There weren't any students like Josh here. These kids didn't struggle with math the way he did, but everyone had their own blocks to understanding, and figuring out what was most effective for them was the most rewarding part of my job.

Between questions, I was working on my own exam review. The difficulty of master's-level classes was exponential. It was tempting to check the game I knew Josh was playing, but I wouldn't do that in front of the class. It wasn't like the game against Minnesota when there was so much on the line.

I'd answered some questions, went through a couple

246

more pages of my own stuff, when the door suddenly slammed open and Andrea stopped just inside, panting.

"Andrea? Are you okay?"

She shook her head. I got up and rushed to wrap an arm around her, trying to calm her while she gasped for breath.

"I...texted..."

I'd turned off notifications. I'd be too distracted with following the game if I let myself open my phone.

Andrea waved her hand, so I picked up my phone from the desk and opened it up. Before I could see what she'd sent, notifications from the game popped up.

Middleton taken off the ice.

Status of #17 unclear after brutal check.

My stomach twisted. It couldn't be. That injury in the preseason, he'd said it had been his first one. His game style was to be fast, to get out of any dangerous situations. He had bruises, sure, after a game, but he wouldn't get seriously hurt, would he?

I swallowed down my panic. "What happened, Andrea?"

She shook her head. "Bad...check." She straightened up. "I know you keep your phone off during labs, but I thought maybe he'd send you something and you would need to know."

I scrolled through my notifications. Andrea's message, game posts about goals—Josh got one—but nothing from Josh himself. "There's nothing. Is that good?"

"I don't know. Teams are really bad about revealing injuries to their players."

"What's going on?" one of my students asked.

For the first time, I realized the entire class was following along, much more interested in this drama than math.

"Her boyfriend was just taken out of the game," Andrea answered tersely.

"Wait, do you mean Ducky? I saw he was out."

"My TA is dating Ducky?" The guy in the back row stared at me in surprise.

"Ducky. Fuck, man, he's been having a great year."

I couldn't handle this. I just wanted to find out what happened to my boyfriend without fielding questions.

"You know Ducky?" The guy in the back row was not letting this go.

I nodded, fingers trembling as I tried to operate the stupid phone, looking for more news. "I was his math tutor in high school."

I'd finally called up a search engine and typed in *Josh Middleton* and *injury* to see what news was out. I scrolled through the hits that came up. Nothing definitive.

"Seriously? Why aren't you at the game?" The same guy.

Nothing online except that he'd been taken off the ice on a stretcher. *Damn it.*

"If you're really dating him, you'd be at the game."

I looked up at that. These kids were questioning my relationship while I was freaking out over whether my boyfriend was alive? Healthy? "For the record, what I do in this classroom is just as valid as what he does on the ice. But I need to find out what the hell is going on with him, so lab is over. Email your questions because I'm done."

I texted and called Josh's phone. Students gathered their stuff and headed out the doorway. There was no answer. I drew in a deep breath. Josh didn't have his phone with him when he was playing, but he always seemed to check it as soon as he was off the ice. He was either still playing, or something bad had happened.

He had to be playing. How did I find out when I couldn't message him and I didn't know anyone at the game in person? I checked the latest game stats online, showing player shifts and time on ice. Josh was not listed, which was a bad sign. There was nothing about Josh's condition. Wouldn't they know if it was bad?

I tapped my phone impatiently. Who else could tell me what was going on? Would Jess or Callie know? They weren't at the game tonight. I needed someone on the team. *Daniel.* He wouldn't have his phone with him, not right now, but he'd let me know when he could. I was sure of that.

I pulled up his contact and started to text.

"What can I do?" Andrea asked.

"Thanks for letting me know, but I don't think there's anything anyone can do. At least no one here. I'm messaging Daniel, Josh's roommate."

"You mean Fitch?"

"Yeah. I hope he'll tell me something when he can." He would, wouldn't he?

"It can't be too bad. They didn't stop the game."

"But he hasn't had another shift."

She bit her lip.

All the students were gone. I had nothing to do but refresh my phone's browser while I waited for information. No point in staying. "I'm going home now. I can worry in private."

"Do you want me to come with you?"

I turned and gave her a hug. "Thank you for offering. But I'll be terrible company, plus you've got exams coming up."

"So do you."

I shrugged. "Until I find out, I won't be able to concentrate." I shoved my textbook and laptop into my bag. "I'll let you know if I hear anything."

She asked me a couple more times if I was sure, then hugged me and finally left. I headed home.

Madeline was gone, so I flipped between sporting channels on the TV, desperate for news. I couldn't concentrate on my textbook and kept pacing as I waited to learn something.

* * *

It was long hours later when Daniel finally got back to me. It had taken him a while to find out himself what was happening with Josh. Emergency surgery on his knee, out for six months.

Josh was going to freak out, missing that much time.

"And that's a guarantee, that he'll be playing again?"

Silence on the other end. Then, "The odds are in his favor, but there aren't any guarantees, Katie."

If he couldn't play hockey…this would devastate him. I thought he'd been smart with his money, so at least he'd be good financially and not desperate for a job. I didn't know for sure; since that wasn't why I was with him, I hadn't pried. But I knew *Josh*. Hockey was his thing. The thing that gave him his sense of worth. I'd been telling him, in high school and now, that there was more to him than that, but he didn't really believe me. What would he do if he was done?

This could be bad. Really bad.

"I need to see him."

"I'm not sure what I can do, but I'll try to get you in. I know he'd want you there. I'll contact you when I work something out." Then he was gone.

I looked around the condo. If Daniel could get me to Josh, I needed to take some things.

My tablet, with all the *Star Wars* material I could put on it, for a distraction when he woke up because he was not a good patient. The hospital would feed and hydrate him, but I'd need a water bottle and some energy bars. Some of my assignments, because there'd probably be a lot of time to wait, and I'd be calling in a couple of sick days. I'd have a lot to catch up on.

It was two in the morning when I got the call from

Daniel. He'd somehow wrangled permission for me to stay with Josh. I had explicit instructions to follow to get into his very private room, and a message he texted me to get past security.

"Thank you. Thank you so much."

"I'm doing this for Ducky as much as for you."

"Still, thank you."

"Just help him. That will be enough thanks."

I'd do everything I could.

* * *

I DIDN'T REMEMBER MUCH about the ride to the hospital. I was exhausted and wired, resulting in everything feeling both removed and immediate. I five-starred the driver and tipped her well before making my way through the corridors, following Daniel's instructions.

I didn't get through easily. Security was tight for a celebrity athlete. I saw people around who I assumed were reporters, so a lot of the checks they made were to make sure I wasn't a member of the press. There were a couple of phone calls to someone higher up to verify I was allowed through, but finally I was in his room.

He was out of recovery, but he was still hooked up to a lot of machines. His knee was in a weird brace/cast, the rest of him under the covers, in a hospital gown. He looked so defenseless, so vulnerable. I dropped my bag in a chair and stood beside the bed.

There were shadows under his eyes and his mouth was pinched, as if the pain under all the drugs was still bothering him. He was breathing on his own, which shot relief through me. No reason a knee injury should be fatal, but my fears had not been logical.

As long as he was alive, we could get through anything else. I ran my fingertips over his forearm and hand, the one not hooked up to the IV. He twitched.

Exhaustion wrapped over me. There was nothing I could do right now, not until he woke up, so I might as well try to get some sleep too. I pulled out my tablet and set it on the rolling table at the side of the bed. Not that he was likely to wake up and want a distraction immediately, but once he was back to himself…

I pulled the chair up beside the bed. I tried curling up in the chair, then leaning back, and finally resting my feet on the side of his bed. A nurse came in and nodded to me. Guess word had gone out that I was okay to stay. Once she'd checked Josh's vitals, she left again.

I watched him breathing, lashes occasionally twitching as his eyes moved behind his eyelids, until my own lids drooped and I slept.

I woke up partially, some indeterminate time later when a nurse came in, but I was tired and not even the uncomfortable chair could keep me awake. I squirmed around, this time leaning forward, head on the bed near Josh's hand, hoping I'd sense it if he came to. I wanted him to see me first thing when he opened his eyes.

That wasn't what woke me up.

"*What* are you doing here?" The voice in my ear broke through the bonds of sleep.

I jerked, and my back and neck let me know they were very unhappy with the way I'd been treating them.

I shook my head and sat up, looking around, and saw the furious face of Mrs. Middleton.

I blinked to make sure I wasn't in some kind of nightmare. When had Josh's mother gotten here?

I was rumpled and groggy and probably looked like shit.

She looked like she'd had a shower recently, and fresh clothes. Her makeup was perfect, but her expression? Pissed.

"Hi, Mrs. Middleton." I stretched my neck and tried to corral any awake brain cells. I desperately needed coffee for this.

"What are *you* doing here?"

Right, she'd asked that earlier. My mouth felt gross. I'd give a lot for a toothbrush. And my bladder was letting me know I needed to get to a washroom.

I rubbed my eyes. "I was keeping Josh company."

Her lips tightened. "Well, I'm here now so you can go."

"Okay. I need to clean up, but I can come back later."

"That's not necessary."

"I'm happy to."

"Yes, I'm sure you are. But you're not needed. In fact, I want you to stay away."

My brain fog was clearing up, much too slowly. She didn't want me here. "Josh and I are together again. Didn't he tell you?"

"No. Which tells you a lot about how serious he is, doesn't it? Now, will you leave or do I have to call security?"

I had no idea what would happen if she followed through on that threat. Daniel had pulled some strings to get me in here, but Mrs. Middleton was right. I had no legal status. And she did. She wanted to keep me away from Josh, and right now, she could.

Until he was awake and aware, right?

I stood up, picking up my messenger bag. "I want nothing but the best for Josh, so I'll leave rather than make a scene. But Josh gets to decide who he's with, not you."

"If you want the best for him, you'll stay away. Permanently. Goodbye."

No confusion about whether Mrs. Middleton still didn't

like me. Now she wasn't bothering to even try to be subtle. I limped out of the room, still achy from the awkward sleep.

I'd be back though. Mrs. Middleton could have this victory now. But when Josh woke up, then we'd straighten things out.

* * *

*J*OSH

I WAS CONFUSED when I regained consciousness. My brain was foggy and I couldn't figure out where I was. With all the traveling we did, I was used to being in new rooms all the time but this one smelled different. The sounds were different too—noisier, with people and announcements. But not like the arena.

A twinge came from my knee and then everything came crashing back. The trade. Getting injured. And this was a hospital.

How badly had I fucked up my hockey career? And what about Katie?

"Josh?" The voice was soft and familiar.

Mom. How much time had gone by if my mother had made it here?

I flickered my eyes open, squinting against the light. "Mom?" The word came out in a whisper.

"Josh, it's so good to see you awake. How are you feeling?"

She put her hand on my forehead, like I might have a fever. I felt pretty shitty, if I was being honest. Some familiar aches from bruises, muscles complaining after playing, but my leg felt heavy and my head was currently throbbing.

"Fine."

"Would you like some water?"

I tried to nod, but that didn't feel good. Mom got the idea and brought me a cup with a straw. I was thirsty and drank most of it.

Mom set the cup down and fussed with my covers. "The doctor will be by soon. But they say everything went well in surgery."

What did that mean? Would I get to play again? Would I be able to play the way I had before?

I needed to sit up and make a plan for what was going to happen. If the trade was still on, how would that tie in? And I had to see Katie. That more than anything.

How could I be this exhausted? I closed my eyes for a moment and then…nothing.

When I woke up again, it was darker, so later in the day. My head was clearer, so that was good, and I was thirsty again. This time it was a man's voice I heard, asking if I was awake.

"Yeah," I croaked.

"Drink?"

"Please."

Allen, my agent. He was an older guy, in his forties, with perfectly styled hair and an immaculate suit. He held out the cup and I took a long drink.

"Your mother went down to the cafeteria to get something to eat."

I nodded and let go of the straw.

He set it back down. "What the fuck, Josh?"

I blinked at him. "What?"

He dropped into the chair. "What were you doing in that game?"

I looked down and plucked at the fold in the sheet around my waist. My eyes continued on to my leg, and I flinched.

He sighed. "Sorry, I know that the knee must be bothering you. But honestly, what were you even doing that this happened? That's not how Josh Middleton plays."

I shook my head. What could I tell him? "I just…wanted to go out with a win if it was my last game in Toronto."

"You know trades are a part of life in hockey, right?"

I did. I'd been traded to Toronto. But I didn't want to leave, not this time.

"Were you trying to fuck up the trade?"

I looked at him. "No, I didn't do this"—I waved toward the contraption on my leg—"on purpose. Am I going to play again?"

I held my breath while I waited for his answer.

"The odds are good. But you're going to have to work harder than you ever have in rehab to get there."

I couldn't have fucked things up any worse. Being traded was bad enough, but traded and not playing? Unless maybe I could rehab here…

"The trade is off. Management is pissed. They're deciding now whether they'll try to replace you or start selling."

I opened my mouth but nothing came out. I hadn't just fucked things up for me, but for the whole team. "I'm sorry."

"You should be. You were in a great place, Josh, even with the trade. Despite the slow start, you were playing well. Seattle would have been a good fit with you."

But not for Katie. "So what now?"

"Now you rehab like your life depends on it. You don't breathe a word about a trade. And if the team finds another winger, you hope he's not as good as you, or more expensive, or older because the next trade might not be as good."

I swallowed. "Are you going to fire me?"

He shook his head. "I was tempted. But the optics aren't good if I do. Plus, for some stupid reason, I like you. And I think you can come back from this." He grinned, an expression that made me think of a shark. "You do that, and negotiations become fun. I like a challenge."

Something relaxed inside. Allen wasn't giving up on me. He thought I had a chance.

Mom came in the room, smiling at Allen. She liked him, because she thought he was taking good care of my career. I wasn't sure Allen liked her, but he never said anything. I was kind of shocked he'd said he liked me. He and I had a business relationship, so I knew at the end of the day it came down to money.

"He's awake again," she said.

Allen stood. "We were talking. But I need to see the Blaze management, and then I have to fly back to California."

"Thank you for coming. We both appreciate it." Mom smiled at him.

She hadn't been told off like me, but I was grateful he'd shown up. I didn't get into trouble so I didn't see Allen often. I'd like to get back to that arrangement. He was unnerving.

Once he was gone, Mom came over to fuss with the blankets and offer me more water.

"I'm fine." Now that my head was clearer, I wanted to hear from the doctors about my knee, and I wanted to see Katie. "What did the doctor say?" Mom had said she was coming by.

"She didn't tell me much. But everything is going to be fine."

Was she coddling me? Had the woman said something bad, and Mom was keeping it from me? Or was I being paranoid? I needed details. Did *fine* mean I'd walk again, or that I'd play? "When is she back again?"

"Tomorrow morning."

I started to fidget and stopped when my leg twinged. I was going to have a whole night to worry about this. I needed to at least talk to Katie.

"Where's my phone?"

Mom looked around and then shook her head. "I don't know. I'm not sure it's here."

Right. It would have been in my stall when this happened and might still be there. What would they have done with my clothes and personal items?

There was an iPad on the table tray thing at the side of the room, the one that could swing over my bed. I recognized the cover. It was Katie's.

I relaxed against the pillows. Katie had been here. She'd be back. That was good. I needed to see her.

"When's Katie coming back?"

Mom stiffened. Yeah, she didn't like Katie, and didn't know we were going out. I should have said something when we switched from friends to dating, but I didn't like upsetting people.

"Katie?" Like she didn't know who I was talking about.

"I know she was here. That's her iPad."

Mom's lips tightened and she picked up the tablet.

"What are you doing? I want that."

"I don't think screens are good for you right now."

Something about the way she spoke made me realize there was more to what she said than the words. She wasn't just talking about the screen.

"Where is Katie?" I repeated.

Mom's chin went up. "I sent her away. I don't know why she was even here, but she had no right."

"When's she coming back?" I needed to see her.

Mom shoved the iPad in a drawer in the bedside table, at the bottom where I couldn't reach. "She isn't coming back, as far as I know."

"Mom," I warned.

"She has exams now, doesn't she? She's busy."

True, but she'd come here, somehow. That meant everything. I needed to speak to her, but Mom wasn't going to budge. And right now I was stuck in a bed, with no phone and no one who'd help me reach out to her.

I'd find a way to get her back here. If Mom hadn't said anything too horrible to her. Would she be upset I hadn't told Mom about her?

I had to make it right. But my head was getting dizzy, and my thoughts were floating away from me. I fell asleep again.

CHAPTER 29

LET'S SEE IF GANDALF HAD ANY ADVICE

KATIE

I WAS EXHAUSTED, sore, worried and irritated when I let myself into the condo. I'd booked the day off sick, so once my shoes were off I headed to my room and collapsed on my bed, fully dressed. I crashed immediately.

I woke to sunlight, a full bladder, and a hungry belly. I stretched out on the bed, and decided peeing and a shower were my top priorities.

Dressed in fresh clothes and feeling clean, I headed to the kitchen for coffee and food. I set my laptop up on the countertop and got back in touch with the world. There was nothing from Josh, but the man had just had surgery, so I had to cut him some slack. I was worried about his mother though. Would she even tell him I'd been there?

I had emails from school, and work to do, but my mind kept returning to Josh. How was he? There was nothing meaningful in the news reports out there. Had he regained consciousness? Would his knee recover? Would he be able to play again?

I picked up my phone and brought up Daniel's number. I sent him a quick text, asking for news of Josh.

Aren't you at the hospital?

Run off by Mrs. Middleton. Haven't heard from Josh.

Let me check and get back to you.

I was still antsy, so I stripped my bed and threw a load of laundry in. Vacuumed my bedroom and cleaned the bathroom. Mindless work that kept me busy but didn't require me to focus.

Jess pinged, asking how Josh was doing and how I was doing. Jayna and Callie sent messages too. I blinked back tears at the unexpected support. I'd been feeling alone, but these women wanted to be there for me.

Callie promised to ask Cooper for any information he knew, and Jess asked JJ, who didn't have anything new to offer. I thanked them and explained that Josh's mother, who was not a fan of mine, had made me leave the hospital.

Finally, Daniel got back to me. He'd arranged with the team to get Josh's things from the locker room and take his phone to Josh at the hospital. He'd give him the phone with the messages I'd sent and promised to tell him I'd been there and wanted to see him again.

It was a relief to know he hadn't had his phone, rather than that he hadn't wanted to reach out to me. By this time, he should be awake and aware. Insecurities still had a grip on me. Josh hadn't told his mother, so maybe he wasn't as serious as I'd thought.

I shoved those thoughts aside and passed the news on to the nontraditional WAG club. Then, mostly through force of will, I was finally able to focus on the things I needed to get done related to work and school.

My advisor asked whether the time I'd taken off as sick was for female issues. Was this something that would continue on an ongoing basis in future, so he could be prepared. *Asshole.* Stupid asshole, since this was December, and I hadn't taken any sick time to date. Unless he thought I was preg—

My brain screeched to a halt. What was the date? It had been a couple of weeks since the non-condom sex with Josh, and wasn't I supposed to have my period now?

Shit. I scrambled to work out timelines. I wasn't regular, but I was late, wasn't I? I opened my calendar and counted. I hadn't definitely missed but if something didn't happen soon…

I curled up in a chair in the living room, clutching my phone in case Josh reached out. *What if…* I didn't even want to think the word. One brief moment of distraction during sex, and this could change my life.

What lousy timing. Josh injured, exams, Christmas break coming up, problems with my advisor—I just wanted to bury my head under a pillow and not come up for weeks.

The sound of the condo door opening jerked me out of my doom spiral. I sat up in time to greet Madeline as she came down the hallway.

As always, she was impeccably dressed—a pantsuit, hair and makeup perfect, carrying a garment bag and rolling a carry-on behind her. You could do a photo shoot for a successful professional with how she looked all the damned time.

"Hi."

She frowned at me. "Are you all right?"

I closed my eyes and sighed. "Honestly, I've been better."

"Wine, ice cream, talk, or rom-com?"

"Not wine." If I was…well, better not wine.

"Let me put this away and I'll be back out shortly."

I puffed out a breath. Should I talk to her, or tell her it

was just one of those days? The NT-WAGs wanted to get together for a support session, but Jayna was out of town and Jess was sick. It would be a few days before we could find a time we were all available.

But my roommate? I could talk to her. If I was going to upchuck every morning, she'd soon know about that particular problem.

Madeline came back down the hallway, hair pulled into a ponytail, cashmere sweats on. I sighed. It wasn't like I couldn't be look more like her if I really worked at it, but I didn't want to that badly. Especially not now. But damn, the woman was put together.

Josh hadn't gotten back to me yet. Had his mother done something, or had Daniel not given him his phone? Maybe he'd heard bad news and he wasn't talking to anyone? Or was it just me?

My brain couldn't focus on any one thing. I was a mess.

Madeline came over with a pint of gourmet ice cream, a couple of bowls and spoons. "Do you want to talk or just turn on a movie?"

"I want to pretend none of this is happening, but I can't. Would you mind if I dumped on you to try to sort things out?" Madeline would never get into a mess like this, but hopefully she wouldn't judge me.

"I won't pretend I'm the best at advice, but I can be a sounding board." She passed me a bowl with salted caramel ice cream and a spoon.

"Thanks."

Once she'd placed a smaller amount in a second bowl, she took the carton back to the freezer. "This is the good stuff, so bring on the problems."

I gave her a half smile. "I have more than one, so be prepared."

"I meant to ask, how is Josh? I'd heard he was injured."

I held up one finger. "That's problem one." I gave her a recap of what had happened with Josh, his mother, Daniel... everything up to now.

She licked her spoon, eyes on me. "For now, that's all you can do, and that's frustrating. When will Josh get his phone?"

I pulled up my own—still no messages. "I'm not sure. Daniel had to go to the arena and get Josh's stuff, including the phone, before heading over. And he's still got his own life, practices and stuff to deal with, so I don't want to bombard him with my own worries."

"Let's finish the list of problems before you reach out again. What's next?"

Next. Well, this was one she could help with. "My advisor is a misogynist, and it's hobbling my ability to do my research project." I gave her a synopsis of the issues I'd had.

"Is there some kind of hierarchy in place so that you can report his behavior?"

I huffed. "Yeah. I wrote an email, but I haven't sent it yet."

"Why not?"

I shrugged. "I don't want to make a fuss? I mean, other women must deal with this. And what if it backfires? He gets pissed and nothing else changes."

She pointed her spoon at me. "I've dealt with this kind of bullshit. I can tell you from experience that ignoring the problem does nothing to help, just reinforces that mindset."

Nora had told me that when I talked to her. If I wanted something I had to push for it.

I grabbed my laptop and flipped it open. "You're right. And this is one thing I can deal with." I called up my email program, found the draft and closed my eyes. "There's no going back if I do this."

"Do you want to go back or forward?"

"Good point." I opened my eyes and hit the send button. "Done."

"How does that feel?" Madeline was watching with a trace of a smile on her face.

I swirled the spoon in the remaining ice cream in the bowl till it became a soup. "Good. But also, terrifying."

"Is there anything more you can do right now?"

I slumped back in my seat. I should study for my next exam, but my brain still wasn't focusing. I needed to talk to Josh, but I couldn't. And if I was… Nope, that one I couldn't handle at the moment. Maybe tomorrow. "If there is, I'm not going to be able to do it."

"Rom-com?"

"Honestly, I'd prefer *Lord of the Rings*." Nothing romantic, no advisors or disapproving mothers. They just had to save their world, and at this particular point in time, that seemed like a good alternative.

"I think I saw those movies when they came out." She didn't sound like a fan.

"We can watch something else, then."

"No, let's give it a go." She shot me a glance. "I think you need this."

I stopped resisting. I did need that comfort. Let's see if Gandalf had any advice that would help me make my decisions.

CHAPTER 30

A DUMB JOCK

JOSH

HOSPITALS WERE NOT great places to stay. I was spoiled, having stayed in pretty nice hotels when we traveled, but the constant interruptions, the embarrassing hospital gown, the tasteless food and the lack of Katie all made me restless and uncomfortable.

And on top of that, more anxiety than I had dealt with in a long time. It was hard to get a proper sleep, despite being exhausted, not only because of people checking on me and the noise and strange smells, but because I was desperately afraid I might not be able to play hockey again. I was only twenty-four. It wasn't supposed to be over yet.

Mom had gone to a hotel at the end of visiting hours. I wished Katie could come, but I knew she had her own stuff to deal with and I didn't have a phone to even message her. Since we'd agreed on being friends again, I'd at least texted her almost every day and had upped that once we started dating. I missed that contact with her. It would settle me, I knew it.

I had a restless night.

In the morning, the doctor came by and I had a chance to get some answers about my future.

She was careful and didn't want to promise something that might not happen, but there were too many technical words and a lot of *probably* and *likely* in her explanation. I wanted a simple answer: Would I be able to play hockey again? And if I did, would I be able to play well enough to be in the NHL?

Worrying about getting traded to Seattle didn't seem as big a deal as whether I'd even be wanted there anymore.

"Bottom line—is my knee going to get all the way better?"

The doctor sighed. "I know you want a guarantee. Unfortunately, I can't provide that. But if you do the therapy without overdoing it, your knee should regain almost one hundred percent of its former strength and mobility."

"But not one hundred percent?"

She shrugged. "The only way to find out is to follow the recovery process and see what happens."

I understood—she couldn't give me a hard promise. Shit happened. But I wanted the best idea of what would happen. "Can you tell me, out of all the times someone has had this operation, how it's worked out?"

She narrowed her eyes. "Do you want me to include the eighty-year-old woman I operated on last month?"

My jaw dropped. "Um...probably not."

"Should I maybe narrow the participants to only include athletic males in their twenties?"

I dropped my head back on the pillows. "I get it. So, there's nothing more you can tell me?"

"I'm sorry. I know this is your vocation. But an athlete in

his twenties has a lot of factors in his favor. If he doesn't overdo it."

There was a lot of talk about not overdoing it. "I hear you. When do I start rehab?"

"You need to recover from surgery, and then someone will assess you. There are *some* exercises you can start right away, and a therapist will be by to show those to you. Your team will help set up a program for you."

That was encouraging. The team was going to work with me. They had to be pissed about me getting injured, but I was still valuable to them.

The doctor left, and I was poking at some sort of eggs that I'd been served when Mom arrived. Right behind her was Fitch. I was glad to see my mother but overjoyed to see Fitch.

"Good morning," my mom said, then turned when she realized the man behind her had followed her in. "Excuse me, who are you?"

"Mom, that's my roommate, Fitch. It's good to see you, Fitchie."

He raised an eyebrow my way but greeted my mother politely. "Good morning, Mrs. Middleton. I'm Daniel Astrom. I brought a few things for him."

"My phone?" I needed to get in touch with Katie.

"Yes, your phone, some clothes, and—" He pulled a hand from behind his back with a bag showing the Golden Arches on it. "Breakfast."

"Best roommate ever," I vowed.

My mom frowned. "Maybe that's not the right thing to be eating, Josh."

I grabbed the bag from Fitch. "It's way better than what the hospital sent me. I'll be back on my meal plan soon." I tore the bag open and groaned at the greasy smells wafting up. I shoved the hospital tray aside and pulled out hash brown patties and a couple of wrapped sandwiches.

"Wasn't sure what you liked, so I got a few things."

I shoved a bite of hash brown in my mouth. "Right now, I like all of it."

He grinned and then passed me my phone. "Clothes and toiletries are in the bag."

I dropped the patty and took the phone, waiting impatiently while it recognized my face and opened. There were millions of notifications, but I made my way to my conversation with Katie. There were a lot of messages from her, but they stopped after yesterday morning. I needed to read them, but I wanted to do that on my own. I quickly sent a message to reassure her.

Just got my phone. I'm okay. Will talk later. Love you.

My mother had taken the bag of clothes and started to put them in my closet. "Hey, I'd like to put those sweats on instead of this stupid gown."

"They won't fit over the brace."

"I'll rip them."

"I brought some shorts—you can probably put those on when you're not all hooked up," Daniel assured me.

Right. I had tubes and needles and some of those were in very private places. "Thanks, Fitch."

"Glad to see you're looking better, Ducky. I've got to get to practice. I'll tell the team you're doing good. They'll be stopping by, if that's okay."

Mom frowned, but I didn't let her fuss. Before talking to Katie, I'd have assumed she was worried about me, but now I was trying to figure out if it was more than that. Katie was probably right that Mom was still a little possessive, but if I didn't like it, it was up to me to tell her to stop. And right now, seeing my teammates was what I wanted. "That would be great."

He smiled and leaned down, as if to fix my sheet. "Katie's anxious. Your mother made her leave." His voice was barely a whisper. He straightened up. "Okay, you should be good for now. Nice to meet you, Mrs. Middleton." He left.

I needed to have a serious conversation with my mother.

"So that's your roommate? He's a little older."

"He was traded from Edmonton this summer. He's a good guy."

She finished with the closet and turned around, frowning. "I still don't understand why you need a roommate."

"I like the company. He's new, so I'm helping him get to know the city. And he cooks."

"That's all well and good, but while you recover, you're going to need a lot of help. I could take care of you…"

There was my cue. I'd put this off, thinking I'd wait till I knew things were serious with Katie before upsetting Mom. But that was just avoiding the problem because talking to my mom was difficult. Katie deserved someone who stood up for her, and I needed to act like an adult.

"Don't worry. I have a girlfriend and she'll help me." And if she was busy, I could hire in-home care.

"You didn't tell me you'd started dating. Don't you think I should meet her?"

"You already know her. Katie Baker."

She froze in place. "Katie Baker."

I braced myself.

"How long has this been going on?" Her voice was accusing.

"I told you when I met her before the season started."

She sniffed. "And you think that was an accident?"

"I know it was an accident." Mom was not going to like this, but I wanted to make it perfectly clear that Katie had not organized our meeting so that she couldn't use it against her. I pushed up against my pillows. "I met someone at a bar and went home with her. She was a hookup. We both knew it was just sex."

Mom's lips were pursed.

"When I got to her place, Katie was there. They'd just become roommates. If you think there's some way Katie made that happen, that I met her roommate at a bar and she asked me to go home with her so that Katie could meet me? You're insane. It was a terrible way to see her again, and I had to work hard to get her to trust me enough to be a friend. And just recently to be more than that."

Mom spoke. "You were too young back in high school to get that serious. I think you're confusing nostalgia for something more." Her arms were crossed, her expression grim. She really didn't like Katie. Was it a control thing, like Katie thought?

"Maybe we were young, but we're not now. She's not taking advantage of me. I've had to deal with people doing that, and Katie is different. Why don't you like her?"

She wouldn't meet my eyes. "I just don't think she's good for you. You have a demanding career, and you need a certain kind of person to support that. She won't do that—her parents have pushed her to put her career first."

That was true, but it wasn't an insurmountable obstacle. "I'm sorry you feel that way. Because she's perfect for me."

"How would you know? You've never dated anyone else."

I closed my eyes for a moment. "I didn't tell you, but do you really think I've spent five years as a professional hockey player and not had a chance to meet women? A lot of women?"

She blinked. "But you never *dated*."

"Nothing serious. Because I could never find anyone better than Katie."

"You didn't really try."

"Yes, I did. I never thought I'd see Katie again, and I

wanted to have what we had back then. I never found anyone who made me feel the way she did. When I saw her that night, I knew I'd do anything to get her back."

Mom didn't answer for a minute. I braced myself for an argument. "You won't listen to anything I have to say, then."

"Not if it's against Katie. She's…when I'm with her, I don't feel like a dumb jock. She makes me feel smart. She doesn't want me to buy her stuff, like a lot of women do. She just likes being with me. She's more interested in talking to me about *Star Wars* than hockey. No one else is interested in that Josh."

"That's why she was in your hospital room when I arrived."

I shrugged. "I guess. I didn't even know she was here, except she left her tablet."

"I might as well leave. Since you prefer her." She stood, gathering her coat and purse.

"I don't want you to go." Damn it, was she really going to do this?

"But I'm not allowed to talk."

"I said I wouldn't hear you say anything bad about Katie. You can still talk."

"Is she coming here?"

"She will. I don't know when, but yeah. If she wants to come, I definitely want her here."

"I don't think there's room for the two of us."

She wanted me to choose between them? Was she manipulating me? I wasn't choosing between them, I just wasn't choosing to leave Katie like she wanted. "That's your decision. But Katie is part of my life now, and I hope for a long, long time to come."

She paused, waiting for something. For me to say I'd make Katie stay away so Mom could be here? Katie had never done anything like that, had she? She'd told me Mom

272

didn't like her, which was true, and said it was because Mom wanted me to need her.

"We should probably talk, you and me and Katie. So we all get along." There had to be a way for that to work, no matter what my teammates thought.

"I'm going back to my hotel room."

And she left.

* * *

KATIE

I COULDN'T SLEEP. Way too much going on in my head.

My brain still wanted to pick over the same arguments. I was confident that Josh and I had a trust strong enough that he wouldn't believe his mother. At least not without talking to me first. But the longer things went on without hearing from him, the more I worried, and my old insecurities tried to push forward.

I should have asked Daniel when he was giving Josh his phone, but I was kind of afraid to check with him in case he told me Josh already had his phone and hadn't reached out. What had his mother told him? Had she told him I'd been there? Did he think I hadn't cared and couldn't be bothered? That I would abandon him if he was injured? I'd left him my tablet, but had she hidden it? Thrown it away? Would she convince him we were better apart again?

Maybe I should just get up and go over there. Sure, it was the middle of the night and visiting hours were over, and he was in a private, secure room, but I could use that message from Daniel again, probably.

But if Josh had his phone and hadn't reached out...

I did fall asleep at some point and ignored my alarm. I

woke up with cramps, so I knew pregnancy wasn't an issue, but it wasn't the relief I'd expected. There were still so many things to consider, and this was not the time. I barely managed to pull a comb through my hair and brush my teeth before I had to rush out the door to proctor an exam.

I arrived just in time to get everything set up. This prof was giving an old-school exam for this group of students, so I had to gather phones before giving out paper exams. The students complained, but it was part of some research he was doing about how students responded to different test settings. There was another exam in the next room with the same questions but on computers, and they'd compare the results.

My job was to sit up front observing, with occasional trips around the room to make sure no one was using contraband. There'd been a calculator provided with each paper, but no internet access. I had confiscated a couple of smartwatches on the desk with the phones.

Once everyone was settled in and I'd done an initial lap, I sat behind the desk at the front of the room, watching everyone else frantically at work. My brain started right back at my problems: school and Josh.

One student moved her hand, and her ring flashed. Diamond, left hand, ring finger. She was an older student. Maybe she'd already had a family and was now going back to school. Was that a better path? It was working for Nora.

I scanned the room again.

My phone buzzed in my pocket. I checked that the students were busy with their exams and decided to walk around again before I sneaked a look. I didn't have the restrictions they had, but it seemed wrong for me to do it when they couldn't. Everyone was still busy. It was early enough in the time slot that no one was close to finishing yet.

I carefully slipped my phone out of my bag as I sat down

and set it on the desk. I tapped the screen with a finger and glanced down, stomach starting to hula when I saw it was a message from Josh.

Just got my phone. I'm okay. Will talk later. Love you.

I covered my mouth with my hand, afraid to let my squeak disturb the students. Daniel must have brought his stuff over this morning. If his mother had said anything, it hadn't convinced him to be done with me. And, *love you.*

He hadn't said that since before we broke up, all those years ago. Was it just a sign-off that didn't mean anything, or was it what he felt? Knowing Josh, yeah. I'd suspected we were both as committed now as we'd been back then. I had a hard time holding in the grin that wanted to cross my face. Not appropriate when proctoring an exam.

I checked the room again. Everyone was fine.

I still wasn't sure about my future here, beyond this semester, and I was even more eager to talk to him. We had a lot to work out. Where did we go from here?

Josh was injured and might not play again. Or he might have a lot of rehab to do. Could he be traded while he was injured? How would that work with my education? Assuming things didn't go terribly with the math department chair.

And if they did?

As if I'd conjured her up with my thoughts, the phone buzzed again with an answer from Dr. Marsden, the math chair. She wanted to meet with me on Friday.

Shit was getting real.

A movement caught my eye. I stood up and walked quietly over to a desk near the back. The student tried to stuff his smartwatch away, but I stood there, hand out, and he finally gave it to me.

I took the section of the exam he'd completed. "I'll let the prof know this part was done with banned technology. Finish the rest, and he can decide what to do with you."

Honestly, I was surprised this was the only incident so far. I'd been given a few different protocols to follow, depending on what happened.

I returned to my desk. Despite the mundane setting, this felt like a big moment in my life.

Nora had redefined her priorities when she got pregnant. Now, I might be facing a crossroads as well. On one side, Josh might need me, or he might have to go to another city.

On the other side, fighting to get my degree, which might be a struggle depending on the results of this meeting.

What should I do?

CHAPTER 31

I'M NOT GIVING UP ON MY DREAMS

Josh

I STARED at the doorway where my mother had disappeared. I kept waiting for her to come back, but after ten minutes she was still gone. She was angry, thinking I was choosing Katie over her.

I guess I was. It wasn't like the two of them were drowning and I had to pick one to save, but Mom wanted me to push Katie out of my life and that wasn't happening. I'd spent five years looking for something as good as Katie, and now that I had her again, I wasn't going to waste time looking for someone else.

Would Katie also ask me to choose between them? I didn't think so, but it was one of the many things we needed to talk about.

I pulled up my phone, anxious to get started on that talk and make sure we were solid going forward.

I stared at the last message I'd sent her. I'd said *Love you.* That was true, but would it spook her? I didn't want to have to worry about that. It was time to tell her I was serious and wanted long-term.

My stomach tensed, because she might not be ready. I'd have to convince her I'd wait as long as she needed. Without the trade I had time, for now. Shit, how long before I was a viable trade option again? Not till they knew if I'd recover, I was pretty sure.

My stomach twisted into knots. The two biggest things in my life were Katie and hockey, and I wasn't sure about either of them. It would be months before I knew if hockey was going to happen again. I could at least do something about the Katie part.

She hadn't answered my message. Was she busy, or had I scared her? The message showed as read. I drew in a breath and sent another message.

Talked to mom. Told her we were together.

She left.

Was that enough for Katie to know I chose her?

Please come. I'll make sure you can get in.

I stared at the messages till they showed as read but didn't see the dots to say she was responding.

Mom had said Katie had to leave because she had exams. I'd have to hope that was all the problem was. I had no idea what Mom said to her, and I was stuck waiting since I was immobilized. Katie had to come to me.

I'd dozed off, phone in my hand, when some of the guys stopped by. Cooper, of course, being team captain. Fitch was with them again, and Mitch, Crash, Oppy and even Petey.

It was a lift to see them, but it also hurt. I didn't know if I'd play with them again.

"Ducky! We brought you a duck!" Oppy grinned, holding out some bizarre Christmas-decorated stuffed bird. The duck was white and wearing a Santa hat and beard. Red coat and a belt, bare-assed and with an evil expression.

"Where the hell did you find that?"

"I do not reveal my sources."

Oppy pushed it up by my face and took a picture with his phone. I didn't want to know what he was going to do with that.

"How are you feeling?" Mitch asked. He looked worried. His girlfriend had lost her hockey career due to a knee injury. What would have happened to them if the trade had gone through?

My stomach knotted again, but I wasn't going to stress the team. They had games to win. I shrugged. "Enough drugs to keep me from hurting too much."

"What did they say about recovery?"

"Six months." But no guarantees.

"You work hard, you play again. I will help," Petey promised, or was that a threat?

Mitch passed over a bag of something that smelled incredible. "Figure you're not watching your weight right now, and hospital food sucks, so..."

"Give me!"

I munched on burgers, listening as the guys talked about the last games, how they'd squeaked out a couple of wins, including the one I'd been injured in, but insisted they needed me back. I couldn't tell them about the trade that hadn't happened, but would management switch to sending someone else out after the holiday freeze? Had they given up on the Blaze's season? Would some of these guys be gone before I was back on my feet?

My phone buzzed.

I'm done with school for the day. Should I come by?

YES

I didn't care if it was shouty. I wanted her to know this was a priority for me.

Fitch smirked. "That Katie?" I nodded. "She coming?"

"Yes."

He deliberately looked around the room. "Get things worked out with your mother?"

Yeah, she was conspicuously absent. I shrugged a shoulder. "I told her Katie was here to stay."

"How did that go?"

The guys were watching me. Some looked amused, some concerned.

"Mom left. Her choice. Like you said, I figured out what was most important. And now Katie's on her way, so you guys have to book."

Oppy pouted. "We like Katie. We want to see her too."

"Another time. We have a lot to talk about."

They teased me, and Petey reminded me not to be distracted by a woman, but they left soon after. I appreciated the visit, but I needed my girl. And while it was great of them to come by, they had stuff to do and I was a reminder of how easily we could lose our careers. I didn't want to bring anyone down.

I finished the food Mitch had brought and tossed the bag at the garbage. I missed but couldn't get up to put it in the can. Oppy had left the duck on the table with some flower arrangements fans had sent, just out of reach. So it sat, staring cross-eyed at me between roses and carnations while I waited. I shuddered.

A nurse came in, checked a bunch of stuff, told me I was doing well, and then left.

I heard footsteps and watched the door till I saw her there. *Katie.* She was wearing a coat, hair messed up from the hat she was now carrying in her hand.

She paused, staring at me while I stared at her. I was trying to figure out what she was thinking by how she looked, and she might have been doing the same. It didn't work, at least for me. She didn't seem to be upset or angry, but I couldn't understand how she was feeling. It was going to take words.

"You gonna come in?" The way she lingered in the doorway made me nervous.

A bit of a smile, just one corner of her mouth turning up. "I picked up some donairs."

Was that our thing now? "Thanks. But you didn't have to. I just needed to see you."

She bit her lip and crossed the threshold, walking toward me. I saw her eyes go to the food wrapper I'd not sunk in the garbage.

"You had something already?"

"Some of the team stopped by. Put the donairs on the table—I want them, but first I want you."

A bigger smile this time. She dropped the bag on the table, giving the duck a strange look. Then she came to the side of the bed.

Finally. I grabbed her hand and tugged her toward me. "Can I kiss you?"

This time the smile reached both sides of her mouth. "Will your doctor be upset?"

"Don't care." I put a hand on her cheek and brought her close enough that our lips touched.

Everything relaxed and my brain stopped worrying. Katie's lips felt a little cold, a little chapped, and totally perfect. I twisted to get closer, and my knee throbbed. I flinched.

She pulled back. "Not going to jeopardize your recovery."

I sighed but let her go. She pulled up a chair and sat down right beside the bed. I reached out my hand and she put hers in mine. Instant relief. We had things to work out, but I was optimistic. We'd get through this. "We have a lot to talk about."

She nodded. "Yeah. I've got some stuff to discuss with you too. But first, how are you doing?"

I ran the fingers of my free hand over our joined ones. "It'll be months before I know for sure about playing hockey again. The surgery went well, but they can't make any promises."

"I'm sorry. Is there anything I can do?"

"Just be with me. I didn't mean to tell you in a text that I loved you, but it's the truth. I love you, and I maybe never stopped. Since I broke up with you, I've never found anyone who makes me feel like you do. Could you give me a chance to make you love me again?"

I'd just put it all out on the line, but I wasn't playing any more games. Clear communication. We were going to be different this time.

Her hand tightened on mine. "What about your mother?"

I shrugged. "When I told her, she walked out. I don't know what she's going to do."

Katie drew in a breath. "I can't say she's my favorite person. But I'll try to get along with her. I don't want to keep you apart."

I felt the smile break out on my face. "So you're staying? Giving this a chance?" I got a partial smile back so I tensed up. There was something coming on her side, something I didn't know about.

"We need to talk about what that means."

My stomach was seriously sore from all the nerves twisting it up. I gripped a little harder on her hand. She didn't let go, so I drew in a long breath, relaxing my grip. "Okay. Let's talk."

"How sure are you that you're staying in Toronto?"

Ugh. "Not sure. I didn't have a chance to tell you, but the team had almost finalized a trade. I found out before the game where this happened. Me being injured stopped that."

Her mouth opened. "So I don't know. If they decide to rebuild the team, I'm probably going."

She closed her eyes. "Maybe it's a sign."

"What?" I was confused.

"I'm having problems at school."

This shocked me. "You were always such a good student."

She opened her eyes, smiling at me. "It's not the work. Not the courses. But my advisor…"

I tried to remember what she'd told me about him. Had he done something? I couldn't even get out of bed to help her. "What did he do?"

"Nothing and everything. Sorry, I'm not trying to be cryptic, but he has some frustratingly old-fashioned ideas about women and academics."

"Can you do something?"

A big breath in. "I wrote to the chair of the department. But I don't know if that's going to help or make it worse."

"Does that mean—what does it mean?"

"Maybe…maybe U of T isn't where I'm supposed to be. Maybe I should just be happy with the education I've got and forget about going further. I could withdraw and help you till your knee is better."

I tried to shove myself upright but my leg twinged. I jabbed at the remote for the bed to lift up my back. I needed Katie's attention for what I was going to say. The thought of her with me, while I went through rehab? Was great. But not great enough.

"I don't *ever* want to stop you from getting your dream. I got mine, and even if I can't play again, I did it. This was what I wanted, and I've had years of hockey and lots of memories. But you've always dreamed of getting more education. Helping people with math like you did me. I don't want you to give that up. We'll work something out."

She was biting her lip. Not convinced yet.

"There are other schools, right? Or wait, you didn't speak to your chairperson yet. Maybe it will be okay. But if not, we'll find a way."

"I'm not sure. Nora said when she got pregnant that it made her rethink her priorities and she decided she wasn't supposed to be a doctor. She's happy, so…"

I gave her hand a tug, making sure she'd hear. "You talked about some problems you have. And that you don't need another degree. But you never said you don't want it. If you do, I promise we'll make sure you get it."

She lifted my hand and kissed it. "You always surprise me. I thought you'd be all over having me at your beck and call while you recover."

"I want you around, don't get me wrong. But you don't have to quit school for that."

She curled up on the bed beside me. "I hate being in limbo like this. Not knowing what's going to happen."

"Tell me about it. But if you're with me, I can wait."

* * *

KATIE

I DIDN'T WANT to leave Josh alone at the hospital, but he needed to heal and I needed to study. I left the donairs for him, because he was stuck with hospital food, and picked up some takeout for myself on the way home. I hoped I could focus on math this evening.

Despite talking everything out with Josh, I still had questions. I was going to see the math chair after my exam tomorrow. Did I want to fight the math department to get my degree? Was quitting taking the easy way out, or was I figuring out what my priorities were, like Nora did?

There were lights on in the condo, and Madeline was in the kitchen cleaning up. She raised her brows when she saw me clinging to my own bag of fast food. "I have leftovers in the fridge but it looks like you took care of dinner."

"I don't have the bandwidth to prep food, not tonight."

She wiped her hands on the dish towel. "Anything get resolved yet?"

Despite all the questions and problems, I smiled. No, I grinned.

"I'm going to guess yes."

"The mother-in-law dragon has been slain."

"Did I miss something? Are you two married?"

I shook my head. "No." But we would be. I knew it. "Josh told his mother he was with me and that it was serious. She left, probably pissed with him. I got to see him, and we talked. Cleared up stuff like we should have the first time around."

"Congratulations. And the rest?"

I pulled out the burger and fries. "I was seriously considering dropping out of the master's program."

"No, Katie." I widened my eyes, surprised at her vehemence. "I'll just say that I've seen that firsthand and it turned out badly."

I opened the fridge to get some water. "Josh told me I shouldn't give up. It might be difficult, but it's my dream."

"Josh is definitely improving."

I sat down and took a bite of french fries. "He is. We are. I'm going to talk to the math chair, see what happens. I'm still considering my options, but I'm not giving up on my dreams."

"Glad to hear that."

I shrugged. "After my exam tomorrow and my meeting with the math chair, I'll have to figure out what my future will be." But it would have Josh in it, so that was one certainty.

Madeline coached me on what I should or shouldn't say in my meeting while I ate my dinner. She didn't admit it, but I think she'd been through something similar in her own life. Then I went to my room, determined to study no matter how much my brain wanted to wander.

I rewarded myself for getting through the material by texting Josh. And finally, I slept.

* * *

I SAT ON MY BED, staring at my phone. It was a good thing my exam was over, because my head was spinning.

I hadn't aced the exam, but I thought I'd done okay. I'd had a hard time focusing since I was meeting the math chair after it, and that meeting had me worried.

For nothing. The woman had understood my issues and knew the prof in question had problems. He was more worried about his own publishing than the career of his students, and his attitude toward women was something the chair had dealt with herself. If he hadn't had tenure, I wasn't sure he'd still be there.

After the holiday break, I was being switched to a new advisor and the chair promised it would be someone I could work with.

That had been an incredible relief. I'd thanked her profusely. And with that hindrance out of the way, I knew I was going to stay in the program. I did want this. And fuck what the purists and applied maths people thought—I was going to teach. To share what I loved about math with others and help the ones who didn't deal with traditional learning to love it too.

I was ready to take on anything, even Mrs. Middleton.

CHAPTER 32

A PLACE FOR YOU IN HOCKEY

KATIE

I'D messaged Josh all day long, keeping him posted on what happened while he told me what was going on at his end. I was going to the hospital to see him, but first there was something I needed to do.

He'd stood up to his mother, and now I needed to let my parents know what was happening.

I let out a breath and called.

"Katie! How was your exam? We're looking forward to seeing you next week."

"Is Dad there?"

Her voice was wary. "I can get him."

"Please do."

Once Dad was on the phone, I started with the good stuff. "My exams went well. I didn't tell you I'd been having a problem with my advisor. I just spoke to the chair of the department today, and I'll have someone new next semester."

"Oh Katie, that's terrible. Why didn't you tell us?"

"I didn't want you to worry."

"We worry anyway. We want to know what's going on with you. Not just the good stuff."

"I know, I should have told you. There was a lot at stake. When I finally reached out to the chair, I was afraid I might be shooting my academic future in the foot. And that would upset you."

Two gasps. "Are you sure you should have done that? What if he found out?"

"There's a process for dealing with this. I didn't think I'd get through the program with my old advisor anyway, so I reached out to the chair with my concerns, and it paid off."

They didn't respond to that right away. My parents weren't big on risks.

"There's something else. I'm dating Josh."

I heard the indrawn breaths again. Then a long pause. "That doesn't seem like a good idea. What with everything you have going on with school—"

"I need to stop you right there. What I decide to do now, with my life, is my choice."

"We just—"

I broke in. "Josh is my choice. And despite what you're afraid of, when I considered dropping out of school, Josh urged me not to give up on my dreams. He supported me, said it was my decision, but encouraged me to keep going."

"Oh. Um, well, that's good." Dad's tone suggested it was also surprising, but there was more to drop on them.

"You may have heard he was injured. His mother flew out and found me in his room. She banned me, so Josh told her I was going to be part of his life, and she needed to deal with that."

Mom snorted. "She's too tied up with her son's life. She needs to let him live for himself."

Did they hear the irony there? Probably not. "We're not

sure if she'll come around or not. I'm willing to try with her, but I'm not sure she'll do the same. Which means I'm staying in Toronto over the holidays to help Josh when they send him home from the hospital."

"What? We've been planning on this. You have your tickets."

"I know, and I didn't decide this lightly. But Josh is important to me, and he needs me. Right now, when we've just got everything worked out between us, we need that time together."

"Do you think he's going to forget you over the holidays? What does that tell you?" Mom was reaching for any argument.

They really didn't think Josh was like that, did they? The only time he'd hurt me was at their instigation. "That's not what I said. I didn't call to discuss this with you, but to inform you. I'm not changing my mind."

"So, that's it? We don't get to see you?"

I held back a sigh. "I'll come during reading week in February instead, when Josh will be able to get around on his own better. I really am sorry to miss Christmas, but even if Josh wasn't in the picture, I don't think I'll be settling in Halifax. We'll have to come up with new traditions."

That didn't go over well. I didn't waver. I wasn't leaving Josh alone or letting his mother poison his mind. My parents had to learn to respect my choices, just like Mrs. Middleton had to do with her son's.

Things were still tense when I ended the call, but I felt good. I wasn't staying in school for my parents, or because it was easy. It was my dream, and I was pursuing it.

Now I had to get to my boyfriend, to support him while his dream was in jeopardy.

* * *

*J*OSH

I MET someone from physio in the morning. There were exercises I could start right away, but everyone was cautioning me to take it slowly. They could tell how much I wanted to get back. I needed to know if I could play again, and having to wait was frustrating.

I believed them when they said I'd walk again. But no one knew if I'd be able to skate. And if I could, if I could skate the same. I had months of rehab ahead, and not till then would I know if I still had my dream, my job.

If it wasn't for Katie, I'd be going out of my mind. And it was difficult enough *with* her. We'd been messaging since she'd left yesterday. She was in an exam now, so I had nothing to do but flip through my phone and try to find a distraction.

I heard footsteps again, and expected someone was coming by to check that I was alive and had blood pressure. But it was Coach.

I shoved myself a little straighter against the back of the bed, wincing as I disturbed my knee. "Hey, Coach."

He paused in the doorway, examining the room.

Fortunately, the scary duck was now hidden among flowers and fruit baskets and other shit people had sent. It was touching, that people I didn't even know cared, but would they even remember me in another year if I wasn't playing again?

"Bet you can't wait to get out of here."

"Absolutely. They'll soon let me go if I have someone around to help me."

His eyebrows lowered. "You room with Fitch, right? He has to travel with the team."

"Yeah, but my girlfriend will stay with me for a couple of weeks."

"She reliable?"

"Absolutely. She's writing her last exam today, so she's free till the next semester starts." Her parents were going to be pissed, but I needed her. And I'd prefer her assistance to Mom's, if Mom was even willing to help now.

"She's a student?"

"U of T. Master's in math." My voice was proud, because I *was* proud of her. Proud that she was mine.

His mouth quirked up. "A smart one."

"Yep."

He crossed to the foot of the bed, staring down at where they kept the chart. Was he going to read it? Was he allowed to? Did he know what that stuff meant?

"We're going to miss you, Middleton."

I swallowed. I hated to leave my team in the lurch. "Sorry, sir. I got a little carried away that last game."

He snorted. "That's hockey. Sometimes people get hurt." He wandered to the chair and finally sat. "You're going to be out a while."

I nodded.

"Thanks to the holidays, we can't do anything about a trade till later. The guys have been playing hard. I hope we can keep on till they can get us some help."

Help meant trading for someone to play on the top line, since I couldn't now.

"Hockey's a business, so yeah, you're going to be replaced. Doesn't mean there won't be a spot for you when you return."

That was a nice thought, but… "If I return."

"You'll be back."

How was he so sure?

"You're young, you're motivated, and you're talented."

I swallowed. "But what if my knee isn't as good? What if I lose my speed?" The size I was, I needed that speed to play with the bigger guys.

"You might. You will at some point, for sure. Everyone slows down as they get older."

Not much help. "But my game is based on being fast."

"It is now." He reached into his pocket and pulled out a folded piece of paper. "Here." He tossed it onto the bed.

"What's that?"

"Those are players who relied on speed when they started. They learned to adapt their game as they lost some of that quickness. You've got a good eye for how the game flows on the ice. You watch these guys, how their games changed, and see what you can work into your own play."

I blinked quickly. "Thanks." I cleared my throat, since my voice was a little tight. "Thanks, I'll do that. I've got lots of time."

He nodded. "The scouts all talked about your hockey smarts when you were drafted. But with that idea you had for the Minnesota game, you've got smarts for the bigger picture too. There's gonna be a place for you in hockey, even when you're not on the ice."

Something inside me lifted, like a weight was removed. "You sure about that?"

"You'll have to work hard at it. Maybe that girl of yours can help you study. If you want to retire and leave it all behind when you're not playing anymore, then it doesn't matter. But I think you've got something. Don't waste it." He pushed himself up out of the chair. "Now I need to convince management that this team can go somewhere this season. Watch the games, and if you get any more bright ideas, I want to hear them."

I stared after him as he left, pinching myself to see if this was real. I held on to that paper he gave me like it was gold.

The months till I could play again were no longer so empty. I'd watch the fuck out of the games and videos of the players he'd recommended. I could even start thinking about a future beyond playing.

Hockey and Katie. I was the luckiest guy—my knee twinged—well, a lucky guy anyway.

* * *

I woke up from a nap to find my mom sitting in the chair this time.

I rubbed a hand over my face. "Hey, Mom."

"How are you feeling?"

I hit the control to bring the bed up. "Not bad."

"Would you like a drink?"

I nodded and rearranged my pillows while she stood up and poured some water in a cup.

"You have a lot of fans." She indicated all the offerings in the room as she waited for me to drink.

"It's nice. I've sent some of the flowers to other patients, and the stuffed animals will go to the kids." Except for that horrific duck. Didn't want to give anyone nightmares.

She straightened. "Where's Katie?" Her voice was level, like she was trying not to let her feelings out.

"Her last exam was this morning, and she had a meeting. Then she had to call her family, tell them she wasn't coming home for the holidays."

Mom blinked. "She's not?"

"She's staying to help me. I didn't know what you were doing, and I need her right now."

She started fussing with the sheets at the foot of the bed. "So, you don't need me."

She was trying not to sound hurt, even though she was. But she didn't need to hate on Katie because she thought I'd forget about her. "Mom, I will always need you. But Katie is important to me as well. She's promised she'll try to get along with you, since, you know I love you both."

She straightened. "I still have my opinion. I can't just turn it off."

This week had been a roller coaster, and here I was, heading down again. "I'm sorry you feel that way, but I'm not changing my mind about her."

"I will give it a chance though. I'm sure she and I will disagree, but I can at least be polite. You're all I've got, and I don't want to lose you."

"You won't, Mom. Come here." I held out my arms and she leaned into my hug.

She wasn't perfect, but she was my mom. She'd done so much for me. I wished she liked Katie better, but if they could try to get along, maybe it would all work out.

"Hello?"

Mom pulled back, and I smiled big as I saw my girl in the doorway. "Hey!"

"Good afternoon, Katie."

"Good to see you, Mrs. Middleton." I shot her a glance, but she didn't look like she was being sarcastic.

"Since you're here now, I'll step out for dinner. And it seems I have some additional Christmas shopping to do, if you're spending it with us."

Katie's eyes went round. "Oh, fu—dge. I need to do that too."

Mom picked up her coat and purse. "I can sit with him for a while tomorrow if you need time."

"That would be nice, thank you."

"I'll be back after dinner, Josh."

"See you then, Mom."

I held open my arms again, needing to feel Katie close. She settled on the side of the bed, leaning into me, her hair under my chin. I let out a contented breath. Despite the hospital and the knee and all the other things I couldn't control, I was happy. Incredibly happy.

"You seem pretty upbeat, all things considered," she said.

"I think Mom's coming around. You messaged everything went well with the advisor stuff. And Coach came by, said some things that gave me some good ideas for the future."

She sat back, smiling at me. "I told you. You have a lot to offer."

It was great to have someone who believed in me, for the times when I didn't. "How was the call with your parents?"

She didn't tense up, so that was good. "They're disappointed I won't be home, but I promised them reading week."

"I'm going to miss you."

"Then you'll know how I'll feel when you're traveling to those away games."

Yes. When I rehabbed my knee and got back on the ice. I believed it would happen now. "You're going to call me lots. And I'll call you. We can do this, if we talk to each other, right?"

"Okay. But that's not our biggest worry right now."

I frowned. Had I missed something? "What?"

She dropped against my shoulder again. "What the hell am I going to get your mother for Christmas?"

EPILOGUE

Don't Freak Out

KATIE

IT WAS a semi-official meeting of PAC—the Player Adjacent Club. We couldn't keep using the anti-WAG name because a lot of us were WAGs. I was with Josh now, so officially a girlfriend, but we didn't want to leave Jess out. We had our separate group from the other WAGS, but we had things in common as well. We weren't in opposition to them, we just had different needs for support than the more traditional WAGs.

It was a cold night in late January, and we, the PAC, were at the Top Shelf, sitting in the hockey player section. The team had just won a home game and we were waiting for the players to arrive. When the timing worked out, we sat together at games to support our fellow adjacents, but that was about the only time Jess bothered to go. Tonight had been a PAC-free game. Callie had a late meeting at the office and hadn't wanted to walk into the game partway through. Jayna had been at a sledge hockey association meeting, and Jess said she'd had a bad day.

Josh was at the tables with us. He'd deemed himself a member, claiming that IR meant he was now adjacent rather than a player. The others had agreed to give him part-time status, which meant he could be with us on occasion, but not always. Sometimes we wanted girl time together. He could argue semantics, but he didn't understand what it was like to be close to a player but not be one.

It was a Friday night, no one had to be up early in the morning, and we'd decided to come out for the after-game fun. Jess had been a little reluctant, but I'd convinced her. I was closer to her than the other two, and I hadn't seen her for a few days.

Josh had another week before he could stop using crutches, and he couldn't wait. I was looking forward to the brace coming off—he complained a lot about itching, and though we'd managed to work around it, it would be nice to have sex without it limiting what we could do.

Though we'd been very creative.

We were on our second round of drinks—none of us had driven, so we were indulging—when the team started to trickle in. They were met with applause for a difficult win.

The team had been slowly, very slowly, climbing in the standings and tonight they'd made it to the wild card slot. There were still months to play, and no guarantees they'd get into the playoffs, but after the horrible start to the season, everyone was feeling optimistic. They missed Josh's scoring though. He felt guilty. He blamed himself for playing more recklessly the night he got injured after the trade news, but hockey was a dangerous sport. As I reminded him, he could have been injured at any time.

Daniel sat across from me. After ordering a drink, he grinned. "Enjoying having the place to yourselves now?"

He'd bought his own place in the same building that Jess and JJ lived in and moved out a week ago. I was going to miss his cooking, but with his departure I'd agreed to move in with Josh. Officially.

"I still feel guilty." Like I had pushed him out. I was at Josh's all the time now. It had started when he got out of the hospital and I was helping him cope with his crutches. I was still Madeline's tenant till the end of the month, but I'd slept almost every night at Josh's.

"It's fine, Katie. My divorce is final and it's time to start fresh."

"Still..."

Daniel tilted his beer toward me. "The real reason I moved out is because I can't carpool with Josh anymore. Now I can drive in with JJ. Nothing to do with the noises coming from Josh's bedroom."

My cheeks flamed and I covered my face with my hands. Josh and I were noisy. After having to be so quiet when we were in high school, it was like we'd gone completely in the opposite direction. I swore we'd be quieter each time, but...

"Still better than having your date ask your brother for his autograph," Jess whispered in my ear. She had a point.

Josh was on the other side of me from Jess, his hand warm on my thigh. He liked to be touching me, and I was happy to indulge him. Even though he wasn't on the active roster, he was still popular with the fans, including the puck bunnies. When he claimed me like this, I didn't have to kiss him every time a jersey chaser considered making a play for him.

Not that kissing Josh was a hardship.

He still had times he stressed about the uncertainty around his hockey-playing future, but so far rehab was going well, and he was spending a lot of his free time studying films of games. Once the brace and crutches were gone, he was going to the practice arena when the team was in town to do exercises with the team trainers, and I knew he'd be talking to Coach as well. I was confident he'd be playing next season and made plans to deal with that.

School was enjoyable again. My new advisor was much easier to deal with. He still questioned and challenged me, but he was willing to offer his advice when I asked for it and never gave me that same misogynistic vibe. And my research project, slightly amended, was a go.

All in all, once we'd gotten through Christmas with Mrs. Middleton, life had been so much better than it had seemed for those few dark days in December. Josh was coming home with me for reading week, and he'd have his turn on the hot seat. Mom and Dad were starting to come around to the idea of the two of us, and once they heard Josh brag about how I was doing at school, they'd end up supporting us.

I'd have never thought we'd get here, Josh and me, after that night he arrived at the condo with Madeline. But I was so glad he did.

* * *

JOSH

KATIE WAS TUCKED up beside me and I'd soon be done with the crutches. I hoped I'd be able to play next season, but I was working on the stuff Coach had talked about. So whatever happened, I'd have a future, most likely with hockey. Conversation swirled around me, and I was happy to enjoy being with my girl and my teammates.

"I swear, that chick was hiding everything in that purse she had…"

"The ref was looking right at him and still didn't…"

My phone chirped, so I pulled it out of my pocket. It was a message from my agent, Allen.

Don't freak out. You're not part of the trade.

Of course I immediately freaked out. *A trade?* No one would want to trade for me till we had a better idea if I'd be able to play again. Or would they?

Don't you know me? Of course I'm freaking out.

It's not you, so settle. Team's getting a goal scorer. It's a rental, doesn't mean they're giving up on you.

Sure, but if that rental did well, they might sign him on again. I must have tensed up, because Katie noticed there was something going on.

"What's wrong?" she whispered in my ear.

"Allen said there's a trade."

Her eyes went wide. "Where?"

"It's not me. They traded for a rental for the playoffs."

Daniel was across from Katie, and we weren't quiet enough. "Who's traded?"

He'd spoken loud enough for Royster to hear. "There's a trade?"

Now everyone heard. "Shit, anyone got a message from their agent?"

"I did!" I yelled.

"No, Ducky! We need you next season!"

I rolled my eyes. "It's not me."

"Who is it?"

Was I supposed to keep this quiet? But if it was a done deal, the whole world would know soon.

"I don't have any names. Allen says there's a trade, for a playoff rental. A goal scorer. That's all I know."

300

"We could use someone to take your place till you're back, Ducky," Oppy said.

I knew that. Didn't mean I liked it. Some of the guys started guessing names, but most of them had a phone out. The atmosphere at the table had turned tense. My fault. Even Cooper was texting—probably his agent.

"I think you've started something," Katie said in a low voice.

"Yeah, I didn't mean to."

She shrugged. "It wouldn't have been a secret for long anyway."

Since I didn't need to check in with my agent—if he'd been going to tell me names, he'd have already done it—I used my phone to check on the Canadian sports network site. They had almost as good connections as Allen and usually were the first to break trade news.

A banner started to scroll through their website. I missed the first words but saw *trade* and *Blaze* and *Los Angeles*.

"I've got it!" yelled Crash.

Katie looked over my shoulder as Crash read out what was on his screen—exactly the same as mine.

"Novak and Olsson from the Blaze for LA's Alek Denbrowski."

Denny? Why the hell would the team trade for him? Guy had a rep in the league as a wild card.

"Are you *fucking* kidding me?"

Everyone stared at JJ in surprise. He was so quiet it was easy to forget when he was around, and when he talked it was normally polite. If the team had an award for player most likely to melt into the woodwork, JJ was the guy. Kind of the opposite of Denny.

JJ bit back whatever he was going to say. "I'm hitting up the head." He shoved his chair almost hard enough to knock it over and strode off without looking at anyone.

Whoa. Did not see that coming. There was bad blood between JJ and Denny? I didn't remember anything from when we'd played LA. This trade looked like it was going to mess up team chemistry. What the fuck was management doing?

"You okay, Jess?"

Katie was talking to JJ's sister. Jessica also looked majorly upset. She didn't come out to team things that often, but she and JJ never caused trouble or attracted attention. Seeing them riled up like this raised a lot of questions.

"What a shitty day. If Justin comes back, tell him I left." She threw some money down on the table and shoved her chair out pretty hard too.

Damn, something big was going on here. Then she was gone.

I turned back to the table. Everyone looked shocked. "What's the big deal with JJ and his sister and Denny?"

Even Cooper shrugged. If anyone knew what was up with JJ it was Cooper.

"When's the new guy arriving?" Crash asked.

We looked at Cooper, because he was our captain and he knew shit. "I didn't even know the trade was happening. With the time change, he won't get here till tomorrow at the earliest. Your agent have any details, Ducky?"

I shook my head. "He just told me I wasn't being traded and not to freak out."

The celebratory mood was gone and everyone started to leave. I hoped like hell management knew something we didn't, because so far this trade was a problem, and Denny hadn't even arrived.

On the TV screens, pictures of Novak and Olsson were on one half, Denny on the other. His photo showed a guy wearing an intense expression, dark hair down to his shoulders and a full beard. Maybe the hair would help him adjust to Canada after being in California.

Jayna and Callie talked to Katie while I called up a ride to get us home. They were worried about Jess. They finally hugged, and Cooper and Mitch led their girlfriends away.

"Do you know why JJ blew up like that?" Katie asked.

I shook my head. "I don't remember him doing anything when we played LA, so not sure why he's so pissed. I mean, Denny has a rep."

"What do you mean?"

"He's got a killer shot and a good eye, but he's a hothead and a defensive liability. Maybe JJ thinks it'll be more work for him?"

Katie tilted her head. "And Jess was upset about that too?"

I tugged her close, holding one hand with mine on the crutch. "I'm sure you'll find out. And we'll do whatever we can to help them. Meantime, the condo is all ours."

"I'm so embarrassed that Daniel heard us."

"What can I say? I'm just that good."

She poked me in the ribs. "It's still embarrassing."

"Now that he's gone, we have to break in the rest of the rooms."

"Break them in?"

I nodded. "We have to have sex in every room."

"We do, eh? It's a rule?"

"Oh yeah. I'm looking forward to that."

She rolled her eyes, but her hand squeezed mine. She was on board.

I'd never have dreamed, back when this season started, that I'd be where I was now. And I hated being injured, missing games and not knowing where I'd be next season. But at the end of it all, I had Katie, and that made everything worth it.

I leaned over to kiss her, here where she'd kissed me to

chase off a bunny. "I love you." I didn't want her to ever worry about another woman again.

Her lips quirked up. "I know."

I waited. Still no ride outside, and Katie didn't say it back.

"Come on. Tell me." I knew it, but some part of me always wanted that reassurance from her.

She grinned more widely but put me out of my misery. "I love you, Josh Middleton."

And all was right with my world.

BONUS SCENE

What happens when Josh wants a pet? Is Katie ready for a duck? Join my newsletter for a bonus scene.

https://www.subscribepage.io/2XnlQH

Next in The Toronto Blaze: Playoff

Pre-Order Now

This is rough – not yet edited so please allow for improvement before it's published.

Alek

I climbed out of my Lamborghini in the players parking lot of the LA NHL facility. The California breeze, lifting my cap, was cool in January. At least, to me. After spending my entire hockey career in Florida, Texas, Nevada and SoCal, my blood was thin. Still, beat the hell out of places like Edmonton and Winnipeg.

The hat twisted around, loose on my head. I'd need to adjust it, now that I'd shaved off my hair. I ran a hand over my newly smooth jaw. I was starting to regret the extreme makeover, but the anger that inspired it was still burning in my brain.

I checked the cars in the lot, a growl threatening when I saw Weasel's Ferrari. Fucking double-crosser. I shut the car door, taking care not to slam it, and stalked to the player's entrance, ready for my closeup. The haircut made a statement, and it would ensure everyone on the team knew what had really happened in our game last night.

I pushed open the door to the locker room, where at least half the roster players were already assembled, changing for practice, shooting the shit, making plans. My stall mates weren't there yet, so I had space on each side, and no one noticed the new me, not at first.

I pulled off my hat, threw it on the top shelf. Hung up my jacket and stashed my shoes. Slowly, the noise level dropped. I reached for the hem of my t-shirt and pulled it off. My full sleeves were on display, but that wasn't what attracted attention.

"What the fuck? Is that you, Denny?" Team captain Marty asked.

I turned around, every guy's stare on my smooth head and jaw. I crossed my arms. "What's the problem?"

"Your hair. What happened to your hair?"

Last night, when we'd left after the game, my hair fell to my shoulders. I often had to tie it back. Not now. The full beard was also gone.

I shrugged. "I lost a bet."

Marty's eyes bugged. "Who...what the hell?"

I turned my head until my glare was pinned on Weasel. "*Someone* bet that I couldn't get away with an illegal stick last night."

The guys were quiet again for a moment, since the resulting penalty had contributed to our loss in that same game.

"That's why you had that stick?" Marty sounded pissed.

I nodded, gaze still focused on Weasel. "It was just supposed to be for the first couple of shifts. Everyone knows that none of the coaches risk stopping the game to ask for measurements." If a coach was wrong, then they'd be assessed a delay of game penalty.

"But you got caught, dumb ass."

I looked at Beano, Weasel's best friend. "Because the guy who bet me told San Jose what was going on."

I heard the sucked in breaths. For a teammate to deliberately give up a power play? That shocked them. Some of these guys believed that their teammates were all loyal. News flash – everyone was out for themselves.

Marty frowned. "Why did you bother shaving then? It wasn't a fair bet."

"Because *I* don't cheat. Or weasel out of consequences. *I* follow through. And now, in case you missed it, some of the guys in this room are not to be trusted."

Everyone's eyes were focused on Weasel.

"Fuck you, Denny." He spat out.

"What the fuck, Weasel? Why would you do that?" Marty was almost as pissed as I was.

Weasel turned to the others, all watching him in shock or anger or disappointment. "He hooked up with my sister!"

This? Again?

"I *told* you, I didn't know who she was." I growled. "You didn't mention that she was visiting and was joining us at the bar. You buggered off with some jersey chaser so how the hell was I supposed to know she was related to you?"

Two months ago, I'd been out with Weasel and Beano and that's when it happened. With the two of them nowhere to be found, I'd been approached by a woman wearing a short, sexy dress, enough makeup that no one could see a resemblance to my teammate, and she'd been all over me. She'd wanted sex, and I'd obliged. If I'd known who she was, I wouldn't have touched her, but I didn't ask for ID.

Weasel pointed at me with a shaking finger. "You don't mess with a teammate's sister!"

"I DIDN'T KNOW!" I yelled, frustrated that he refused to listen. "Maybe you should tell your teammates who she is. Or, what the hell, tell your sister not to mess with us. She wanted it."

Weasel lunged for me. I loosened my arms, ready to vent my anger with my fists, but Beano pulled him back.

Marty, wearing most of his gear, stepped between us. "For fuck's sake, the two of you. That stunt cost us a goal. Denny, apologize, and Weasel, let it go."

I'd apologized to Weasel before, once, and I wasn't doing it again. It obviously didn't take, though he'd pretended everything was okay. "What am I supposed to apologize for? Do I have to ask every bunny I come across if she's related to Weasel?"

Some of the guys muttered. The fuckboys, the ones who didn't ask questions if they found someone willing were on my side. The ones with female siblings were more inclined to support Weasel.

Yeah, teams really were just one big happy family.

The assistant coach came in through the door, and noticing the tension in the room, narrowed his eyes. "Better not be late, men. And Denny, Manager wants to see you."

My teammates turned to me, curious about this unexpected summons. Weasel had a smirk on his face, so maybe this wasn't so unexpected.

"Now?" Coach was out for a couple of days with a family situation, so our assistant should be the one with the task of calling me out. The team manager didn't normally deal with the players directly. He nodded, so I shrugged and pulled my shirt back on.

This was my third year in LA, my longest stay with a team so far. Weasel had been signed at the start of this season on a one-year deal. I wasn't all rah-rah kumbaya with my teammates, but Weasel and I had got along. Neither of us had families, and we liked hooking up. We hung out together on the road, since we were looking for the same things. I'd thought he was as close to a friend as I had on the team.

I should have known better. That dare, which he'd made into a bet, whether I could get away with Drako's stick for a shift - he'd been planning to mess things up for me the whole time. Fuck him.

This was why I didn't buy into the whole team is family bullshit some coaches liked to spew. At the end of the day, we were co-workers, often competing for the same job. The only family the team resembled was one of those fucked up ones that sent people into therapy.

I had time to consider possibilities as I took the elevator up to management offices. My contract expired in a few months, at the end of the season. If this was good news about a new contract offer, I'd have heard from my agent. I was the top scorer on the team, so they weren't sending me down to the farm team. By a process of elimination, it must be a trade.

THANK YOU

For reading *Replay*. Extra thank you's for leaving a review. This hockey series is a new project for me, so I appreciate anyone who spreads the word!

About the Author

Kim Findlay left hockey country, (Canada) to sail the beautiful waters of the Caribbean, finally landing in Sint Maarten (SXM). She balances a husband, dog, writing reading and accounting, while missing family back home. (Not the weather though)

Website: www.kimfindlay.ca

If you'd be interested in more frequent updates and would like to help name characters and assign their jersey numbers, join me in my Facebook group: Runaway Romance. (Link)

I'd love to hear from you, so please reach out at kim@kimfindlay.ca

Logo links:

FB https://www.facebook.com/AuthorKimFindlay

BS (Blue Sky) https://bsky.app/profile/authorkimfindlay.bsky.social

IG https://www.instagram.com/authorkimfindlay/

Bookbub https://www.bookbub.com/profile/kim-findlay

Goodreads: https://www.goodreads.com/author/dashboard?ref=nav_profile_authordash

Also by Kim Findlay

Cupid's Crossing Series, Harlequin Heartwarming
A Valentine's Proposal https://books2read.com/u/ml6A7Y
A Fourth of July Proposal https://books2read.com/u/3Rw6vB
A New Year's Proposal https://books2read.com/u/bWYQOD
A Country Proposal https://books2read.com/u/3y9KwJ
An Unexpected Twins Proposal https://books2read.com/u/br9wAk

MooU (College hockey multi-author series) Heart Eyes Press
Halftime https://books2read.com/u/4E7lYz

Inspirational Suspense (as Anne Galbraith)
Out of the Ashes https://books2read.com/u/bQpyOD
Kidnap Threat https://books2read.com/u/3JLpvJ
Hidden Evidence https://books2read.com/u/ml6ARY

Out of Print: (waiting for reissue!)
Crossing the Goal Line
Her Family's Defender

The Toronto Blaze Series:
Playing to Win https://books2read.com/u/mVY0n2
Playmaker https://books2read.com/u/bMExpk
Coming Next:
Playoff (Denny) https://books2read.com/u/4NVZr8
Frozen Play (Bongo)
Played Out (JJ)